Adrift on Stony Beach

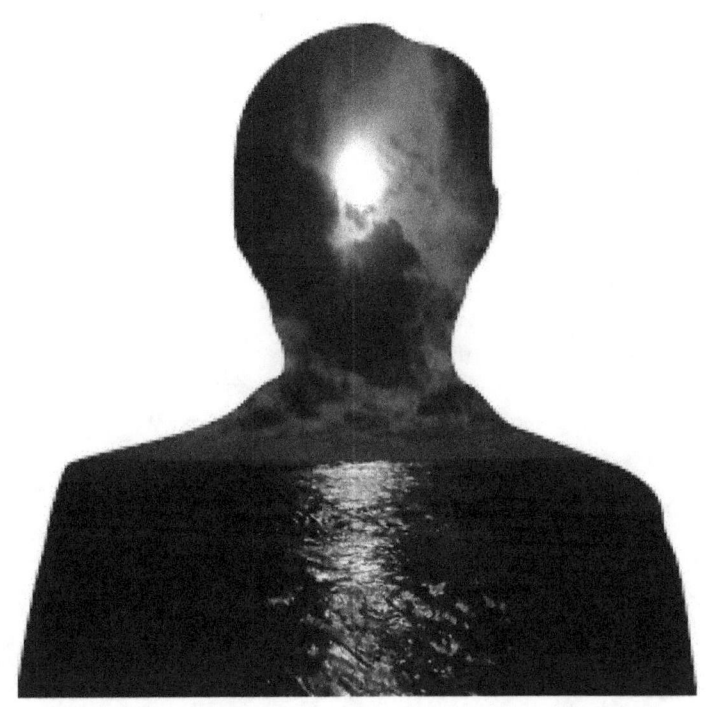

~~~ TWISTED THREADS ~~~
A Novel
SHERYLL O'BRIEN

ISBN 978-1-939351-43-2

WOODWIND PRESS

Printed in United States of America

Mom,

I am a writer, and yet,

Words fail me.

I love you,

Sheryll

A heartfelt thank you to my team:

Andria Flores ~ Editor extraordinaire.
Nancy Pendleton ~ Goddess of the publishing world.
Jessica Champion ~ Web designer and manager.
Guidepost Creative
Jessica Champion ~ Cover design

Acknowledgement:

My team, my friends:

Andria Flores, a soft-spoken, lovely woman who has said her fair share of, "Oh dear," in response to my very salty language, in my work and in my life. The thing that mattered most to this writer was having an editor who pushed and praised, and who acquiesced when I made up words and insisted on using them. I love that she trusted the journey I set my characters on and held tight to my hand as I put them into peril and graced them with joy. I appreciate all that Andria has done, including becoming my friend.

Nancy Pendleton, a bawdy, hot-shit of a woman who has said her fair share of, "I just spit my coffee, water, or cocktail across the room at the wonderfully ridiculous things you do in your work and in your life." The things that mattered to this writer was to have a publisher who saw the value of my work and made sure it was presented in the best light—which she did. I appreciate having had the opportunity to follow Nancy along the publishing path – appreciate ever so much the friendship we forged from afar.

Jessica Champion, a sassy, highly creative woman who has said her fair share of, "Trust me, I've got your vision and I can make it better." The things that mattered to this writer was to have a social media professional who saw the intricacies in my work and made sure they were showcased with subtlety or grandeur. Step by step Jessica introduced me to the world of technology, then continued walking into a valued friendship with me.

I am very grateful to have had the opportunity to get to know these women professionally and personally. Each has brought me joy and I will be forever grateful for their presence in my life.

Muah!
Sheryll

Additional acknowledgements: For the Spanish flair in my Stony Beach books I would like to thank Jessica O'Brien, Andria Flores, and Nancy Pendleton. Gracias, muchachas.

For a complete list of Sheryll O'Brien's books,

Please visit pullingthreadsnovella.com

Adrift on Stony Beach

~~~ TWISTED THREADS ~~~
A Novel
SHERYLL O'BRIEN

REVENGE IS BEST SERVED WET
Friday, July 21
Waning Crescent – Illumination 4%

Laire and Heir
Together Again

LAIRE

Your fate is sealed, Edward Kingston IV. As sure as you killed the mother of your unborn child, a right turnabout will be yours. Before next morning light, I'll be rising up and giving you what for. But should you deliver your own fate, by your own hand, I'll welcome you to my watery grave, in a right fine way, then toss your heap upon Stony Beach.

Edward

The twenty-five year old Heir to the Kingdom of Whisper has drifted at sea for days. He hasn't eaten or slept, or altered his plan for a quick end to a life he fucked up, with help from others, of course. Lots of help. The young man who'd been raised in a world of privilege rails at the universe, "What did you fucking expect from the offspring of Edward the third? Maybe if I'd had a different father. Maybe if I'd been raised in a different home..." He shakes his head and forces himself to remember the hands wrapped tightly around the necks of innocent girls were his; to remember it was he who heard their final plea, who felt their struggle to live, who watched their life end.

Edward Kingston IV lifts the loaded gun that rests on his lap, enjoys the feel of it in his hand, admires the power it holds. He talks to it, confessing his sins, "Christie and Laire, I killed them. I took the life of one during a fit of rage and the life of the other on a bent knee of weakness. I deserve to rot in Hell." He cracks open a bottle of whisky, pulls a gluttonous lot, and reminds himself during the cough and burn, "I carry the sins of the women I killed, but the sins of Danielle and Joe, they belong to another." He raises the bottle high, "Here's to you, brother. You played me well." He pulls some liquid courage. "My deeds have caught up with me. I pray that one day you bear the weight of your own murderous acts, and when that time comes, I'll welcome you to the pits of Hell." Heir Kingston lets loose a madman's laugh that ends at the sudden rise of sea. The boat lifts high, then drops hard. Edward bangs upon the deck and struggles mightily to hold on—a final act to live. When waters calm, he crawls the deck looking for the gun, the symbol of his strength, the means to his end. He stops cold when he hears her voice.

~~VENGEANCE BE MINE~~

Edward Kingston IV collapses. He raises his arm to shield himself from the blinding sun, then offers a pitiful acknowledgement, "We could have made a go of it, Laire. You, me, and the baby." He begins to cry.

~~LOOK AT ME YOU COWARD~~

He thuds his arm on the deck and smiles wide when he sees the beautiful young spirit lift on a wave, "Laire." The man who killed the girl draws his final breath, welcomes her crash over him, and surrenders his soul as she pulls him to the depths. And when Edward's lungs fill with the water of her grave and his life is no more, Laire MacTavish has her say.

~~HAPPY ANNIVERSARY,
MATHAIR FUCKER~~

A King, an Heir, and a Spare

Edward Kingston III knows deep in his soul, should such a place exist, that the son he raised as his own is dead. She delivers the news on an ice cold whisper.

~~HEIR IS DEAD~~
~~ASHORE ON STONY BEACH
HE WILL BE~~

~~LONG LIVE THE KING~~

The self-proclaimed King of Whisper stares at the horizon where darkening sky and water meet, where waves moved by powers unseen begin their long journey. The breaking man chooses a lifting, curling swell from countless others and follows it as it builds and crashes hard upon the shore a stone's throw away. He finds the horizon and begins the process anew, though none of it really registers. What holds his mind's eye is the ghostly image of a young woman rising in the sea; what deafens him to the hypnotic push and crash of ocean water is the echo of her brogue. The shell of a man is desperate to enjoy his final night on earth, wanting nothing more than to sit in his favorite rattan at the shoreline of his estate and get lost in the sights and sounds of his ocean. He pulls a shaky breath, the kind that lingers after a good cry, lumbers to lift his arm and takes a swig from a near-empty whisky bottle. Edward Kingston III takes hold of the gun that rests on his lap, feels its weight, admires its power. The act helps clear his head of her and fills it with one word, "Brother." He scoffs, then angers, then slurs at his son, "You **do not** have a brother, Edward. You were fed a line of bullshit. You should have asked me outright and not in some half-assed way." A memory floats to the top of his saturated brain…

Edward met King at the marina for some shop talk and an early dinner. "I'm going to chew and screw, King. I'm meeting Quinn and her law partner for drinks in Portland at 8 PM."

King raised his glass, "She's a beautiful woman, Heir." The father expected pushback at the name, he received none. "Have you settled into your birth title?"

Edward laughed, "No. I hate it, but I've reconciled that you won't stop calling me that any time soon."

"Well, you're my son. My only Heir."

"Yeah. Lucky me," he laughed big, then pushed in a bit on that comment. "Why didn't you and Mom have other kids?"

"Kathleen had an emergency hysterectomy right after your birth. She never wanted to consider other options."

"Like surrogacy or adoption?"

King gave a little nod, "Kathleen's greatest joy in life was being your mother, but she didn't want to have children through other means."

The son pushed beyond normal boundaries, "But you would have had other children? By other means?"

"Yes. But that wasn't in the cards."

"You sure about that? Your dalliances are legendary. Maybe there's a sibling out there who can share the kingdom with Heir Kingston."

The King pulled a good long gulp and paid the price with a good long burn. "I assure you, Edward, you are my one and only. And I assure you, I'd be more than happy with a bunch of snotty grandchildren tagging along, so find a broad and knock her good." **The father noticed the change in his son.** "I'm sorry, Edward. I didn't mean to push the bruise of Laire."

~~YOUR SON IS DEAD~~

King shivers at the sound of her voice and pains at the excruciating reminder of his son's fate. He gets up, stumbles down a set of stairs to the shoreline, and continues unsteadily along until he leaves his property. With each step toward Stony Beach the sands become firmer and the shoreline becomes littered with rocks. He rests on one before moving on, locking his gaze on his bay. A memory grabs on tight and won't let go…

"A fucking bone washed ashore at Echo."

"Don't touch it!" Chief Banks barked into the phone.

King checked over his shoulder before speaking again, "I should throw it back."

"Don't fucking touch it, King. When we hang up, you're going to call WPD and report it."

"Whose bone is it?"

"Is there any flesh on it?"

"Jesus, Vern. No."

"Then it's Christie Anderson's."

King hangs his head, "And now I'm sitting on this godforsaken strip of land waiting for my son's body to wash ashore. Edward, you are my only son," the words cut deep—they should. The words of a King to an Heir sever the final tie that binds. Loss and regret push him toward madness. He laughs until he cries, chokes on his spittle, and loses a bit of booze and bile. He calls out again when he sees the body of his son bobbing toward the shoreline, "Edward!" he howls. He gets up and stumbles toward the bend, raises the gun to his head, rights himself on a large boulder, then steps behind when a man shouts and rounds from the other side. He recognizes the face from a picture in a file from Edward's office, the file labeled, **Brother**.

"Dale Jacobs," the name ignites a hellish burn. The King of Whisper shows himself, raises his gun, and shouts, "You lying fuck!" He shoots the retreating man in the back, bangs hard against the stone pillar, takes shelter behind it, and loses the rest of himself in a puddle of puke. A beginning rain rouses his senses, reminding him of what sent him to Stony. He's readying for his final act when he hears a scream. He peeks out from his hiding place, watches a young woman run to the prone man, strip off her sweatshirt, press it to his back, and scan the beach for something—someone.

As soon as she pushes herself upright and makes her way back around the bend, The King of Whisper abandons his death wish and spits the remnants of his murderous rage on the beach of Stony. Before turning the corner onto his property, he takes one final look at the tumble-tossed body of a man he raised from childhood, then at the man he cut down in his prime. He pockets his gun, lights a menthol, and heads back to his kingdom.

Three Months Later

Welcome to Murder Island

Esmé Baxter is behind the wheel of a Honda CRV inching along the main street of Whisper Island, a tiny strip of land located in Casco Bay, Maine. The backseat passenger, Esmé's daughter Marin, refers to the isle as Murder Island. There are very legitimate reasons for the renaming. During the earliest days of the Baxter's arrival, one year ago – a teenage girl went missing, the second in as many years – a young woman was strangled in her beachfront shack – the bone of one of the missing teens washed ashore – the husband of Esmé and father of Marin died at the base of a cliff on the backside of the island – and Marin and a guy named Dale almost died when their unconscious selves banged relentlessly against massive rocks at high tide.

Marin knows the broad strokes of what happened that night because she's heard bits and pieces while in rehab and because she's been getting her memory back in dribs and drabs. The crux of those events, however, is lost somewhere in her battered and bruised brain. When Marin Baxter finally recovers those memories, she may very well wish she could forget what happened on a beach named Stony on an island named Whisper.

The driver takes frequent looks in the rearview mirror at her daughter who objects frequently to those looks, "I'm still here, so stop checking."

"I've been thinking how good you look."

"Uh huh."

"No really, Marin, you look really good, and once you get some fresh air and sunshine, you'll feel really good, too."

"Uh huh."

"Jenny and June called earlier and said they have your bedroom all set, and they've put your telescope onto the balcony."

"I'm staying at Sand Castle."

"Marin, I don't think—"

"Mom, I'm staying at Sand Castle."

Esmé silently finishes her daughter's sentence. *I'm staying at Sand Castle because you're forcing me to stay on Murder Island ... I'm staying at Sand Castle and there's nothing you can say to change my mind ... I'm staying at Sand Castle because I need to be alone.* The mother is ready to concede. The daughter doesn't need concession. She's already moved on.

"Have you seen Tom?"

"No."

Marin searches for a time-marker, something she can use to calculate how long it's been. She finds one in the blaze of autumnal color, then does some mental math, or she tries to. *July 21ˢᵗ. Mom said that was the day Dale and I went to Stony Beach, the day I paid a little side visit to Hell. It's autumn now. A new season.* "What's the date?"

"October 25ᵗʰ."

Marin counts on her fingers, July. August. September. October. "Was I in rehab for three months?"

"Yesss." The sighed word ushers away some of the heavy load this mother carried as she watched her child face death, then obstinately deny its hopeful claim by battling her way back inch by inch. "Marin."

"What?"

"Nothing. Just wanted to say your name."

Marin circles back to her original question, the one she asked in her head, but may not have asked out loud, "When was the last time you saw Tom?"

"July 25ᵗʰ."

Marin counts on her fingers, July. August. September. October. "That was three months ago."

"Yesss."

"Does he know I'm out of rehab? Did he know I was in rehab?"

Esmé tears, "I'm not sure what Tom knows. We haven't spoken."

"Why?"

"I don't know." She lies. She knows.

Marin Baxter silences and looks out the car window at the autumn sky. She pulls the only real memories she has of *that* day. The memories are hers and she comforts in them…

Dale playfully hip-chucking as they walked the shore, and laughing at something she said, and running his hand through his flaxen, wavy hair, and rolling his seaweed-green eyes, and lying beside her on the sand, his hand close enough to touch.

Jacobs Jolly

Injured police officer Dale Jacobs groans when his physical therapist knocks on the front door. The patient's mother, Connie, a throwback to the 1950s, practically skips to greet the arrival. Her son gives an eyeroll when she singsongs a hello to the barbarian filling the doorway, then groans loudly and repeatedly while the asshole sets his massage table in the basement workout area. *Can't escape – can't get my hands on my gun,* he silently grouses. The men grunt their greeting and get on with it. When the door closes behind 'Conan The Crusher', 120 grueling minutes later, Dale's mother delivers some news in her drippingly sweet tone, news that is sure to hit a sour note with her son. "Esmé Baxter called.

She said Marin is home from rehab and settling in at Sand Castle."

The young man of nearly twenty-five, the guy who'd give anything to be tooling the island on his Harley, the dude who's living at home with his mommy, the guy who misses the girl, and his job, and the great outdoors, pushes from the table at which he just sat for lunch. He limps to a screen door, slams through and hobble-storms across the backyard to an Adirondack chaise set on a shaded veranda. He lowers himself onto the seat, slides his cell from his pocket and thinks about calling the only person he needs and wants to talk to—then thinks about what that call would be like. *Hey, how are you? I heard you took quite the bump to your head. OR. Hey, about what happened on Stony, I'm really sorry I fucked up your protection and you almost died. OR. Hey, I heard you had to withdraw from the marine institute. That sucks. OR. Hey, it must have been fuckin something when a dead guy nearly drowned you.* "Nope. We can't talk about that because she doesn't remember that. And I only know about the dead guy because I was told what happened after I was shot. There's nothing about that part of our day banging in my head, and what does bang there is a bunch of drug-induced freaky shit. Nope. There's no reason to call," he slides his cell back into his pocket.

Dale Jacobs looks at the autumn sky and pulls the only real memories he has of that day. The memories are his and he clings to them…

Marin playfully shoulder-nudging as they walked the shore, and laughing at something he said, and flipping her shoulder-length, wavy, chestnut hair, and rolling her hazel-blue eyes, and lying beside him on the sand, close enough to touch.

There is so much more for them to remember.
They will—in time.

Day One
Thursday, October 26
Waxing Crescent – Illumination 38%

Marin wakes to find The Three Women 'cramped' out on the tiny deck at Sand Castle, her pale pink, waterfront cottage on the sandy side of Whisper Island. She groans loudly to get their attention, "Why are you here?"

"We've missed you," Esmé and Jenny unison.

"I haven't," June snarls, "and your morning bitchiness is Reason Number One."

"I hope you'll be leaving soon."

"Marin!"

Jenny touches Esmé's forearm, "It's because of the brain bump."

Marin snarls, "It's because of the moderate traumatic brain injury, the one I got from my head smacking against monolithic boulders on that fucking stony shithole."

June cracks up. "OMG, she's hilarious!"

Marin cracks up. "I kinda like you. Do you want to hang out after these two leave?"

"Hell, yeah!"

Esmé gets off her chaise, "Sas! We'll go get donuts."

"Make sure there are two jelly for me and two honey-glazed for Miss Bitchiness."

"I don't like honey-glazed. I want plain."

"You the fuck do not want plain donuts."

"Yes. I. Do."

"Suit yourself, but mark my words, when your brain bump gets better you'll be back on the honey-glazed."

"What makes you think my BB will get better?"

"Your BB?"

"The whitecoats in rehab said I should label things, that it would help me organize my thoughts, so my brain bump is now known as BB."

"This could be fun. Let's label the shit out of everything."

"Okay. Let's start with you."

June rolls her eyes, "Can't wait to hear this one. By the way, I'm a lesbian, in case you forgot." She eyes Marin for a good long minute, "You do remember what a lesbian is, right?"

"Oh, for fuck's sake, of course I know what a lesbian is."

"What?"

"It's one of those long-necked furry barnyard animals."

"That's a llama, you nutcase."

Marin cracks up laughing, "Your new label is LL."

"For lesbian llama?"

"Yesssss."

"Oh. My. God. You just did an Esmé yes thingy."

"Yeah. I sound like her from time to time, but it's way better than sounding like Eeyore. I sounded like him for weeks."

"I heard about that. I cracked the fuck up when Es told me."

"I bet you did, Lesbian Llama."

"I thought you were gonna use LL, you know, cause you're labeling things."

"I think Lesbian Llama is funnier."

"Yeah, it's a hoot."

Boardwalk

Dale thought about leaving the donut shop when Esmé and Jenny walked in, but he knew he wouldn't be able to limp out unnoticed, so he turned toward the window, quietly sipped his coffee, and stared in the direction of The Promise, Esmé Baxter's home and art gallery. The guy who needed to get out of the house, but who didn't want attention, might have gone unnoticed if Donna Abbott, the police dispatcher, hadn't seen him.

She steps out of line and hurries his way, "Dale Jacobs, you are a sight, I tell you, you're looking good."

Every eye in the joint turns his way. "Take a seat, Donna, please." He pulls his ballcap a little lower.

"Sorry for calling attention to you, but I'm really happy to see you."

"Yeah, you, too." He looks beyond her and nods in Esmé's and Jenny's direction.

They smile wide, place their order, then head his way. Donna leaves with a smile for the ladies and a touch to Dale's hand, "I'm keeping your desk free from the riffraff."

"Yeah, thanks, Donna." He points to the seats across from him, "I'd get up, but I'm a bit stiff."

Jenny takes the seat nearest the window, Esmé kisses his cheek before sitting across from him, "You look good, Dale."

"General consensus, I guess."

There's a minute, or maybe one hundred minutes of awkward silence accentuated by frequent looks onto Main Street before Esmé breaks the tedium.

"Do you feel like talking about—"

"Nope."

She smiles, "You don't know what I was going to say."

"It doesn't really matter, Esmé. I don't feel like talking about anything."

"Do you feel like listening?"

He gives his head a shake, lets out a long sigh, and looks out the window toward The Promise. "How is she?"

"Different."

"Aren't we all?"

"Yesss. If it would help, you could come by and—"

"And what? Tell Marin I remember her when I don't. Of course, that'd be a lie because

I remember her in my dreams, but most of those are pretty fucked up." He gives his head a good shake, "I'm hoping the nightly shit fests are byproducts of a drug-induced coma because otherwise I'm a homicidal maniac." He turns away.

Esmé touches his hand. He takes hold then lets go.

"You were one of the good guys, Dale. You hunted the homicidal maniac, remember?"

"Nope, but that's what I hear—every damned morning, midday, and evening during the news programs, and during every other waking minute when the June Cleaver lookalike tells me how proud she is of her son. It took me a damned month before I honestly knew she was my mother."

Jenny smiles at the Beaver Cleaver mom reference, pains at the other stuff, then lets her lawyering-self take over, "The press coverage is going to intensify when the inquest kicks in."

"Yeah. Can't wait for that."

Jenny does something outside the norm; she speaks without forethought. "If you're able... If you want to," the usually articulate lawyer begins inarticulately, "my place in Oxford hasn't sold yet—you're welcome to head there and hang out, away from everything here."

"Oxford?"

A dawning hits Jenny, "It's a little town in Massachusetts."

He smiles. The women follow suit.

Esmé reaches across the table and tries the whole hand holding thing again. "Dale, you look really good." He gives a gentle squeeze and a shrug. She continues, "You look like the guy I knew a few short months ago—a guy who I miss having in my life. You should stop by and see Marin. She looks good. Seeing that for yourself might help."

He ignores Esmé's suggestion, removes his hand and addresses Jenny. "Thanks for the Oxford offer. I'll think about it."

When the women are nearly to the door he calls out, "I don't remember much, Esmé, but I know I miss her."

WPD

Vernon Banks steps to his office door when Donna Abbott blows into the squad room with a couple dozen donuts and an enthusiastic story about seeing Dale Jacobs at the Boardwalk. He gives her time to gush to the cops then waves her to him, "He looks good?"

"He really does. He was sitting so I'm not sure if he's still limping about, though I did notice a cane, so there's still some issue with his leg, but he looks really good, Chief."

Banks glances at a paper in his hand, then back at his dispatcher, "How's his memory?"

"Not sure how to gauge that, but he remembered me outright, and he knew Esmé Baxter and Jenny Stuart well enough to sit and chat for a bit."

"Good to know, Donna. Really good," he nods.

She leaves, and the chief gets back to work. He places a call and leaves his umpteenth message, "Mr. Kingston, this is Chief Vernon Banks calling with a reminder that the inquest into the criminal matters of Edward Kingston IV will begin on Monday, November 6th, at 6 PM, at Whisper Island Town Hall. Your attendance is requested by the Council. I suggest you give me a call prior to the meeting. Thank you."

He returns to the matter at hand, more precisely, he returns to reviewing the paper he holds in his hand, "There's isn't enough evidence to link Edward Kingston IV aka Heir Kingston to Christie Anderson, not yet, anyway. There's substantially more evidence to tie him to Laire MacTavish. And as for the killing of Danielle Rayburn and death of Joseph Baxter, there's a lot more digging that needs to be done." He tosses the handwritten To-Do list onto his desk and grouses, "My lead detective retired from the force, my rookie detective is fucked up and out IOD, the inquest is around the corner, and I'd better get on this shit."

Echo
Edward Kingston III, better known as, The King of Whisper Island, is sitting in early morning light near the dock of Echo, the Kingston family estate on the far westerly end of the three-mile-long, two-mile-wide island in Casco Bay. The

sixty-year-old man swirls his Glenlivet on rocks, takes a long pull, then takes a long drag from his cigarette and flicks the remaining nub into the ocean. He grabs hold of his chirping cell phone from the side table, listens to the voicemail, and scoffs at the chief's message. "I don't give one goddamn about the inquest, or the criminal charges being considered against my son, or the Council's request that I appear." He takes a pull of booze, lights another menthol, and continues his rant to no one. "Edward Kingston III cares about one thing—payback. And when I deliver it, you can damn well believe it's going to be a fuckin bitch."

Primrose Priscilla

Tom Martin, recently retired detective from the Whisper Police Department, is sitting on a big-ass recliner in a room that used to be his den, his special place in the yellow bungalow he once shared with his wife, Priscilla, better known to him as, Miss Prissy. The den was recently converted to a downstairs bedroom for Priscilla, a beautiful Mary Tyler Moore clone who captured Tom's heart and never let it go, until her death, that is. When Priscilla was diagnosed with a rare blood disorder, Tom relocated his wife to the first floor of their adorable abode with fieldstone walkways, yellow primrose bushes, and hearty crabgrass lawn. Leaving their marital bed was a change the husband *needed* to make;

sticking close to home while Miss Prissy adjusted to her new life was a change the devoted man *wanted* to make. As things would have it, those changes came with a loss and at a price.

In the early evening hours of July 21st, Thomas Martin found his sixty-two-year-old wife unresponsive in their four-poster, mahogany bed having suffered a stroke. At 12:12 AM on July 22nd, Priscilla Louise Martin died, having never regained consciousness. The man who spent nearly four decades loving Priscilla is grateful he spent the last hours of her time on Earth holding her hand, reminding her of their most treasured days together – all of them – and singing the chorus of her favorite song, *Let It Be Me*, the one they danced to as a newly married couple. The husband was where he wanted to be and should have been on *that* night, but the recently retired detective knows he should have been elsewhere. For months, he's been carrying the burden of not responding to several emergency voicemails from Esmé Baxter, the first of which expressed some concern that she hadn't heard from her daughter, Marin, or from Dale, the man who was charged with protecting her. The last of her eight calls was a desperate plea from a mother barely holding on…

"Tom, it's Esmé, again … it's a little after midnight … Marin and Dale still haven't returned to the bungalow from a walk on Stony … they haven't answered any calls or texts for hours … June and Jenny stumbled along the shoreline … but it's high tide now … so they're back at Wind. We've checked The Spot … and Watch … and The Promise … and even Jacobs Jolly … and nothing. Please call. Tom, please call."

He shakes those torturous thoughts free, grabs hold of one of Priscilla's journals and begins reading the poetic prose of a woman who woke each day with an ache to be a mother and retired each night in the arms of the man who couldn't make that happen. The easily distracted man barely makes it through a page or two when memories and regrets of July 21st begin anew…

Tom Martin raced toward Cliff Road shortly before 1 AM, bounded onto the porch, and pushed into the house.

"I'm sorry I missed your calls, Priscilla—never mind, tell me about your last communication with them."

"They texted late afternoon saying they were headed to Stony to spend some of Marin's last day cliff side on the beach. They were going to text us their food order and we were going to eat at Wind. We never heard from them."

Tom got back into his truck and raced to the public access ladder. He followed a flashlight beam to the cliff's edge, the crash of waves drowning his shouts. He tried to discern shapes on the hauntingly black beach, followed the moving water as it crashed then receded below. He strained to find something in the dark of night. A sliver of moon offered no help, shone no light on what happened on Stony Beach or elsewhere on Whisper. He looked skyward, begged for her help, "Please, shine bright. I need to find Marin."

FLASHES OF LIGHTNING BLAZED THE SKY

AGAIN AND AGAIN AND AGAIN SHINING UPON HER, AND HIM, AND HIM

The Promise

Esmé and Jenny never expected Marin to be in earshot when they got back from the donut run, but she was, and she had a rather explosive outburst to what she heard. "Oxford? You told Dale he could crash at your place in Oxford? My Oxford? Shit, Jenny, why don't you let ME go home?"

Esmé starts to answer. Marin cuts her off.

"I didn't ask you. I asked Jenny. God, Mom, you need to stop with the butting in and pussy-footing around. I'm a big girl now." The words do a ricochet sucker-punch when an awareness pushes in, "Oh. My. God. I'm eighteen. I turned eighteen! And I missed it!" She holds up her fingers and silently counts, *July, August, September, October.* "Last month?

A month ago? I missed my eighteenth birthday! Well Happy Fucking Birthday, Marin. The universe gave you a fucked up brain as your gift."

Esmé ignores the outburst and concentrates on the words. "Yesss, Marin, you missed it. We haven't celebrated, but we will. Until then, I have a gift for you. It's in my gallery. Do you want to see it?"

The very pissed eighteen-year-old wants to go back to her cottage, but somewhere in her addled brain she knows it's important to her mother that she look at whatever it is, "Sure," she groans.

Esmé leads the way, swings open French doors, takes hold of her daughter's hand and ushers her in. She wraps her arm around Marin's shoulder and points, "There."

"What?"

"*Moonlight Over Midnight Ocean*. I matted and framed your collection."

"My collection?"

"Yesss. You drew those pictures." She pauses, "You don't remember them?"

"No. I'm sorry. I don't." She hears the disappointment at the end of her mother's sigh, feels the emotional and physical separation between them become greater. "You did a very nice job framing them. Thank you." Marin turns and leaves. Before she's back at Sand Castle, something loosens in her brain. "Do I remember those drawings?" She cautions herself with words from the rehab whitecoats, "Don't try to grab hold of a memory-thread, just let it dangle and unravel itself, then follow it if you can." A flash of memory twists the loosening thread, she follows it to a lovely bramble on a cliff overlooking an ocean, "I used to sit there and draw." A shiver runs her spine. She looks around for something, someone—she finds she's still alone. A cold wind pushes off the water and grips her, unleashing a good, long heebie-jeebie. "It's getting colder by the day. My mother is going to make me move inside the main house at the end of October." She shakes her head, "How do I know that?" A memory lifts...

"Marin you need to weigh in on which room you want at The Promise. The wives are taking the master suite and I'm taking the bedroom suite right off of the studio, so that leaves two upstairs bedrooms facing the bay, one has a balcony off a set of French doors, the other has access to the widow's walk and a fireplace."

"I want Sand Castle."

"Huh. I never thought about the cottage." Adult eyes started finding one another. There were a few nods, a shrug or two of shoulders, a smile or two, or three, then a silent consensus, "Sas, but only through the end of October. After that you need to move into warmer digs. So choose your winter residence."

"The room with the balcony. My telescope will fit and I'll be able to hop out of bed to look at the moon instead of using my preferred mode of exit, climbing out a window."

"I used to sketch the moon? I used to climb out windows? Bet there's a story there."

Day Two
Friday, October 27
First Quarter – Illumination 48%

Marin wakes early and makes her way to the end of the dock, plops her ass onto a plank and dangles her feet over the end. She turns her head toward the public beach and stares at a particular square of sand. Her mind releases a memory-reel of a young man, wet and breathing hard from a vigorous swim…

The flaxen-haired, physically fit guy swam from the public beach to The Promise several times before seeing Marin sitting on the dock. He headed in her direction, "What are you doing here, alone?"

"I remembered something, then thought about something, and the women said I should tell you."

"Should I come out, or is it something quick?"

"Out. Nothing about me is ever quick, Dale."

"Right." He put his hands onto the dock and pushed himself up bringing a good amount of ocean water with. She got a good splashing and a good eye of his physique. If he noticed her reddening cheeks, he didn't let on. He sat next to her on the edge and nudged, "Okay, spill."

"I was thinking about the Celtic Five Fold and the star symbol."

The memory ends. The young woman looks out at sparkling ocean waters, "Maybe another memory will roll in with the waves." She sighs when a new puzzle piece fills her headspace...

"Ancient Greeks believed everything was made up of earth, water, air, and fire—except Aristotle who believed there was a fifth element, ether, because it seemed strange to him that stars would be made out of earthly elements. He was wrong of course."

Dale laughed big, "Aristotle was wrong? How?"

"Stars are made up of many elements found on earth, and they burn with the heat of fire, all the time, so that is their element," **she realized she'd veered off track, so she pulled herself back on.** "Bottom line, every visible thing in the universe is made up of some combination of earth, water, air, and fire. Hippocrates went on to theorize that the four elements describe the four basic temperaments of human beings, you know, if someone is grounded they are like the earth, if someone goes with the flow they are like water, if someone is untethered or flighty they are like air, and if someone is intense and quick to burn with emotion they are like fire. He believed that a bit of all temperaments are needed for a person to be in balance, to be mentally and physically well."

She loses the thread, drops her face onto her bent knees and analyzes what she's remembered so far, "Aristotle. Hippocrates. God, I'm a dork. Was I always a dork?" The next part of her memory sneaks in…

"The four elements are prevalent in Shaky Town. He might be from there, or they might have met there."

"Who is he? Who are they?" Marin groans and buries her face.

June interrupts the newest round of 'Hey, there's a memory-thread you may want to pull – but just let it dangle'. She nudges Marin with her knee, "So, who is he? Who are they?"

"What?"

"You said, 'he might be from there, or they might have met there'. Who were you talking about?"

"Seriously, LL?" she rolls her eyes.

June nudges. "Right, you don't know shit." She nudges again, "I'm going for a walk."

"Thanks for the update."

"Do you want to come?"

"How far are you trekking?"

"To the ferry dock and back."

"The Abenaki."

June nudges, "You remember the Abenaki?"

"Nope, I heard a docking announcement on the way home from rehab the other day."

"Still, you remembered the ferry's name without using one of your alphabet labels."

She smiles, "I guess I did, LL."

June offers a hand up, then wraps her arm around one of her most favorite people in the world, "Come on AH."

"Oh no, you've given me a nickname and then converted it to a label."

"Uh huh."

"What's AH stand for?"

"Ass Hat."

"Great."

Primrose Priscilla

Tom grabs hold of the recliner handle and pulls. The bang of the footrest closing is loud enough to be heard from outside.

"Good, he's home."

The words have barely found air when he opens the front door, "Miss Carmichael."

"Detective Martin."

"Retired."

"Yes, but I think you have a little work still to do on a case of yours."

"Retired."

"I know the timing is terrible, but—"

"Retired," he slams the door in her face, then heads back to Priscilla's room.

Roxanne plops her ass on the front stoop, takes a notebook from her messenger bag, and reads the notes she took during her visit with Lachlan MacTavish at the prison in Portland the day before. She is still perched upon the detective's front porch when he comes around the side of his house and gets into his F-150 for his daily trip to Hillcrest Cemetery. He rolls his eyes when he sees the perched reporter, gets out of his truck, leans against the bumper, and waves the plucky young woman his way, "Miss Carmichael—"

"Roxanne."

"Roxanne. I know what you want—"

"You need to—"

"No. You need to tell Lan to wait it out. The inquest begins on November 6th. It shouldn't take much time for posthumous charges to be filed and guilty findings rendered against Edward Kingston IV."

"Detective Martin, with due respect, Lan MacTavish needs to be released from prison. He needs to mourn the loss of his sister. He needs to feel the sun on his face and to breathe fresh air known to free men." She gives him a chance to respond. "Given recent events in your life, you know the importance of walking through the steps of grief, the need to ache while sitting at a gravesite, the comfort of attending a prayer service, the unburdening of talking to a friend. Lan needs all of those things, and you need to finish what you started. You need to make sure the inquest leads to justice for the people Heir Kingston killed, but more importantly, you need to make sure the people in that inquest room don't fuck Lan MacTavish a second time. If you trust they won't, then sit your ass in this lovely little bungalow, otherwise, get your ass to Town Hall on November 6th." She makes a move to leave, but he steps into her path.

"I'm going to visit Priscilla. You're going to get some grub from the Beach Bum and meet me back here. Then you're going to remind me about this case. For months, my heart has been running the show, so you're going to have to get my head back in the game."

Roxanne touches his hand, "I heard Mrs. Martin was a beautiful soul."

"You heard right."

Beach Bum

Roxanne breezes into the bohemian bistro and heads to the Order Counter. "Two grilled veggie pockets, one with cheese and into that one, tuck some sort of cooked creature."

"How about some chicken?"

"I'd really rather not know." She takes a casual look around and sees Ruby Norman huddled in a back booth, deep in conversation. "Huh, I thought she lived on the mainland now. Maybe she's back for the inquest?"

The surfer dude behind the counter interrupts, "You talkin to me?"

"Nope, to myself."

"My babe does that. Must be a woman thing."

She laughs, "Careful with the gender labels, cause ya never know."

"Whoa. Right." He eyes her for good measure. "There's a whole lot of alphabet labeling these days, but I'm thinking you're a good-ole double X chromosome." He cuts the Syrian pockets, wraps them in parchment, shoves them into brown bags and hands them off. "Peace."

Jacobs Jolly

Dale is on the veranda when his boss walks around the side of the house. "Is this a social call, Chief?"

"Some, but we need to talk about Edward Kingston IV."

"That's the young one, right?"

"And the dead one," the chief adds.

"Right. I heard some shit about the dead part, but so far, I haven't heard how he got that way."

"His death is still a mystery."

Silence. Lots and lots of silence.

"So Dale, would I be wasting my time having a sit down with you? I've got some questions."

"About?"

"An investigation you and Tom Martin worked on."

"Why don't you ask Tom?"

"He's grieving Priscilla."

"Yeah. That sucks. Still, his head is screwed on better than mine right now. And if that's not the case, if he can't give you information, why don't you just read the damned police files?"

"The investigation you two did wasn't for WPD."

"No?"

"No. It was a rogue investigation."

"See. I don't remember a thing about any rogue investigation. You feel like telling me who we were looking into?"

Silence. Lots and lots of silence.

Dale breaks the silence. "Are we about done here, Chief Banks, cause I need to piss and I need enough time to get there." He taps the handle of his cane.

"Connie said you're getting better."

"Connie would know since she's here 24/7."

The Promise

Marin has been in her mother's gallery since she returned from her walk with June. She's popping a squat on a footstool set in front of her framed collection of drawings. From time to time she reads the labels then scoffs a bit, "Waxing and waning this—full and new that—gibbous and crescent." She gives the memory that's trying to break free all the room it needs…

Marin was on the widow's walk staring at the tiny sliver of moon. She startled at the voice from behind.

"The sky and ocean are so dark."

"Because the moon is at 10% illumination. **I know most people love the full and waxing gibbous phases,** but I'm all about the crescent phase. The thinner the better."

She stepped away from the scope and moved to a lawn chair. He joined her there a few minutes later. "I need to talk to you about something, Marin."

She noticed the gun and gun belt for the first time. "What's wrong?"

Esmé touches her daughter's shoulder, sending her nearly through the ceiling.

"What. The. Fuck? Jesus, Mom, you scared the crap out of me!"

"I'm sorry, really I am. I didn't mean to scare you," she begins crying and tries to explain through her sobs, "I heard you say the word *gun*."

"I did?"

"Yesss. I didn't know why. I thought you might be remembering things. I didn't want you to be alone when," the concerned mom leaves that one hanging.

"When what?"

"Nothing."

"When what?"

"I'm not supposed to help with your memory recall. And I wasn't going to, it's just that you seemed so far away."

Marin walks to a bank of windows overlooking the bay, "I had a memory of Dale and me on the widow's walk, but not the one here."

"No, not here."

"Then it must have been at Wind Ledge."

"Yesss."

"We were talking about the moon. I was telling him that I like the crescent phase the best."

"You always loved the sliver."

Marin hesitates before telling about a previous upsetting memory. "I saw the image of a girl rise on a wave. I think her name is Laire."

Esmé reaches out to touch her daughter, but pulls her hand back when Marin shrugs her shoulder away.

"I know what I saw."

"Mija, it was probably an oddity of the ocean."

Marin shakes her head.

Esmé tries again. "Maybe part of what you're remembering happened and parts are hallucinations from your time in the hospital. You were heavily sedated."

Marin shakes her head. "No, it was real." She looks at the bay again and asks a pretty big question. "Did someone put Laire in Casco Bay?"

Silence.

"Mom, help, please."

"I can't tell you that, mija."

"But you know."

"Yesss."

A memory from her time in rehab pushes through…

Her mother rushed into the room, "I heard you've been upset all day." She ran her hand across Marin's head, barely received an awareness of her presence. She pulled a chair close and took hold of her daughter's hands. She examined her eyes, rubbed her fingertips, "Your hands are freezing." She leaned forward and wiped a tear, then two. "Can you tell me what's upsetting you?"

"Laire. She's dead."

Esmé leaned forward and gently squeezed Marin's hand, "Yesss."

"Who's Laire?"

"A girl from the island."

"And she's dead."

"Shhhh. No one knows that."

Marin dipped her head to one side, "I know that?"

Esmé nodded.

"And you know that?"

Esmé nodded and looked around for eavesdroppers.

"I don't understand."

Esmé put her finger to her lips, "I'll be right back." When she returned, she had a pillow and blanket, "I'm camping out with you tonight."

"Why?"

"Because you were upset earlier and I thought it'd be good for you if we could talk—if things surface."

Marin let the weeds tumble about in her head, "Because you don't want me talking about Laire with anyone else."

"Yesss. It's best that you not mention her."

"Ever?"

"Not until you're home."

"I started remembering things about Laire when I was in rehab."

Esmé nods.

"And you didn't want me talking about it then."

Another nod.

"You said we could talk about her when I got home. I'm home and you still won't tell me what happened."

Nothing.

Marin leaves without further word.

Primrose Priscilla

Roxanne follows a fieldstone path around the back of Tom's place. She finds him sitting at a round, wrought iron table beneath a bright yellow sun umbrella. She hands off a brown bag and tosses hers onto the table, "I'll go get drinks from inside."

"Help yourself, Roxanne," he chuckles.

"I will. By the way, you'll never guess who I saw at the Beach Bum."

"Who?"

"Guess."

"You said I'd never guess."

"Try! But you'll never guess." The screen door slams, then opens again, then slams again. "Did you guess?"

"Ruby Norman."

"No. You. Did. Not. just guess that." She puts a pitcher of lemonade and two ice-filled glasses onto the table. "You need to come clean. Who told you?"

"No one. I strung your clues."

"I didn't give you clues."

"You went to the Beach Bum, so you were in Shaky. Whoever you saw was a big deal. You had the whole, 'I just saw a celebrity' thing going on. The inquest is coming up. There's no way Ruby Norman, the former live-in sex toy of Edward Kingston III, isn't going to be questioned about the comings and goings at Echo —— and tell me what's in this sandwich?"

She shrugs, "A bunch of grilled veggies, some American Cheese, and some sort of creature, I think the dude said it was chicken."

"You're a vegetarian?"

"Vegan."

"No wonder you're skinny."

"I'm not skinny."

He laughs.

"What?"

"There was a time when a woman would have killed to be thought of as skinny."

"Yeah, when?"

"Does the name Mary Tyler Moore mean anything to you?"

"She can turn the world on with her smile," she sings.

He chuckles. "She sure could. Anyway, Ms. Tyler Moore was skinny and women wanted to look like her."

"MTM was thin and toned. I think she was a dancer. I don't think she was a vegan."

"Probably not, but you're missing the point."

"What's the point."

"Damned if I remember."

"I think you were suggesting that consuming plant-based foods leads to a skinny physique."

"Yeah, that's my point."

"You're in shape, do you eat a plant-based diet?"

"Hell, no."

"That's point number one, now for point number two. You ever see a cow, Detective? Cause I'm pretty sure they are girthy beasts that eat a plant-based diet." She surveys the crabgrass lawn around her, "Bet you could grow a herd of skinny-ass cows here."

They clink a glass, bust a gut, and finish their sandwiches in silence.

As soon as the last bite is swallowed, they fill their glasses and move to the chaise loungers, Roxanne notices there are only two, "I don't have to sit on—"

"As much as I'd like to be sitting here with Miss Prissy, I'm enjoying your company,

Roxanne, so go ahead and sit and tell me about your concerns."

"I'm going to bottom line this. The inquest board isn't taking the cases in order; first up is the murder of Danielle Rayburn. As you'll recall, that happened after Christie Anderson's disappearance and murder, and Laire MacTavish's disappearance." She gives her head a good shake, "I can't believe Laire's murder and disposal is still a secret."

"The people on our team who know the circumstances of Laire's death either can't remember she's dead or have very good motivations for keeping her death secret."

"There has to be others who know she's dead," Roxanne pushes in.

He nods. "And they have better incentives for secrecy than we do. The whole island of Whisper would know by now if Marin and Dale hadn't gone to Stony Beach that night." He quiets a minute, "I suspect Laire's death will come to light pretty quick now."

She scoffs.

"What?"

"If the news comes from your hodge-podge team, Detective, I'm not sure people are going to give much credence to the breaking news."

Silence.

"Word around town is that Officer Jacobs is having a lot of trouble with memory and won't be questioned at the inquest about any cases he worked on. Marin Baxter saw what happened on

Casco Bay the night Laire MacTavish went missing, but no one knows that. If Laire's death and dumping comes to light, the star witness is suffering greatly from her near-death experience and isn't going to be any help whatsoever."

Tom takes a sip, a good run of condensation spills from his glass and finds his lap. He wipes the droplets free, "Damn shame about that girl. One of the smartest people I've ever known. And Dale, he had a real ability at pulling threads and pushing an investigation along."

"I heard Dale was seen in town at the Boardwalk, so things might be moving in a good direction for him."

"Good to know. Continue with your bottom line, Roxanne."

"The explanation floating for the order of things is that the Council doesn't want to be accused of leaving a man languishing behind bars by doing a 'first things first' presentation against Edward Kingston IV. What it really means is there won't be a chronological thread for the 'powers that be' and the 'public at large' to pull and follow. On top of all that, they won't hear a full accounting about the night Christie Anderson went missing because Fred Fuller, the former owner of Diggers, the guy who might have seen Heir with Christie, is missing."

"For how long?"

"Weeks, maybe more."

"He's dead."

"Probably. I'm not finished bottom lining."

"Continue."

"Again, since the Council isn't starting from the beginning, and they're jumping directly to Danielle's murder, they aren't going to hear the shit about Laire MacTavish, either. Like how the underage teen might have met Heir Kingston at an employees' gathering at Echo, or that there's evidence the teenager entered into a relationship with someone shortly before she went missing, or that she purchased birth control pills, or that she received a very expensive pair of earrings most likely belonging to the late Kathleen Kingston. Basically, the Council isn't going to have anything that suggests Edward and Laire were involved with one another. And even if that salient information is entered as fact, Marin Baxter isn't in any condition to testify about the man in the boat and the body in the bay." It's Roxanne's turn to take a sip and get a drip. "Marin's home from rehab, you know."

"Didn't know, but that's really good to hear."

"She's not the same."

"Wouldn't expect she would be, but then again, who is?"

"Lan MacTavish sure the hell isn't. He's starting to unravel. He really needs a visit from you, Detective. I'll go with if you want, but he needs to be talked off the ledge. He knows about the slated order of the inquest, and he knows that without a straight line leading from Edward Kington IV to Christie to Laire to Danielle, the evidence and testimony against him stays the same. If the Council starts pulling threads at the Danielle Rayburn strangulation without first connecting Heir to two underage girls, Lan still looks good for Danielle's murder. I'm telling you right now, come the day after the inquest, Lan MacTavish, an innocent man, will stay in prison to serve out his 25 year sentence."

"Sure wish I could bang all of this around with Dale."

"You should try."

Tom drains his glass, "Do me a favor, Roxanne, take this stuff into the house. There's a key under the mat, lock up when you leave. I need to head out."

Roxanne smiles wide. "Welcome back, Detective."

Jacobs Jolly

Connie gives Tom a hug then sends him around back, "He's surly, Tom."

"Then he'll be in good company." He grabs a stone from the gravel drive and tosses it toward the resting guy. "Wake up, Sleeping Beauty, we've got work to do."

"Shit, what is it with the ghosts of Whisper PD haunting my ass."

"The chief came by?"

"And I ran into Donna at the donut shop."

Tom laughs, "They were the warmup act for me. Sit up and listen up. Roxanne Carmichael just spent the last couple hours laying out a compelling case as to how and why certain elements are conspiring to keep Lan MacTavish in prison for Danielle Rayburn's murder."

"Is that shit supposed to mean something?"

"It doesn't?"

"Shit, Tom, the names fit in my headspace, but it's probably because I've been hearing non-stop crap on T.V. about the inquest. I'm not sure if what I hear is something I knew, or remember, or some hellish combination of the two."

Tom thinks. Dale closes his eyes. Tom taps the young man's foot, "Oh. No. You. Don't. I need you on this case. Look, maybe you don't remember everything or even much of anything, but I'd be willing to bet your instincts are still intact. I can fill in the holes with information and we can process the case. It's worth a shot, right?"

The reclining man shrugs a shoulder and closes his eyes. Before Tom gets to the corner of the house Dale calls out, "You never asked why Banks was here."

Tom returns, "Yeah, well, I'm a little off my game, too."

"I'm real sorry about Mrs. Martin. I know it must be a tough one for you, Tom."

"Yeah. Miss Prissy was special, and she liked you, Dale."

"Sure appreciate knowing that." Dale pushes up on the Adirondack, "The Chief said he had some questions about an investigation you and I worked on. I asked why he wasn't asking you the questions, and he said you were grieving. I suggested he give you a shot since my head wasn't exactly screwed on right. Then I asked him why he didn't just look at the WPD files. He said it wasn't a WPD investigation, it was a rogue one that you and I did. I asked who the subject of our investigation was. He left without comment."

"Shit. If you can remember all that then there's nothing wrong with recent memory recall. So this is how things will work. I'll tell you the old stuff and then we'll move on to new parts of our investigation and get Lan MacTavish out of prison."

"This MacTavish guy, are he and I friends?"

Tom laughs, "Friends don't put friends in jail."

"I helped convict him?"

"Yeah, but you had lots of help."

"Well, fuck, then. I guess I owe him."

"So you're in?"

"For what I'm worth, I'm in."

Tom leaves.

A memory pushes…

The young, fair-haired man in uniform gave his head a shake, "No, Mr. MacTavish. Dispatch should have mentioned that we can't start a formal search for your sister until 24 hours of notification, but ...." the officer paused way too long for Lan's liking.

"But, what?"

"We had a teen go missing two years ago, so we want to get ahead of this."

"This?"

"May I come in, Mr. MacTavish?"

"Lan. My name is Lan."

"Dale Jacobs, I'm an officer and rookie detective with Whisper PD. I'm stepping out of order by coming here, but I'm concerned about a possible connection between the missing teens."

"Missing teens." The words hit Lan like a sucker punch. He doubled over and tried really hard to squelch his emotions. He failed. Miserably.

Day Three
Saturday, October 28
Waxing Gibbous – Illumination 57%

Chief Vernon Banks doesn't bother knocking on the front door, he just heads to the backyard, the one with better greens than most pro golf courses on the Eastern Seaboard. He's surprised to find King's preferred seat, a high back, cushioned rattan chaise, vacant. He turns when King talks from behind.

"Get off my property." The owner of the estate is sitting at a patio set on a shaded veranda having his morning belt and butt. "I said, get out."

"This will only take a minute."

"What do you want, Vernon?"

"We need to talk about the inquest."

"I'm not interested in the Kangaroo Court's attempt to frame my son for a few dead bitches, so get off my property."

"Give me five minutes. There are things you don't know."

"You said your piece months ago, Chief Banks," he laughs and slurs a bit. "If memory serves, you told me then how things were going to go down. If you forgot your threats, let me remind you. You have all you need to put my ass in jail for the rest of my miserable life, and you've made damned sure none of my shit will blow back onto you." King pulls a gulp and takes a puff. "That's the gist of it, although I omitted the part where you said it would be better for us if Heir was dead."

"King. You need to listen."

"You need to leave. And be forewarned, Vernon, the next time you pull a loaded weapon on me, I'll blow your fucking head off." King lifts his hand from under the table and points a gun at the chest of the chief of Whisper PD.

"Is that new, King?"

"Yup."

"Is it loaded?"

"Yup."

"Is that supposed to scare me?"

"It's supposed to send a message."

"What's the message, King?"

"Get the fuck off of my property, and if you come back, Vern, you'd better be wearing Kevlar."

The chief walks away, glancing upward when he sees gossamer silk sheers flap in the breeze at open balcony doors. He waits several seconds—time enough for him to see Ruby step outside. "For fucks sake, why the hell is she back in King's bed?"

Ruby places her hand onto a tiny baby bump and shrugs.

The chief shakes his head and storms away.

The Promise

Marin insists on going for a walk by herself, "I'll only go to the public beach and back." June offers to do lookout from the dock – Marin readily accepts the offer. "I think my first go of this should be monitored. Make sure to get me off the beach before high tide," she scoffs.

"Got your back, Marin. Head off."

When she gets to the beach, she walks the shore a bit then plops her duff onto Dale's spot. She gets totally captured by the glint of ocean and almost misses a memory, a continuation of one she'd recently had, or dreamed she had, or wished she had...

Dale sat next to her on the edge of the dock listening about the Celtic Five Fold, and Aristotle, and Hippocrates, and through it all, she thought about him. She liked him, in *that* way. She wanted to reach out and run her fingers through his wet hair – wondered whether he thought of her in *that* way or in any way at all. She wanted to frolic in the ocean, in his arms, the water hiding her inhibitions, his desire.

"There wasn't any frolicking, just fantasizing." She bends her legs, wriggles her feet into soft sand, wraps her arms around her knees, and hopes for some more memory-threads, or lusty dreams and wishes. She turns her attention to the Abenaki that's moving closer and closer to the Whisper shore. "The ferry comes from Portland. So this is the sandy side of the island, the other side is the cliff side. Was I told that, or did I remember on my own?" She sits quietly watching the bright blue boat cut through the water. "I must have taken that ferry from the mainland." She startles when a voice comes from behind—knows instantly the voice is *his*.

"Unless you swam over."

She shades her eyes with her hand and looks up.

"I didn't mean to scare you. I just wanted to say hi."

"Dale," the word catches with emotion.

"You look good, Marin."

"Yeah. Good. You look good, too." She notices the cane. "You hurt your leg."

He laughs big, "Yeah, and a whole lot of other shit." He notices some sort of wrist thing. "You hurt your wrist."

She laughs big. "Yeah, and whole lot of other shit, mainly my head, but I don't need to wear the protective helmet anymore. I sort of miss it."

He laughs, then stops short. "Shit, Marin. I'm really sorry."

"For what?"

He cautions himself. He knows she needs to remember things on her own. He changes subject, "When I got here, you were talking about taking the ferry."

"Yeah. The Abenaki. I know I'm originally from Oxford, that's on the mainland in

Massachusetts somewhere, so I had to have taken the ferry to get here."

"Yeah."

"And you, are you from here?"

He pauses.

"You can answer simple questions, Dale. It's the big stuff, like what we were doing on Stony Beach that day, that's the stuff I'm supposed to figure out for myself." A memory bangs the fuck in…

Marin began to stir at raindrops hitting her face, then shot to her feet at the sound of a gun. She looked for Dale, panicked when his spot on the sand was empty. She reached into her pocket for her cell, slapped at each one, remembered leaving it at the bungalow. She looked up and down the abandoned beach for him, for anyone, then turned eyes to the ocean, fearing he went for a swim and maybe … panic pushed hard and she wondered if she really heard a gun being fired. She started for Wind, then stopped hard, "No, Dale is my protection. He wouldn't have left me." She turned around and moved toward the bend, saw him lying on the wet packed sand far from where she stood. **"Dale!"** She ran to him, screaming when she saw blood seeping from his back. **"Shot!"**

The memory-thread breaks. She's staring at her hands as though she'll find blood—his blood. "You were shot."

He nods.

"That day. On Stony Beach."

He nods.

"Who shot you?"

Silence.

"Dale! Tell me! Who shot you?"

"I can't tell you."

"Because I need to remember on my own?"

"No, Marin. Because I don't remember." Dale sees movement beyond the young woman who is breathing hard and spiraling down. He waves to June who'd been watching the interaction and who'd gotten to her feet when things became tense. She runs from the dock to the beach, sliding to a stop at a heaving Marin.

"What happened?"

"She started remembering what happened."

"That day? At Stony?"

"Yes."

"What did she remember?"

Marin answers the question, "Raindrops. Gunshot. Blood."

June pulls her close, then to her feet. "Come on, Marin. Let's go home."

"To Oxford?"

"Maybe." June turns to check on Dale, but he's already limping away and caught by his own memory...

They plopped onto the sand, huffing and puffing from their jog and playful shoulder-nudges and hip-chucks. He watched her breathing regulate and take on the soft in and out of approaching slumber. "She's beautiful."

And just like that a fragment of a different memory pushes. Maybe...

Dead eyes stare right through him.

Echo

King has been in his office since shortly after Vernon Banks left. His eyes haven't veered from the four things resting on the massive desk at which he sits. A loaded gun, two pregnancy sticks, each showing a bright blue plus sign, and a file folder with a hand-labeled sticker that reads, **Brother**. There are two things in King's hands—a beautiful crystal tumbler, full to the brim, and a near-empty bottle of Glenlivet. His mind is spinning a conversation he had with Lan MacTavish when the young Scotsman first started working at Kingston Marina...

"Read your file, MacTavish. You're from Speyside, Scotland."
"True, but no need to hold it against me."
"Your family business is in Glenlivet."
"Scotch whisky or sheep. A young man's workin path leads to one or the other."
King laughed, "So your path lead here."
"Did indeed."

"Tell me, Mr. MacTavish, if you were to brag about a particular Glenlivet for my personal stock, what would you mention?"

"I'd tell ya that Speyside-Scotland is the Glenlivet Master Distiller. It has a wealth of casks to choose, but I'd be suggestin the XXV for its nutty spiciness and subtle sherry tones. It's a silky elegant single malt."

King reads the label on the bottle he's holding, "The Glenlivet. Single Malt Scotch Whisky. Batch No. 04199G." He pulls a belt. "The Scot was right about this drink. Bought cases of the twenty-five-year-old shit so Heir and I could crack a seal and celebrate his twenty-fifth birthday." He pulls a lot and swallows it hard. "We had that celebration in early February. It's October and my son is dead." He pulls a long gulp, eyes the big-ass gun, takes a puff of his butt, then flicks the dying smoke out an open window.

He leans toward the desk and grabs hold of the pregnancy sticks. "This one has the DNA of Laire MacTavish and Edward Kingston IV. This one has the DNA of Ruby Norman and *someone* with the name Edward Kingston – could be the third or the fourth." He laughs hard. "The bastard inside that bitch could be the offspring of the King or the Heir. Fucking bitch thinks I don't know she rode my son. She sure the fuck doesn't know I told Edward to bed her and spread her. Now she's here under my roof because she's carrying a Kingston." He laughs again, pushes spittle across his chin with the back of his hand, takes the file folder from his desk and heads outside to his rattan.

Once seated, he opens the behemoth and removes a sheet of paper. He reads Heir's handwriting. "King – Connie Jacobs – Dale Jacobs – Brother." He closes the file, talks to Heir as though he's sitting next to him, "I found this shit in your office the night before your body washed ashore on Stony Beach. I'd just been put on notice that Chief Banks was going to bring you down, so I checked your office for things that might help his cause, things you wanted kept from prying eyes. I was going to destroy whatever I found." He laughs, then moans long and low. "That's before I found this fucking file, and the fucking piece of paper with Connie's and Dale's names and the accusatory word, *brother*. Like a bolt, I knew the conversation we had at Mulligans wasn't idle curiosity. You didn't want to know if I would have had other children, you wanted to know if I **had** other children."

King eyes the big-ass Brother file sitting there, taunting and haunting him. He abandons the conversation he's been having with his dead son and starts one with himself, though he's sick and tired of hearing his own voice, sick and tired of working through this mess. "Heir spent a long time researching and assembling information on Edward and Kathleen Kingston and Matthew and Constance Jacobs. The question is: why?" King taps the file with his finger, flips the cover open then shut, open then shut. "Heir got down and dirty on the state of my marriage, went deep on rumor and innuendo." He looks out at the sparking ocean and reflects a bit, "I wanted Miss Kathleen Beckwith of Kenilworth, Illinois, from the minute I saw her, and I did whatever it took to get her out of Vernon's bed and into mine. I should have waited for her monthly stain before bedding her. My impatience set the stage for the uncertainty about Edward's parentage." He gives his head a good shake before continuing. "I should have left things alone when I found out Kathleen was pregnant, but my hubris demanded answers to questions. And once I knew the truth, I assuaged my battered ego with booze and broads, until it nearly cost me my marriage." He does a mental review of the trail of women chronicled by Edward, "I bedded each and every one of those whores." He snarls at the glaring omission, "there's absolutely nothing in Edward's digging that put me in the bed of Connie Jacobs. Granted, I wouldn't have turned down the June Cleaver's cleavage if opportunity arose, but she wasn't the type to mess around. Or was she? And if she was, did we fuck?" He sits with those questions for many minutes then asks another, "Why was Connie Jacobs singled out for research? Edward didn't just wake up one day and start wondering who Dale Jacobs' father is and whether I could be the guilty party. He had to have heard the bullshit paternity line from someone and that someone is probably Dale Jacobs. Did they know one another? I never heard any mention of Dale from Edward, but someone made the link between me and Connie. Someone made the suggestion that Edward and Dale were brothers ……. Who?" King slogs through his booze-soaked brain. "I talked to someone about the Jacobs' kid recently ……. Who? Who?" The memory surfaces…

Detective Tom Martin was on a lean-to against a big-ass weeping willow on the perfectly manicured lawn at Echo. He had his eyes trained on the happenings at the shoreline, stopped his glare at the throat-clearing from behind. He looked over his shoulder, "Good to see you King," he lied, "though the circumstances—"

"Suck."

"I'd say so. Who found the bone?"

"Yours truly. I was heading to the dock to check on the tarp on Heir's boat." King slid a pack of cigarettes from his pocket, tapped the bottom several times, flipped the top, pulled a filtered menthol, and lit it.

Tom lived vicariously through the process, "Damn, that still smells good."

King laughed, "Nowadays, the only men who smoke are widowers. Be thankful you've still got Priscilla chasing your ass on this habit cause these are gonna kill me."

"Thankful for Miss Prissy every day, King."

The owner of the estate pulled a long drag and gave his head a tilt, "Have you been to the shore yet?"

"Nope."

"Has news hit the airwaves?"

"It hadn't when I got here."

"Did the chief call you?"

"Nope. I heard about it from Dale Jacobs."

There was a pause and a tilt of the head. "That's Matt Jacobs' kid?"

"Yeah."

"Last I heard the kid lived in Portland with his mother .... what's her name?"

"Connie."

"Right, Connie."

"Seems I knew some about the Jacobs woman. Seems someone else knew enough to wonder about Connie and me." King pushes into that for all it's worth, "Edward had to have heard the paternity line of bullshit from Dale—who else would know or care? Once that suggestion was floated, there was absolutely no way Edward wouldn't have investigated. I should have followed his lead, I should have investigated what I found in the Brother file before acting out. Instead, I bellied up with booze and went off the deep end. I let my anguish over the death of Edward push me to want to end it all on Stony. And when I got there, I put a bullet into the back of a young man—one who could be my biological son." He sits with that for quite some time, drains his glass, then tosses it across the lawn. He finds the smallest pleasure when it hits the stone wall and smashes to smithereens.

He clears his mind, lets himself get lost in the push and pull of waves and glint of sun off bright blue waters. He closes his eyes and when they fill with tears he admits, "I knew you were dead before you washed ashore, Edward." He sobs then moans, "She told me."

"Who told you?" Ruby asks from behind.

Primrose Priscilla

Dale knocks on the back door, gets no answer, so he takes a seat in the screened-in porch. That's where Tom finds him when he's back from a walk to Hillcrest Cemetery. "Hope you're comfortable, Dale."

"Comfortable enough."

"You're early."

"I wanted to talk to you about some things before the reporter gets here."

"Shoot."

"I don't want my personal shit on the news."

"Everything will be off the record. What else?"

"I saw Marin at the public beach earlier."

Silence. Lots of silence.

"She's so different, but man, she's the same, too."

"How's her memory?"

"Pretty fucked, but she's getting some stuff back. When I first got to her, she was thinking she must have ferried to Whisper on the Abenaki because she remembered she was from Oxford on the mainland. Then she asked me where I grew up. I didn't answer because I know we're supposed to work through our memory issues by ourselves. She pushed back and said I could answer a simple question like that, but I shouldn't tell her the big stuff like what happened on Stony. Within a second of her saying that, she got quiet. I could tell she was working through a memory. When she wound down some, it was clear what the memory was about. She got agitated and was looking at her hands for blood. I could tell she was still digging deep for a thread to pull, so I waved to June who was watching from the dock at The Promise. By the time she got to us, Marin remembered I'd been shot. She became really upset that I wouldn't tell her who shot me. I explained I couldn't tell her because I can't remember who put a bullet in my back. By the time she left, she was repeating three words over and over."

"What three words?"

"Raindrops. Gunshot. Blood. She was really upset, Tom. Ever since this morning, I've been thinking how messed up she's gonna be when she remembers she was almost drowned by a dead guy."

Roxanne Carmichael rounds the corner and is greeted by sudden silence. "Can't tell you how often people stop talking when I arrive."

"About that, Roxanne, you need to give some assurances to Dale and me that everything, every word, every look, every sigh is off the record."

"Done. I'm not here for a story, I'm here to get Lan MacTavish out of prison."

"Is he a friend of yours?"

"Yes, is he a friend of yours, Mr. Jacobs?"

"The name's Dale, and based on some fragmented shit in my head, I'm wondering the same thing. I think we might have been friends, then maybe not."

Tom pushes in, "You and Lan and I were working Laire MacTavish's disappearance and spent a lot of time together. When WPD set their sights on Lan for Danielle Rayburn's murder, your job put you and Lan at odds. When Lan was put in prison, you and I started reworking the case. I'm not sure you remember this, but a week or so before the Stony Beach crap, you went to see Lan in jail, that might explain your confusion about where the two of you stand."

Dale shakes his head, "Not sure you should have filled in that many holes, Tom. Though now that you have, I'm understanding things better."

"Don't want to overstep with information, Dale, so maybe you should tell us how we should work your memory issues?"

"My traumatic brain injury was scaled as mild to moderate. By the time I left rehab, I'd remembered some things about how Marin and I spent the early part of that day on Stony, but most of what I know about Heir Kingston and his murderous life I learned from listening to Ms. Carmichael's never-ending reports."

She smiles, "It's big news, Dale. It's not every day the Heir to a kingdom is an alleged serial killer."

Tom raises a finger to his mouth and Roxanne silences when Dale takes on a distant look…

"Straight up, Dale, WPD made a mistake on the Rayburn case, or worse. Lan MacTavish did not kill that young woman."

"I know you think that, Tom."

"How about you? Do you think he was a good arrest and prosecution?"

"Arrest. Maybe. He put himself in the shack with her that night, but everything about their relationship seemed real friendly, caring, maybe even loving. I definitely don't think their relationship was on again, off again like the press said." **He thought a minute or so,** "I think there was enough of a connection between them that it could have tied up a juror or two and kept him from being convicted. Bottom line, I think Lan's problem was Christie's bone washing ashore right after he was arrested for Danielle's murder. The heat on WPD to make an arrest was intense, and there was just enough rumor-shit for the press to use against Lan. I think that's what moved things in his direction."

"Yeah."

"But."

"But, what?"

"But I hate to think an innocent man is in prison and the real killer is roaming free."

"Yeah." **Tom mulled a bit then asked,** "Are you on duty today?"

"Nope. I just started a two-week vacation. Why?"

"I could use some help finding the person who killed Christie, Danielle, and Laire."

"What the fuck!? Laire MacTavish is dead? You know that? How the fuck do you know that?"

"I'll tell you—if you join my investigation." **The detective read the young officer's face,** "This is the deal. You give me two weeks to prove Lan isn't guilty of shit. Maybe we hit paydirt and find a suspect, maybe we don't. At the end of two weeks, I'll let you take whatever we find to the chief or the press or anyone else you want."

Dale paced a bit, then extended his hand to Tom. "Deal. For two weeks I'll bust my ass working this case with you. I won't say shit to anyone until my vacation is over. And even then, I'll give you a say in what I tell."

Dale addresses Tom when he connects to the here and now, "The rogue investigation you and I were working, it was about a dead woman in a shack."

"Danielle Rayburn," Tom nods.

"Lan didn't kill her."

It should have been a question.
It wasn't.

Day Four
Sunday, October 29
Waxing Gibbous – Illumination 67%

Ruby Norman is settling herself poolside with a book and a blanket when King heads away from shore in Heir's mint-green and white catamaran. Ever since the events on Stony, he's been heading out on early morning runs as a way to work through Edward issues, then spending the rest of the day and night working through a bottle of booze. Today's bay excursion will take him from Whisper to Peaks, and the issue King will work through is: Whose Baby Is It? "I've been playing this fucking game my whole adult life, and I'm fucking sick of it. Whose Baby Is It, Kathleen? Whose Baby Is It, Connie? Whose Baby Is It, Ruby?" He opens the Cat, and his mind, and waits for some mental pieces to fall into place…

"Edward, I'm staying on Peaks tonight."

"Do I care?"

"You do if you want an alibi for the night Laire MacTavish went missing."

"Connect the dots, King."

"When Ruby comes to your bed, take her in. The bitch won't be able to say shit to the cops if her mouth is wrapped around your dick."

Ruby spent that night in Edward's bed, he spent the night in Ruby, and King spent the night in the guesthouse. Father and son met on the rattans just after dawn, one was sipping a coffee, the other was already one finger into his morning libation. King raised his glass to his son...

"Getting Ruby into your bed took less time than I thought."

Edward gave his head a good shake, "Are you sure you want to let this one go? I mean damn to hell she's good."

"I'm not letting her go, Edward, I'm just sharing her. You sex her good from time to time, make her think you two are clandestine lovers, she loves that shit, toss a few trinkets and promises her way, and she'll give you a good alibi, a good blowjob, and anything else you want."

The King bemoans that decision. "Edward enjoyed the fuck out of my whore for more than a damn year. Ruby bounced between our beds and when Heir brought Quinn Hughes to Echo as his supposed yearlong girlfriend, it put my bitch back in my bed with a vengeance. She damned near drained me dry. Could be one of my swimmers tagged her."

A sudden swell and gust of wind lifts the Cat and knocks the man to the deck. He tries to right himself but stops midway when the image of a young woman rises on a wave then crashes over the boat. "What the fuck?" The man who thinks he's King is rolled from one end of the boat to the other several times, then slams hard when the Cat comes to a rest on eerily calm seas. He starts to right himself, then crouches low when her voice lifts.

~~YOU KILLED MY SON~~
~~I KILLED YOURS~~

The memory of Chief Banks' call telling him Edward had washed ashore, and the grotesque image of his body lying at the water's edge pushes in. King empties his stomach. Two hours later, Edward Kingston III convinces himself that grief and booze are to blame for the crazy shit at sea. Three hours later, he vows to scale back his whisky consumption. And four hours later, he resolves to find out whose kid is on the way. "If Ruby is four or more months pregnant, the kid could be mine or Edward's. Either way, I'll be raising that child and calling it my own. As for Ruby, she'll be dead before her baby is a day old." He docks the Cat, heads into the guesthouse to shower and change, then joins the expectant mother poolside, "You're looking good, Ruby."

"Thanks, King." Her hand automatically finds her baby bump. "I think I felt a flutter this morning."

"Yeah? It seems soon."

"The pregnancy books," she waves the one she's currently reading, "say that 'quickening' can start as early as 16 weeks, so I'm right on schedule. Of course, the fluttering last night might have been a tummy roll from the taco I ate."

"You hate tacos."

"Cravings."

He rubs her thigh, gets up and kisses the top of her head, "If you and the kid want a taco, have a taco, hell, buy a whole taco stand."

Jacobs Jolly

Dale gets up really late because he got in really late from Primrose Priscilla. After Roxanne dropped him at the curb, he sat outside for hours banging the shit he heard through his battered brain. The process helped him reconcile some of the stuff he'd been recapturing on his own and put into context things he heard on T.V. and elsewhere. His biggest takeaway was that he was a cop in the thick of things and privy to investigations and crime scenes. The invigorated young man throws himself into a shower, asks Connie for a lift to town, gets out at the beach near The Promise, and heads to the shoreline to pop a squat. "Okay, Tom said the Danielle Rayburn killing is first on the

Council docket, so let's see if I remember anything." He tries to find a mental-thread for a couple minutes, surrenders to the roll and crash of frothy waves, the call of seabirds, and the warmth of a lowering sun. His relaxed state bangs him into a memory...

A petite young woman with
light blonde hair and fixed dead eyes
stares right through him.

"What the fuck?"

The Promise

Marin has been watching Dale sit on the beach for more than an hour. She has her legs bent, her head resting on her knees with her arms wrapped around them, and her right hand supporting the weight of her braced left wrist. The warmth of the setting sun feels good on her face; the move and sparkle of the ocean lulls away worry and opens her to easy thoughts. "I wonder if he knew I—" She doesn't flinch when footfalls from behind announce a visitor onto the dock. She can tell from the catlike movement that it's her mother coming to check on her. "I'm fine," she preempts.

"I know."

"You do?" she turns her head and scootches over.

Esmé takes a seat and dangles her legs over the side, enjoying an occasional splash from the lifting seas. "There's a storm expected."

"I want to stay at Sand Castle."

"I know."

"But ……. it feels like there's a but coming."

"I have my concerns, but the cottage is your home. More importantly, Marin, it's where you want to be. You spent months being where people told you to be, doing things people made you do. You need to be where you find comfort, so this is the deal. You can stay at Sand Castle, but if the cottage loses power, you agree to come to the main house."

"Deal."

"Jenny and I made chicken soup and June is making one of her brown breads for dinner. We're serving at seven, don't be late." She gets up, notices Dale at his spot, and tosses him a wave. Esmé smiles wide when he returns the gesture. "Dale is welcome to come, if that's something you'd like." The mother gives her daughter a hand up, "How's your wrist?"

"Really painful today. Maybe it'll be my personal barometer."

Esmé smiles, "Mija, you've been through a lot." The mom drifts off in thought, casually brushes her daughter's wild, windblown hair, and starts, then stops, a sentence.

"What?"

"Your verbal recall was something the rehab team remarked on often. You struggled with capturing memories, but when you got them and spoke about them your vast vocabulary and understanding of universal things was intact. It really comforted me knowing you were still in there." She tears, wiping the few that fall away, "I'm sorry, I try not to—"

"It's okay, Mom. I know this is hard on you. It's okay if you show it, and it's okay if you do a little pushing back if I piss you off."

"If?"

"When."

Esmé takes her daughter's injured hand in hers, "Your fingers are swollen. Make sure you wiggle and stretch them, and take a pain pill if you need one, Marin. Don't tough it out."

She nods, waits until her mom is near the main house, then waves to Dale. She points toward the main road, then heads there.

It's just after six when Dale and Marin enter The Promise. Casual greetings take place, then Marin leads him to the gallery while dinner prep continues in the huge eat-in kitchen.

He reads the name over the door, "Clemente."

"It's my mother's maiden name."

He nods, "I think I remember that."

She lets him mosey the space while she stands at a bank of windows overlooking Main Street. She turns when there's a lengthy pause in his walking and finds him standing at the wall that holds her collection.

"*Moonlight Over Midnight Ocean*. This is your work. I remember seeing it ... in some sort of notebook? I think we were at Wind Ledge." He pauses in thought, "Were these pictures in a fireplace?"

She laughs. "Are you suggesting they should be burned?"

"No, I'm thinking they were lost, and I think someone said they were in a fireplace."

She laughs even harder, "It's not nice to tease someone who's—"

June pushes into the room and the conversation, "He's not teasing. For a while your collection was missing, hidden, actually," she stops herself from filling in any more details. "Dinner is ready when you are." She leaves.

Marin goes quiet. Really quiet. For many minutes...

"There's something else."

"Okay."

"I took your sketchpad and hid it."

"Why?"

"Until I know what's going on and can tell your mother everything, I can't risk her finding your work and learning that you were sneaking out at night. I'll take very good care of the pad and will return it to you in time."

"Okay." She went off in thought for many minutes then pushed in, "The cottage isn't very big."

"No."

"But you found a hiding place that Mom won't find."

"Yes."

"Cottage or shed."

"Nice try."

"Did it work?"

"Nope."

"Daddy hid my sketchbook." She gets quiet again…

"The book you were skimming when I arrived, it's the one with your sketches of the moon?"

"Yes."

"Can I look?"

She shook her head and gave a shoulder shrug.

After several minutes and several passes through Dale remarked, "Honestly, Marin, these are so lifelike. The detail, and the way the moon shines, or glows, or makes me think it does. I don't know how you did it, but the drawings have an illumination? Is that possible?" He flipped through again, "I don't know if you ever tried to touch the moon when you were a kid, but holding this book is like touching the moon."

"Thank you," she responds to the story in her head, blushes when she realizes she's in that suspended place where the now and then— the past and present of her life try to share space.

He smiles. "You're remembering the night on the widow's walk at Wind Ledge, when I first saw these pictures."

A shiver runs her spine. It's immediately followed by another and the sting of her eyes.

"Are you cold?"

"No, just a little freaked out."

"About?"

"How the hell should I know?"

Day Five
Monday, October 30
Waxing Gibbous – Illumination 77%

The group enjoyed piping bowls of soup; butter-slathered, hot from the oven, crisp on the outside, fluffy on the inside baked bread; and hours of easy conversation. After dinner they played several games of Uno, had late night cups of hot chocolate, and waited for a break in the rain before Dale walked Marin to Sand Castle. It is well after midnight when he takes a seat next to her on the covered deck.

"Believe it or not, this actually brings back memories, real ones—the kind that are just there, without any work."

"Yeah. It's why I wanted to live here and stay here through the storm. I made a deal with Esmé that I'd head to the main house if the power goes out."

"So you'll be here alone? All night?"

She notes his concern. "Sure. I'll be safe. Nothing bad ever happens on the sandy side of Murder Island."

Another flash of the dead woman with dead eyes fills his head.

After a few minutes of quiet Marin asks, "You got awfully quiet. Where'd you go?"

"I saw Tom."

"In a memory, just now?"

He laughs, "No, last night at Primrose."

She smiles wide. "I remember him and his yellow house on a pretty tree lined street. Esmé says it's interesting that I remember Primrose Priscilla when I only ever went there once."

"It's a nice place. Maybe you really liked it or something."

"How is he?"

"Good."

"Esmé said he stopped coming to the hospital on July 25th. I did the math, that was only four days after Stony Beach. Anyway, I was out of it and I don't have a good recall, but I know he was at my bedside. I think. Holding my hand and wiping my tears. Maybe."

They sit on chaise loungers watching waves lift and curl before hitting hard. When booming thunder sounds and flashes of lightning cut the night sky, Dale gets up and extends his hand. "You should get inside, Marin."

"What about you? Did you drive?"

"Not driving yet."

"You can't walk in this storm."

He takes his cell out of his pocket, "I'll call for a ride."

"No you won't. You can stay on the couch."

Silence.

"I'd like the company. Come on."

They head inside. He calls his mother. She calls hers. He tends to the fire. She gets blankets and a pillow.

The storm intensifies.

Primrose Priscilla

Tom is kicked back in his recliner, a mug of tea and three Figgie cookies are on an end table beside him. He hasn't taken a sip or a nibble because his nose has been pressed between the pages of the sixth journal of a seventy-six book collection written by his recently departed wife, Priscilla. He stops reading long enough to marvel at his wife's dedication. "Two journals a year for thirty-eight years. Your tomes will certainly keep me busy, Priscilla, and entertained. I'm enjoying the references to your favorite tunes: '79, *Baby, It's You*, '80, *Lost In Love*, '81, *Don't Stop Believin'*. Your musical taste certainly framed our love story. I'm half-way through 1982, so I don't know your favorite song for that year, but we were three years into our marriage, and your written words are showing concern that we hadn't had children, or even a hopeful delay in your cycle." He closes the journal and places it onto the empty bed nearby when the houselights flicker and dim. He ignores the approaching storm outside, focusing instead on the one that's moving through his heart and head. "I was the reason for our childless state. It took years of trying and testing to get our answers, and when we did you turned the page on that chapter of our lives, never again mentioned your need and want for children—never made me feel diminished in any way." He runs his fingertips over the leather and the gold word, Journal. "I spared you my sorrow, but it was there, and it was profound, my love."

A sudden howl of wind, pound of rain, and nearby crack of lightning pulls him from his chair. He steps onto the screened porch, watching in silence as Priscilla's shade trees, full of colorful autumnal leaves sway and struggle to stay complete, their burdened branches bending toward the ground. Deep rolls of thunder warn of things to come; vivid lightning proves it right. Tom steps inside, just as a strike hits Priscilla's favorite oak and sends a thick branch toward the ground, its many offshoots scraping along the roof and down the pretty yellow cedar shakes before it thuds loudly and symbolically. The brokenhearted man stands frozen in the center of the kitchen weeping for the woman he loved and lost.

Echo

Ruby wanders the private floor of the estate wishing King was home, "He's on Peaks again, with his newest plaything. I hope he's keeping her safe and sound." A flash of lightning and simultaneous crack of contact, followed immediately by another and another terrifies her, "It's right overhead." She puts her hand to her belly and races into the master suite, stands near the balcony, gripping a gossamer silk sheer. She jumps at each boom of thunder, counts the seconds between the flash of lightning and it's announced strike, "Two seconds. Two miles. One second. One mile. It's circling the island and coming back this way." She watches the docked boats rise and fall, bang and pull, and rock to and fro. She begins to cry when Heir's mint-green and white catamaran pulls free and crashes hard against the stone retaining wall that runs the edge of the lawn. "Edward," she sobs. She falls to the floor when the cold touch of death skims her flesh and grips her deep.

The Promise

Esmé, Jenny, and June are pacing the floors with worry. They should be concerning themselves with the raging storm, but their anxieties are about Marin and Dale. "There's an attraction between those two," June reminds.

"He's too old," Esmé reminds.

"We've had this conversation before, but let me restate the facts. Marin is eighteen and Dale is almost twenty-five That's the same age difference as you and Joe, and don't give me the whole 'things were different back then' speech. Back then or today, it's the same story—girl likes boy, boy likes girl—as long as everyone is of legal age, it is what it is. Period, end of story." She pauses before launching Round Two. "If they met on a college campus, I'm not sure there'd be a ton of discussion about this, you know, shared experiences and all. So let's come at this from that angle. Marin was definitely crushing on Dale before the Shit Fest at Stony, and though he never did anything back then, things are different now—there's an age difference, sure, but their life experiences level the playing field and bond them in ways we won't ever understand."

Esmé nods, "That's what I'm worried about – them having feelings – real feelings – and responding to them."

June cracks up, "Of course you're worried about it. You're her mother. If it helps, I doubt anything is going to happen tonight, so stop worrying about them and worry about the storm that's raging." The women move to the kitchen windows and pretend to watch the storm, but their eyes never really stray from the tiny cottage known as Sand Castle.

Pleasantvale Care Center

Connie Jacobs is stretched out on the visitor's couch in her former husband's room at the tiny, residential, long-term care center. The staff insisted she not venture out when the storm pushed onto shore earlier and harder than expected. She sits in a near-dark room, staring at the man she married and divorced all those years ago, the one who is locked in a world of his own. "I wonder if he remembers how in love we were." Connie gently sweeps back her hair, leans into her perch upon the couch, and watches the storm rage outside his bedroom window, "It's a bad one, Matt. It reminds me of that storm when we were first married. The one that sent you home early to check on me. You knew I was terrified, so you gave me something else to think about..."

The newlywed paced her new home for more than an hour, finally taking refuge in her husband's den off the kitchen. "Matt. Come home, please come home." She sat stone-still as lighting hit here – there – everywhere, and thunder went from distant and rolling, to prolonged booms of doom. A sudden flash and simultaneous crack, and the gust of noisy wind sent her flying to the kitchen and under the table. That's where her young husband found her, comforted her, kissed and touched her, and unwound the hell out of her. "Oh, Matt, I hope it storms every day."

Connie throws a blush. "You were a rascal, Matthew Jacobs." A very close crack of lightning sends her from the couch to the chair near his bed. She pulls a long slow breath, and releases it in a quick push. "I'm sorry this is the way of things for you, but in some ways you're spared painful memories. We caused one another so much pain and sorrow." She silently pushes at the bruise that still pains, then moves on. "I don't think I mentioned, but Tom Martin came by the house the other day to see Dale. He recently lost his wife, Priscilla. Remember, he used to call her Miss Prissy. I always thought that was wonderful. She was wonderful. They were wonderful. I envied their unabashed love and adventurous nature. They were such as nice couple. Anyway, Tom's visit put some life back into our son – **our son**." She pulls a choppy breath. "I got a call earlier from Dale. He's fine and is spending the night at The Promise. You'd know the place as Sand Art, but Jasper Crane recently sold it to an artist named Esmé Baxter, and she's renamed it." Connie takes hold of the silent man's hand, "I've decided to stay the night, so it looks like you've got me as a roommate."

Matt Jacobs looks at his former wife and quietly says one word, "Good."

Echo

Ruby is on the floor inside the walk-in closet with a pillow beneath her head and comforter thrown over her face, trying to remain calm. She is failing. She pushes the plush blanket off her head when she thinks she hears the sound of the main entrance doorbell. She crawls from the closet, then pushes herself to her feet when the constant push against the bell beckons. She rushes the length of the hall, down the center staircase, across spit-polished marble floors, and yanks open the front door. She is beyond relieved to see Chief Vernon Banks covered head to toe in raingear. She steps back as he steps forward. "King called from Peaks and said you were alone. He asked for a wellness check. Dispatch called me. It took more than an hour to get here, but here I am."

A sudden boom of thunder and crack of lightning sends her into his arms, her head presses tight against his chest. Her tremble and choking cries put him on alert, "Ms. Norman, you need to calm yourself. King mentioned your pregnancy." He moves her body away and assesses, "You're white as a ghost and cold to the touch." He strips himself of his gear, drops it onto the foyer floor, wraps an arm around her, and leads her to a nearby den. He's no sooner seated her when the lights go out.

"Ms. Norman, stay on the couch." He grabs a blanket from the back and covers her. "The emergency generators will kick on in a minute or two. I'm going to the kitchen to see if there are flashlights. Are any of the staff still here?"

"Cook only comes when King is in residence, and the last I saw Mr. Downing it was sometime after midnight. He was trying to secure a few docked boats. Heir's Cat had come free from the dock and hit the retaining wall. I think Mr. Downing was afraid others would follow. I'm not sure if he's still out there, but he shouldn't be, not in this."

"Why the hell did King leave you alone? What the fuck was he thinking?"

"He was thinking about his Peaks Island plaything, Chief Banks."

He shakes his head and steps away. "Okay. I'll be back in a few minutes. Don't leave that couch, Ms. Norman."

"Ruby."

"Vernon. We may be stuck here for a while, so let's get comfortable." He's back in several minutes, the generator already lighting a few areas of the massive estate, one of which is the den. He hands her a plate, "Sliced cheese, fruit, and a granola bar. Eat. We can't afford you passing out from hunger." He hands her a water and a sport drink, "Keep yourself hydrated." He moves to an electric fireplace set in the corner near a small sitting area, flicks a switch and nods to the quick amber flame and blast of heat. "Good. Come sit on one of these chairs. The fireplace should keep you warm enough. The storm is expected to last through tonight's high tide, so get comfortable. We're gonna be here for the duration." Before he finishes his sentence, the expectant mother falls into the sleep of the dead.

Sand Castle

Marin spends time in the shower, then heads back to the living area, all comfy-cozy in a pair of flannel pajama bottoms and long-sleeve tee. She shuffles past her roommate, sets herself on the shorter side of a sectional couch, the one with a built-in recliner and towel-dries a mess of long chestnut waves. Dale is stretched out on the long end of that couch trying hard not to respond to the perky mounds and budded nipples covered by her well-worn, curve-hugging top. She calms and quiets after several minutes of finger-combing and hair-twisting. She quickly finds the sweet spot of slumber, goes deep and stays deep until the hard slam of high tide wakes her.

Dale senses her anxiety, pushes himself to a sitting position, experiencing just enough pain to remind him of his leg injury, "Marin. What is it?"

"High tide. Look," she points to the wall of windows. Enormous waves push toward shore, gaining strength and volume before cresting in ash-colored froth that crashes hard against the dock, then ride the shore.

"What time is it?"

"Seven antemeridian."

He laughs, "Well, at least you remember that."

"Esmé said the whitecoats found it interesting that I retained my vocabulary."

He laughs, "Whitecoats. That's perfect." He checks the tide schedule on his cell phone, "It's not quite high yet, so it's gonna get worse before it gets better."

He turns in her direction when he gets no response, immediately realizing she's in some sort of fugue state. He lets her be, but moves closer to her corner of the couch. With each crash of wave, she flinches, and her breathing accelerates until she's gasping for breath.

She angrily pushes aside her cover and starts clawing at her clothing, "Get off. Please get him off." She tumbles from the couch, bangs across the floor as though trying to free herself from a dead man's clutch.

Dale joins her, pulls her to his chest, wraps his arms around her body, trying to protect her head. "Marin. It's Dale. Marin. Open your eyes." She does, but her stare is locked beyond him at the tide that rages just outside the windows. She flashes back, reliving the memory that could break her...

"Dale! Blood! Blood! Oh My God. There behind a rock. Help! I need to get help. Go to Wind ... no ... run Cliff Road."

Her breaths take on the pant, pant, pant, of someone running. She collapses into Dale's arms and buries her face onto his chest. "Oh, Dale. I remember. I remember. You were gone. I tried to find you. You were around the bend. On the ground. Shot!" She pushes away. "I got scared and started toward Wind then veered toward the cliff. It was raining and the wind was picking up. I couldn't see all that well and stumbled through the rock field, and when I got to the access ladder I reached up and started climbing. Then my hand slipped and I fell back onto the rocks below. I landed hard and lost my breath. As soon as I could, I crawled toward the shoreline. I tried to call out, but I couldn't get enough air. I thought you called my name. I tried to get to you, and when I got to the shoreline I collapsed. The waves were pounding and the rain was beating hard. I was desperate for you. Then I felt your embrace. You were lying on my back, your arms wrapped tight. I relaxed into you, and we just rode the push and pull of waves. But I remembered you'd been shot. I moved my hair away and tried to move out from under you, to help you, but it wasn't you … it was … Edward Kingston … he was trying to kill me, drown me, but she wouldn't let him."

"Who is she?"

"Laire MacTavish. She saved me."

Dale pulls her close, kisses her temple, "Marin." He rides the pain of her sobs, comforts her with a kiss to her head and a stroke of her hair. "I know how hard that was, remembering all that, but you did it, and I'm here, and I won't let anyone ever hurt you again. I promise." After many minutes, he feels the relax of her slumber. He holds on, then eases her to the floor, grabs a pillow and blanket and tucks her in. He lies next to her, rests her head in the crook of his shoulder, welcomes her nestle, her arm around his waist. He holds her for hours, breathes in the fresh, fruity smell of her hair, willingly suffers through the cramping of his leg and the strengthening of his desire. When the pain of both becomes too much, he limps to the kitchen to make two phone calls.

Primrose Priscilla

Tom uses the brief calm before the second part of the storm to inspect damage to Miss Prissy's mighty oak. He shakes his head throughout his walk around the back yard, "Oh, Priscilla, I'm not sure I'll be able to save Bessie. The mighty one lost a massive knotted and gnarled branch." He marvels at the size of the downed limb, "Damn near covers a whole corner of the yard." He realizes how fortunate he is that it didn't fall more to the left, "It would have taken out the screened-in porch and maybe part of the den. I'm going to have to have Bessie removed." He laughs at the sweetness of Priscilla naming all of their hardwoods. "They became your children. Let's hope Irma, Eloise, Meredith, and Seraphina fair better this next go around." He heads back inside, just in time to take a call from Dale.

"How's the east side, Tom?"

"It's been better. I lost one of Priscilla's oaks, and it looks like Round Two is gonna crash headfirst into another high tide. How's Jacobs Jolly?"

"No clue. I was at The Promise having dinner with Marin and the rest and ended up crashing at Sand Castle. That's why I'm calling. Marin had a huge breakthrough this morning. Her memories crashed at the same time as high tide."

"Did she remember Edward's death hold on her?"

"Yeah, and she has questions about all that, and unfortunately none of us can answer them. When the storm settles, I think you should touch base with her. And heads up, Tom, she wonders why you haven't been to see her. I've been wondering the same thing. Is it because of Mrs. Martin?"

"Some. But it's mostly because of guilt."

"Suck it up, old man. If there's anyone who's responsible for what happened to Marin it's me, and I'm not letting guilt keep me away."

Day Six
Tuesday, October 31
Waxing Gibbous – Illumination 85%

Whisper Island is pretty much torn to shit when the nor'easter finally pulls away two days after she arrived. Trees and power lines are down, roads are blocked and flooded, countless boats at the marina are ruined or adrift, trollies are sporadic at best, and the ferry line is closed until further notice. The good news is there are no reports of casualties, though several islanders suffered injuries of varying degree. Those brave enough to venture from their homes have congregated on Main Street and have entered into a debate about which was worse: Round One that packed a wallop with thunder, lighting, and wind, or Round Two that was all about the ten-foot storm surge during each of the high tide cycles. The residents of The Promise and Sand Castle haven't weighed in on the discussion; they've been busy counting their blessings. Both properties sustained minimal damage, though the people inside have taken a few emotional hits.

Marin heard most of Dale's phone conversation with Tom. When it was over, she got up without word and headed to the shower to work out the kinks from sleeping on the floor. When she returns, she brings with a shower-fresh smell and puffy-red-eyes from an obvious cry. Breakfast smells waft from the kitchen, and a warm push comes from the recently tended fireplace. She takes a seat on the recliner part of the sectional.

"Breakfast is ready."

"Thanks, but I'm not hungry."

"You need to eat while we have power, and breakfast is ready." He grunts a bit when he pushes off the counter.

"Did you sleep on the floor?"

"Yeah."

"Because of me?"

"Well, yeah."

"Your leg. I'm sorry."

He takes a seat next to her on the couch and puts his arm around. She nestles into his shoulder space and smiles when he kisses the side of her head. "Nothing to be sorry about, Marin. We got the fuck knocked out of us, but we're still here. You made a huge memory recovery last night. We can pull at a few memory-threads if you want, or we can spend the day being Marin and Dale."

"Can I be Dale?"

He cracks the fuck up.

Echo

Ruby is standing at a window overlooking the circular drive, not really focusing on anything. She has the blanket Vernon gave her draped long across her back and pulled tight at her neck. She turns when she hears movement from behind. "Chief, the generator must be out because the fireplace stopped working a few hours ago."

"You've been up since then?"

She nods.

"You should have woken me."

She shrugs.

"Are you feeling okay?"

"I'm feeling scared."

"Of King?"

"And you."

He nods. "You should be afraid of King, especially if that baby you're carrying isn't his. You don't need to be afraid of me. My sights are on King, and he is going down for everything. Mark my words."

"He'll take you with him."

He pushes from his seat, "No, he won't. King's arrogance has him believing that he rules without impunity. His hubris will be his downfall. I'm going to take a few hits here and there, and rightfully so, but I will walk away pretty much unscathed."

"Unless he puts a bullet through you."

He nods, "I could warn you of the same."

She nods and turns back to the window.

He moves near. "You've lived here a long time."

She nods.

"You've heard things."

"Yes."

"About Heir."

"Yes."

"Is he the father of your baby?"

"Yes."

"King is going to kill you when he finds out."

"Then my days are numbered."

"Why is that?"

"He has my pregnancy test strip in his office. Mine and someone else's."

Vernon knows who the other strip belongs to…

The chief was readying to leave The Claremont after an extensive search of Edward Kingston IV penthouse condo—the one he nearly destroyed in a fit of rage. The manager of the building stopped Vernon before he made it to the door, "One last thing, Chief Banks."

"Yes."

"Please shut the door. The walls have ears they say."

"What is it?"

Henri reached into his pocket, "I found this in the penthouse and removed it for safekeeping. You should have it. Perhaps it will explain why Edward was upset."

The chief took the pregnancy test strip.

And…

The rulers of Whisper returned to Echo after an unsuccessful search in Portland for Heir. Each had a plan. King headed to Ruby's suite to tell her to leave. In a suite down the hall, Chief Banks was searching for something that might explain where Heir might have gone. More importantly, he was leaving behind something that would tie Edward Kingston IV to the dead pregnant teen on the floor of Casco Bay. 'The only man going down for the crimes committed on my island is a fucking Kingston. I don't care who his father is."

The chief gets into Ruby's space. "Do you know where those pregnancy test strips are?"

She nods, "In King's middle desk drawer."

He stares her down. "Ruby, you're at a crossroads. You can pack a bag, come with me, and tell me everything you know—"

She shakes her head, "He'll kill me."

"No he won't. You'll stay at a secure location, one he'll never find. OR. You can stay here, be called to testify at the inquest and choose to tell the truth or perjure yourself. If you lie, you'll get a prison sentence imposed by me. If you tell the truth, you'll get a death sentence imposed by King."

She places her hand to her baby bump and lets the tears flow.

"Ruby, listen to me. If you're correct and King already suspects you are carrying Heir's child, then he is keeping you around and alive for one thing, and one thing only—to lie on the witness stand. He'll want you to sow doubt with a jury about Heir's crimes. Once he has that from you, there's only one other thing he'll want—and you're carrying it."

Ruby drops the blanket to the floor, "Let's go."

"Pack a few things. I'll check with dispatch on road conditions and plan a way to get you out of here." While the chief waits he heads to King's office, takes what he wants, then returns to the foyer. He sits on the bottom step and replays a recent conversation with King, and a long ago conversation with Kathleen…

The chief tossed a plastic bag onto King's desk, "Look familiar?"

The man who purchased a pair of earrings just like the one in the bag gives a snarl with his answer, "Where did you find that?"

"In Laire MacTavish's bedroom."

"Where's the other one."

"Don't know." He lied. "I'm guessing from your reaction Edward gave them to the girl."

"They were his mother's." He reflected a minute. "Heir said he was really into this girl. He must have been serious about Laire if he gave her something of Kathleen's."

Vernon shook his head, "That woman was too good for the likes of you."

"Still pining?"

"Stopped pining twenty-five damned years ago, you miserable son of a bitch. All I can say now is I'm glad she isn't here to see what a colossal mess you did raising her son."

"Fuck you."

And to a deathbed whisper...

"I should have chosen you, Vernon."

He patted her hand, "You followed your heart, Kathleen."

"I followed the money." **She teared, struggled to take his hand and weave her fingers with his,** "Please ... please take care of our son."

Vernon froze at the words then, breaks at the words, now. When Ruby joins him at the bottom stair, he gets up, sucks it up and gets her settled in the back seat of his Rover, "You need to lie down and stay down. I don't want anyone to know you are with me. When King comes back to Echo and asks if anyone checked on you, I'll tell him the roads were unpassable and no one knows where you are."

"Where will I be?"

"Hopefully, you'll be staying with the most honorable man on Whisper Island."

Primrose Priscilla

Two hours later, after navigating a circuitous route across the three mile long island, Chief Banks parks on the front lawn of Tom Martin's home. Vernon surveys the secluded cul-de-sac on his walk to the front door, "This will work. The only traffic coming this way is whoever's visiting Tom or banging a U-turn." He eyes the deep grove of trees along the sides and behind the place. "A determined someone could come up from the shore, but that'd be some work." He knocks on Tom's door and gets right to it when it's answered. "I need your help."

"Don't work for you anymore, Vern."

"Whisper is going to be looking for my replacement in a few weeks."

"That so?"

"Before I leave, I want to bring King to his knees."

"Tall order, Vern."

"I've got the goods, Tom, but I need someone clean – cleaner than me, to deliver them."

"That's where I come in?"

"Yeah, but that's only part of it." He waits … finishing when Tom remains silent. "I need a place to hide a witness."

"Nope," Tom starts closing the door.

Vern blocks it from shutting, "There must be something you want."

Tom opens the door, "There is."

"Name it."

"I want the inquest to start at the beginning. I want a chronological presentation of Edward Kingston IV crimes."

Vern is shaking his head, "That's not gonna happen. King got to the Council members. Danielle Rayburn's murder is first on the docket. King is convinced Heir didn't kill Danielle, and unless there's compelling evidence proving otherwise, Edward will be exonerated. King thinks it will help down the line if Edward is cleared in the Rayburn murder and Lan MacTavish stays in jail."

"I may have found a motive for Danielle's murder and it involves the marina. With some digging WPD might find some evidence to support my theory. If you want me to babysit your witness and help you put King behind bars, then you'll let me prove Lan MacTavish didn't kill Danielle, and you'll let me do it *after* a direct link is established between Heir Kingston and Christie Anderson and Laire MacTavish. Those are my terms. Take them or get off my front porch."

"Done. I'll change the docket, but until then, you and I will be the only two who know we're working together."

"There'll be one other person on our team."

"Nope."

"Vern, you and I can't be seen together, and our communication can be limited at best. We need someone to act as an intermediary."

"Who?"

"Roxanne Carmichael."

"Jesus, Tom. I can't be seen with her."

"You won't be, but you'll be accessible to her by burner. She'll relay information and arrange meetings if need be."

The chief nods. It ends with a shake of his head.

"You need to change the inquest start date as soon as you drive away. There's no way Whisper will be up and running in six days, so move it out at least a week beyond November 6th, and get Christie Anderson at the top of the docket."

"Done."

"When does your mystery witness arrive?"

"Now." The chief opens the back door of the Rover, helps Ruby Norman out and into Primrose Priscilla. "Tom, this is—"

"Ruby Norman." He turns his attention to the man who neglected to mention a few things, "Miss Norman is pregnant."

"She is."

"With King's child?"

"With Heir's child."

"Dammit to hell, Vern. You might have mentioned that."

He makes introductions, "Ruby, this is Tom Martin."

The young woman, wearing a pair of sweats and a long-sleeve tee, her hair pulled-high in a ponytail, and sans a bit of makeup, looks every bit like the former Shaky Town girl she used to be. She extends her hand. "Chief

Banks said you are the most honorable man on Whisper. I appreciate you taking me in, Mr. Martin. I'm in some trouble. I hope I don't bring too much of it to your doorstep."

"Miss Norman, do you have a cell phone in your possession?"

"Yes."

He extends his hand. She takes it from her purse and hands it to him. "Wait here." He takes it to the kitchen, grabs a hammer and smashes the fuck out of it. He tosses the pieces into the trash.

"That could have had evidence on it, Tom," the chief reminds.

"It definitely had tracking on it, Vern. Hopefully the downed lines and cell interruptions kept King from tracking her movements during the storm." He smiles at his houseguest, "For the time you are here, Miss Norman, you are prohibited from contacting anyone. Is that clear?"

"It is."

"Good. So long as the three of us keep our mouths shut, no one will know you're staying at Primrose Priscilla."

Almost before Tom finishes his sentence, Vernon's cell rings. "It's King." The room silences, "What can I do for you, Mr. Kingston?"

"Where the fuck is Ruby?"

"No clue. At your request, a wellness check was attempted, but the roads were impassable."

"Are they passable now?"

"Some."

"Then get to Echo and break the fucking door down?"

"Mr. Kingston, WPD is not in the habit of entering a property without an invitation or a search warrant, especially your property. Are you authorizing entry into your residence without your presence, Mr. Kingston?"

The call is ended.

"Okay, I need to get out of here. Tom, you need to arrange the communication setup we discussed. Tell our contact to call me at 2 PM tomorrow. That's the only time I will accept her call."

"When she calls, you'd better tell her Christie Anderson is first on the docket."

The chief turns to leave, stopping at Tom's next question.

"Are you sure you want to go down with King?"

"I've got some shit to answer for, but I should be okay, unless King blows me away."

"He's carrying now?"

"Yeup." The chief leaves. The detective and his pregnant houseguest head to the kitchen. "Are you hungry, Miss Norman?"

"Ruby, please."

"And I'm Tom."

"I have a craving for tuna."

"I have a few cans, how about I mix some up?"

"May I?"

"Have at it. I'll be right in there if you need me."

Ruby needs him more than he could ever know.

Around The Bend

Roxanne Carmichael is gathering a bunch of crap that washed onto her waterfront property located on the far end of the eastern side of the island nearest to the bend onto Stony Beach. Her pale coral cottage, Carmichael Corner, is surrounded by dunes, and is currently covered with clumps of wet sand, most with tall blades of dune grass sticking out. She's been doing a fair amount of grousing with her gathering. "The side of the house and porch is covered with a shitload of cement-like sand that actually made it through the window screens. This will take weeks to clean up." She thinks about Lan sitting his ass in jail for a crime he didn't commit, "Could be worse, a lot worse."

She drops the garbage bag she's dragging to and fro and answers her cell. "Hi, Tom. How did Primrose Priscilla fare out?"

"I lost a mighty oak, the porch is missing a side of screening and the house is missing several shakes, but all in all, I was very lucky." He pauses, w.a.y. t.o.o. l.o.n.g. for the reporter on the other end.

"What's going on?"

"I can't tell you everything right now, and everything is completely off the record." He waits for her agreement, then continues, "Chief Banks is joining our team."

She cracks up laughing, "God, that's some funny shit."

"No joke. Banks and I have teamed up to get Lan out of jail and to put King inside."

"Holy the fuck, what?"

Tom cracks up laughing, "Well that's a new one. If you want to be part of our team, and you should think long and hard about it before you agree, Roxanne—"

"I'm in."

"Seriously, Roxanne, by the time the shit hits the fan, Banks said he'll be out as chief, which mostly likely means he'll be implicated in a crime or two. Heir Kingston will be posthumously convicted of one, two, three, or four murders, and The King of Whisper will be leaving the island handcuffed to a rail on the Abenaki."

"I. Am. All. In. Just tell me what my role is."

"Conduit. Vernon and I cannot be seen together, shouldn't even be communicating with one another, at least not directly."

"Got it. You'll talk to me. I'll talk to him. I'll talk to you. Good plan. What about Dale Jacobs?"

"He's out of the mix. He's spending time with Marin Baxter and she's starting to have some memory breakthroughs. He and I will do a back and forth on anything important."

"Got it. And Lan?"

"As soon as the ferries are up and running, I'll make a trip to the prison and remind him I said I will have him out of that hellhole by the end of the year, and I will. Any chance you can get to my place?"

"I'll have to walk."

"I'll see you at 7 PM. Use the front door, or be prepared to climb a downed tree to get to the back entrance. Be careful."

"See, ya."

As Tom ushers one young woman through the front door, the other one closes the door to her guest room upstairs. Ruby moves quietly about the room, thinking about how much it reminds her of her grandmother's place in Vermont, "George Washington spread on a four-poster bed set high enough to need a stepstool." She examines all the pretty things lying about, then heads to a bookcase and chooses, *1st To Die*, a Women's Murder Club book by James Patterson. "I've read Patterson's Alex Cross books, but none in this series." She checks the shelf, counts the spines, "Fifteen. Not sure how long I'll be staying, but these ought to keep me busy." She climbs onto the bed, nestles down, and starts in. She's still awake three hours later when there's a knock on her door, "Come in."

"I wanted to make sure you settled in alright."

"I have. The room is very comfortable, and I found a very good book to read. I hope you don't mind."

"You have free range of the house, Ruby, except for the den that's set as a bedroom off the kitchen."

"Okay, Tom. I can't believe how relaxed I feel not being at Echo."

"You were there a long time."

"Two years ten months, minus the months right after Edward's death. I spent those on the mainland. I shouldn't have gone back to the estate, but King saw me when I came back to Whisper to prepare for the inquest, and insisted we discuss the baby bump—we never really discussed it, but I think he's starting to question if the baby is his or Heir's. Edward and I weren't always discrete, and King may have heard things, or seen things. I've been thinking his doubts are probably why he's holding onto the pregnancy test strips."

"Strips? Did he make you take two tests?"

"No. I'm not sure who took the other test but King has a woman on Peaks, so maybe she's pregnant, too."

He nods. "Well, goodnight, Ruby. If you need anything, just holler." Tom reaches for the door then reaches for a memory...

"I found a package of birth control pills in Laire MacTavish's room. The prescription was filled at Peduzzi's on the 5th of June, but none were taken before she went missing a couple weeks later. I don't know enough about contraception to venture as guess about what that means."

Dale laughed at the old guy, "Well don't look at me. All I know is they prevent pregnancies if they're taken correctly. We should ask someone on our team about them. Probably Esmé. I'm guessing she's the only one who might have actual experience with birth control." Dale looked at the man who'd suddenly gone v.e.r.y. q.u.i.e.t. "Hey, Tom, where'd you go?"

"Pregnancy. You don't suppose Laire could have been pregnant?"

"Shit, I don't know, but I guess anything is possible."

Tom bangs that a bit, "My original theory that Edward got rid of Laire because he tired of her could be wrong. Heir might have killed that poor girl because she was pregnant." He shakes his head at the cold-heartedness of such a man. "I would have given the world to learn Priscilla was pregnant."

Week One Comes To An End
Wednesday, November 1
Waxing Gibbous – Illumination 92%

Tom hops off the trolly across from The Promise. He crosses the empty street and stands in front of a large window that allows a peer into Clemente. His eyes find and stay glued on Esmé's painting, *Girl on a Rock*, "Marin," he smiles.

The owner of the gallery knocks on the glass then makes her way outside. "Tom Martin." She wraps her arms around and holds on and on and on. She steps back and touches his face, "You look good. You're breathing through the pain, now."

"Yeah. I miss the hell out of her, but there's work to do, and I'm ready to do it. I need to do it."

"Marin is in The Castle. She'd love to see you."

"That's where I'm heading. Say hello to June and Jenny." He waves to them both when he passes by the kitchen window, sprints around the corner of Marin's cottage, smiles wide when he sees her sitting on the porch, "Permission to come deck side?"

She pushes from her chair and flings herself into his open arms, "I thought you forgot me?"

"Didn't bump my head."

She laughs. She cries.

He takes her hand, "I would never – could never – forget you."

"But you've been gone so long."

"Let's sit."

Many minutes of silence pass, she breaks it, "You sat at my hospital bed."

"I did."

"You held my hand and dried my tears."

"I did."

"I wanted you to help me."

"With what?"

"The dead man. Edward Kingston was on top of me, pulling me toward the ocean. He was trying to drown me," she begins a bit of ugly crying. "I knew about the dead guy way back then, but I just remembered it was Heir Kingston." She looks at the waves for a minute or two then asks, "Did you tell me I was safe, and that I should listen to the machines, and to push the memories away?"

"I did."

"I think I pushed them too far away. But they're coming back now."

"That's good, Marin."

She wipes her tears and sniffles a bit, "I've tried to think about why you left me in the hospital, why you never came to see me at rehab," her crying ratchets up.

"I know." A tear slides down his cheek, then another, then another.

She reaches her hand his way and wipes them. "It's okay, Tom. I made it through. It's just that I missed you."

He takes hold of her hand and squeezes it. "I'm sorry, but I had to leave. I had to stay away for a bit."

"Had to?"

"I lost Miss Prissy. That night. She passed away. That night."

"Oh, Tom, I'm sooooo sorry. I liked your wife very much, and I already miss her." Marin looks to the ocean. "That was a horrible, horrible night. Dale and I almost died, Miss Prissy died, and Edward Kingston washed ashore on Stony Beach." A thought bangs really hard in Marin's head. "Wait. How did Edward die?"

"That's a very good question, Miss Baxter. So far as I know, the cause of death hasn't been determined or released to the public."

"How did Miss Prissy die?"

"She had a stroke."

"Because of the Polycythemia Vera."

"You remember that?"

"I guess. I'm really sorry, Tom. Miss Prissy was a really nice lady, and she loved the Figgie cookies you left her."

He laughs really big, "You remember that?"

"Yeah, it took me months to remember some dead guy on top of me, but remembering a plate of cookies you brought your wife, no problem." She pauses then adds, "Just so you know, the dead guy memory sucked big time."

"I bet."

She looks back to the ocean, "You know, I could go for a Figgie right about now."

He laughs, "I sure did miss you, Marin Baxter."

"Right backatcha, Tom Martin."

Outer Banks

Chief Banks has been in his home office since 5 AM reviewing documents stored on several USB drives he removed from an upstairs wall safe. He just opened the file labeled Christie Anderson and the document labeled Lachlan MacTavish: Timeline. The chief reads Detective Thomas Martin's summary. "Mr. MacTavish first met Christie Anderson on July 20, 2014. The two individuals spent the day at the public beach on July 21, 2014 and again on July 22, 2014. Mr. MacTavish went to Diggers on July 24, 2014 for a drink. He sat at the bar. No one inside the bar put Christie Anderson with Lachlan MacTavish the night she went missing." The chief pulls up a document labeled, Lachlan MacTavish: Timeline Addendum, and reads the summary he prepared.

- The new owner of Diggers, Max Trainor, stopped by WPD and made a statement that he remembered seeing Christie Anderson with Lan MacTavish at the bar the night she went missing. Mr. Trainor said he was there that evening, but left the island the next day, and wasn't interviewed by anyone from WPD when he returned.

- A vacationer, Camilla Stephian, contacted WPD and made a statement that she and her family were vacationing on Whisper when Christie Anderson went missing. Camilla said she met Christie in Shaky and was with her when they first met Lan on the beach. She said Lan took an interest in Christie and suggested she meet him at Diggers. According to Ms. Stephian, Christie told Lachlan MacTavish straight up that she was underage. He supposedly told her Diggers let underage vacationers in and that they should both go.

The chief puts the USB drives away, grabs a sheet of paper and jots a To-Do list. <u>Create a timeline for Edward Kingston IV</u> for the dates of: July 24, 2014, (date of Christie Anderson disappearance); July 21, 2016, (date of Laire MacTavish disappearance); July 27, 2016, (date of Danielle Rayburn murder); July 31, 2016, (date of Joseph Baxter death). He reviews the list and asks the most important questions. "Did Heir commit these crimes? **All** of these crimes? Baxter's death may have been an accidental fall, but he could have been pushed, so this needs further investigation." The lawman chews around the edges a bit, "If there's a hole in the timeline, if the Council can't tie Heir to ALL of the crimes, will they find him guilty of ANY of the crimes?"

The chief heads to WPD. When he gets there, he locks himself in the storage area, starts pulling files, and looking for threads.

Primrose Priscilla

Ruby Norman rushes upstairs when she sees a shadow move across the side yard. She is squatting in a tight space between a triple dresser and the wall when her bedroom door opens.

"Ruby, are you here?"

"Over here," she waves her hand, "I could use a pull."

"Hope you haven't been stuck a long time," he pulls her free by both hands.

"No. I saw a shadow on the side drive and got scared. I guess I'm a little on edge."

"I don't want to add to your concerns, but King's looking for you. He has eyes and ears all over this island, and he's got money enough to payroll a private dick to look until you're found."

She begins trembling, steps onto a stepstool, and plops her ass onto the bed. "I should go back. I should just go back. The chief said if I stayed with King, I would have a choice, tell the truth and suffer at the hand of King, or lie under oath and face charges brought by the chief."

Tom nods.

"If I lie, I might go to jail for perjury."

"Yes."

"I'd be safe in prison." She reads the detective's expression. "I mean I'd be safe from King." She tears when the detective shakes his head. She lowers hers, "I don't have a choice, do I?"

"Your choices suck, Ruby, but whatever you do is going to affect your baby, so why don't you make your decisions based on what's best for your little one."

She raises her head and smiles. "Little One. That's what I'm going to call the baby until it's born." She stiffens her spine and gets off the bed. "Okay, Tom, what's next?"

"We play Two Hundred Questions. Let's go."

Tom moves some things around on his injured porch, tacks and tapes some of the ripped screen, places a call to a tree removal company only to find they are booked solid for the next week, and heads back inside. He helps Ruby carry their lunch and drinks to the porch, grabs a legal pad and pen from his office and gets to work. "I'll ask the questions. You'll answer them. But make sure you eat and drink. We can't afford you getting sick and needing medical attention. Understood?"

"Understood." She takes a bite of the ham and cheese omelet on toast. "Mmm, if I do say so myself."

When the first half is eaten, Tom asks, "Do you think Heir Kingston had a thing for underage girls?"

The woman carrying Heir's child leans back, takes a looks around the backyard, and lets a memory filter in…

Ruby took advantage of an empty house and headed to Edward's suite. She snuck through his bedroom to his office, shut the door behind her, ran her fingertips over the mousepad, only to find the computer screen stayed dark. "That was a bust." She pulled open a few desk drawers and flipped through a few Kingston Marina file folders. She was ready to abandon her search when she saw a lone piece of paper on the printer tray. She raised a brow when she read it, "Baxter Family." The section on Marin Baxter was bolded in red print. "Date of birth September 1, 1999, so she's almost seventeen. She's from Oxford, Massachusetts, but lives at Wind Ledge with her parents, Joe and Esmé." Ruby put the paper back, and snuck out of Edward's suite, an uncomfortable question gnawing her headspace, *Why is Edward researching a teenage girl?*

Tom sits quietly while Ruby does her thing. And when she's done with that memory, she heads off to another…

Ruby was stepping into the shower when she heard a news report about two missing teens, Christie Anderson and Laire MacTavish. She walked butt-naked to the bedroom and bumped into King. "Did you hear that report—about the missing girls?"

"Yeah. Days ago. Where've you been, Ruby?"

"You know I don't watch T.V. When did they go missing?"

"The Anderson girl disappeared in 2014, and the MacTavish girl went missing sometime last week."

"MacTavish? Why does that name sound familiar?"

"The girl's brother works at the marina. You probably heard me or Heir mention him."

Ruby headed to the shower and began questioning, "Did Heir take those underaged girls? Did he get them on a boat and maybe stash them somewhere … like Portland? He makes the run from Whisper to the mainland all the time, and he supposedly has a woman there—who **no one** has ever seen. What if he's keeping a couple of underage girls for shits and giggles—wait, the first girl went missing in 2014 when she was seventeen. She's no longer jail bait. So maybe she left Heir and he needed to replace her and took the second girl. That fits with the timing. Is that why he's looking at Marin Baxter? A replacement for next year?" **She shook her head and set herself right,** "For Christ sake, Ruby, Edward Kingston IV can have any woman he wants. There's no way he wants juvies. You're stringing a whole lot of shit together based on nothing but a piece of paper with information about Marin Baxter. That paper also mentioned her parents, Joe and Esmé Baxter. The research could be on the parents, or the whole family. That makes more sense than the juvie crap. Although, King only bangs young women, really young women. Could be a father/son fetish."

When Ruby comes around, she says an unequivocal, "Yes, I think Heir Kingston had a thing for young girls," then she tells Tom why she thinks so.

After he's written down everything Ruby said, he sits back for a think.

Ruby pushes in with a concern, "The chief used to come to Echo a lot. He and King spent hours in closed door meetings, most of them were loud and angry. Should we be trusting Chief Banks?"

Tom puts his pen down and shoots from the hip, "The stakes in this are high, not only for you. The bottom line is this, we don't have a choice but to trust Vernon. The way you and I handle this, we stay in our lanes. We only reveal what we have to, and we ask the questions that we need answers to. We leave all the other shit on the side. The good thing for you is that you're here. You're working with me. I get to choose what gets said and to whom. You don't talk to anyone else. Is that clear?"

"Yes."

"Good. Now, tell me when you started sleeping with Heir Kingston."

Her eyes mist, her hand goes to her baby bump. "I'll be right back." She returns with a

2016 and a 2017 pocket calendar. "I don't really need these, but I thought you might want them."

Tom flips through while she gets lost in thought...

Edward bolted upright in bed when something very soft brushed his cheek. Light from the moon illuminated a naked Ruby. "Jesus, put that shimmer robe back on. If King finds you here, he'll kill the both of us."

"King isn't coming home tonight."

"Why not?"

"He has business in town. We both know what that means."

"You think he's with someone else? A woman?"

"Of course, a woman. There isn't a woman alive, or dead, who's managed to keep King faithful." Ruby crawled onto the bed, slid her hand beneath the sheet and took hold of Edward's very hard dick. "So much bigger than King's and I don't have to wait a half-hour for the little blue pill to do its job. Now, speaking of job."

"July 23rd."

"What year?"

"Two-thousand-sixteen."

"What prompted the affair?"

She gets really quiet, thinks a bit, then asks a question, "When did Laire MacTavish go missing?"

"July 21, 2016."

She gets quiet again, really quiet...

120

The sound of a motor pulled her from sleep. She glanced at the clock, "Twelve-seventeen." She went to the balcony, saw King sitting on his rattan having a belt and a smoke, saw Edward securing his Cat.

"Those things will kill you," Edward IV said as he stepped onto the dock, referring to the cigarette in King's hand, the one glowing a red tip and wafting the smell of menthol smoke his way.

"Gotta die someday, somehow."

Ruby headed inside, "I should freshen up, in case King wants to pound my pussy a bit." She moved back to the balcony many minutes later and saw Edward pacing the shoreline, "What's with Mr. Calm, Cool, and Collected? He's all amped up, whipping driftwood, and … is he talking to himself?" She watched from on high as he moved back and forth, back and forth, as he did a quick sit upon the rattan and a jog to his Jag. "Where's he going? Huh? Nowhere?" They made eye contact when he headed back toward the house.

"I saw Heir dock his Cat shortly after midnight on July 22nd. He exchanged a few words with King on the lawn, then spent a lot of time pacing the shoreline talking to himself. He headed toward the Jag, but turned around when he saw me on the balcony. Later that day, he raced into Echo and nearly knocked me off my feet rushing through the foyer. He apologized for not looking where he was going. I told him not to worry because I was watching everything that went on at the estate. The next day, King planned a night away. I spent the night in Edward's bed—a place I'd tried to get into for more than a year."

Tom mulls a bit, "Would you have given a false alibi for Heir if he hadn't slept with you?"

"I would have been vague, like I saw him around the estate that evening, but once I had him in my bed, I would have said anything to keep him there."

"When did you stop sleeping with him?"

"Technically, I didn't know our affair ended. Edward was spending a lot of time in Portland, but whenever King went off Whisper for business, Edward 'boated the bay for a lay' – that's what we called it. On July Fourth, out of the red, white, and blue, Quinn Hughes was introduced as Edward's yearlong girlfriend."

"Quinn Hughes. So Heir *did* have a mystery woman in Portland?"

She shrugs a shoulder and gives a little head shake, "I'd heard the rumors, but there was absolutely nothing to suggest he was involved with someone else until she showed up."

"What do you know about Ms. Hughes?"

"She's in her early thirties, originally from Alvarado, Texas, a graduate of Harvard Law, and the managing partner of Hughes and Creighton. The firm has two locations, one in Portland, Maine, and the other in Portsmouth, New Hampshire."

Tom makes a note; actually he makes several notes. "Okay, that's enough for now. I need to make a call, and you can't stay out here without me."

"No problem. I'd like to rest upstairs." That's where she heads.

He notices the sadness in her eyes as she rounds the staircase. "God, I hope she's alive to see that kid's birth." He gives his head a shake as he heads to his recliner to make a call.

It is answered practically before it rings, "Hello!"

"Hello, Roxanne."

"God, Tom, it's almost two. Did you forget that I'm calling the chief today?"

"Nope. Just getting some things in order. The short story, off the record, is that I'm doing a favor for the chief, a rather big favor. In return, he has assured me he will present the cases to the Council in chronological order."

"So he'll start with Christie Anderson's disappearance?"

"Yes. It's going to be tough linking Heir to Christie without Fred Fuller's testimony, but during a prison meeting with Lan, he remembered that Christie had a minor bump into a new waitress carrying a tray of drinks."

"We need to find that waitress."

"We will. Right now, you need to dig in with the chief about Christie Anderson. If you read the files I gave you then you know what I found during the investigation. Make sure you let him know we talked and I told you there wasn't any hard evidence against Lan MacTavish. Ask him if there are any new developments or witnesses. The chief doesn't know Dale tipped us off months ago that two new witnesses supposedly surfaced and they had testimony unfavorable to Lan. Feel the chief out. Let's see if he's forthcoming."

"Got it, Detective."

"Stop by my place tomorrow night at seven. We can discuss your conversation with the chief, and I want to introduce you to a very important team member—probably the most important team member we have. Be smart and careful, Roxanne, and don't be late."

Week Two – Day One
Thursday, November 2
Waxing Gibbous – Illumination 97%

An almost unrecognizable Lan MacTavish enters the prison meeting room. Tom is hit hard by the urgency of the situation facing him, so he goes in hard and straight, "Listen the fuck up, Lan. I gave you my word, and I am a man of my word. I will have you out of here by the end of this year. Eight weeks. Hold on for eight more weeks."

Lan puts his cuffed hands onto the table, hangs his head, and hopes to hell Tom has something he can grasp onto. "Heard the storm stopped the ferries."

"Yeah. Parts of the island took a real beating, shut down ferries, trollies, and just about everything else."

"You're not drippin, so I'm guessin you didn't swim the bay."

"I have friends. They have boats."

The prisoner makes eye contact and sits straight in his chair, "My regrets at the passin of your wife."

Tom nods and moves on—because he has to. "I'm sure Roxanne filled you in on what happened on Stony Beach."

"Some. Grateful that Joe's daughter fared better than Laire."

"Marin is out of rehab and back home with her mother."

"That's right news, Tom. I heard there's to be an inquest beginnin Monday."

"It's pushed back a week."

He scoffs, "No rush, I guess."

"Look, Lan. I'm working the case again. I made a deal with the devil so I could get the Council to look at the cases in chronological order. That's the only way they'll be able to connect Heir to all of the crimes. I needed an extra week to put some shit together."

"Am I to put my faith in some demon? Cause if that's the path we're travelin, then my prayers to the man upstairs are misdirected."

"You keep your prayers set, let me deal with the devil. Now, for some questions. I want answers, even though you've answered them a hundred times already. Where did you meet Christie?"

"At Diggers."

"And you spent the next two days at the beach with her."

"Right."

"And on the second day at the beach you learned she was underage."

"Right."

"So you left."

"Straight up."

"Then you saw her at Diggers the night she disappeared."

"Yes."

"She was sitting on some guy's lap."

"Yes."

"But you never saw his face."

"Right."

"And Fred Fuller saw you at the bar."

"Yes."

"You said Christie walked past you on her way to the Ladies' Room."

"Yes."

"And she bumped into a waitress carrying a tray of drinks."

"Yes."

"And during the cleanup the waitress mentioned she was new."

"Yes."

"Did she say her name?"

"Not that I heard."

"What'd she look like?"

"A tree sprite. A bit of a thing with brown hair and a mess of freckles."

"Pretty good description for a tray-carrying-new-girl-waitress."

"I'd been watchin her some that night, doin her comin and goin from the bar with orders. I remember wonderin if she was shaggin Fred on the side. Friendly the two were."

Tom gets up, "I gotta go. You need to hang in there."

"Before you push off, how'd Roxanne do with the storm?"

"The east bend took a hit, but she's fine. She's heading to my place tonight for a team meeting."

"Sure appreciate your work, Tom."

"Eight weeks, Lan."

Mooring

Tom bellies to the bar and orders a draft and a plate of smothered fries. He offers a trite apology heavenly, "Sorry for grub, Miss Prissy. But when in Rome."

"What's that?" the bartender asks.

"I stopped in to see Fred. I heard he bought this place and wanted to congratulate him."

Bartender Man leans back against a counter and folds his arms across his b.r.o.a.d. chest. "Fred the fuck who? I own this place."

"Yeah? Since when?"

"Since none of your fucking business, Old Man."

Tom stands, moves his jacket aside, making sure Bartender Man sees his badge, the one he's no longer supposed to be wearing, and his Glock, "Could be the business of you and me, or we can give Portland PD a call and have a group meeting. I'll even share my loaded fries with the boys in blue." Tom stops talking when the bar door opens and a bright glare of light shines in. It brings with it a little bit of a thing with brown hair and a mess of freckles. "Tree sprite," he smiles wide, takes a swig of beer, approaches the woman, shows her his badge, and leads her out of Mooring.

"Where's Fred Fuller?"

She tears, "I don't know."

"What's your name?"

"Sherry Flynn."

"Show me your ID." He takes a picture with his cell phone. "Okay, Sherry Flynn, when was the last time you saw Fred?"

She looks over Tom's shoulder at Bartender Man and clams up.

Tom reaches into his pocket, "How much would you make today waiting tables?"

"Maybe fifty bucks."

"Here's two hundred. Let's go."

"Where are we going?"

"Whisper Island."

She smiles warmly, "My grandma lives on Whisper."

Tom walks her down the pier, helps her into his friend's catamaran, starts the engine, listens to the Cat's gentle purr as he inches it away from the dock, then acknowledges Sherry's last statement. "That's nice, but you won't be seeing grandma this visit."

"Why not?"

"I hope you'll be too busy helping me with a case."

"A case? Like an investigation?"

"Yes."

Silence.

"There's a man sitting in jail for a murder he didn't commit. I think you might be able to help him."

The young woman nods, "Lan MacTavish. This is about him, isn't it?"

"Yes."

Sherry might have asked Tom to take her back to the dock if she hadn't seen Bartender Man glaring and shaking his head in warning.

Primrose Priscilla

Ruby and Sherry are waiting upstairs in separate bedrooms when they hear the front doorbell. They wait ten minutes as they'd been asked before coming downstairs.

Roxanne is just finishing her recap of the phone conversation she had with Chief Banks, when the women appear. "Ruby Norman," Roxanne exhales on a whisper, then turns wide eyes to Tom, "She's on our team?"

"She is."

"And who's that?"

"Her name is Sherry Flynn, and I'm hoping she'll be joining our team."

The Tinkerbell clone smiles, "If you can keep me safe from Rodriquez and whoever he works for, I'll join your team."

"Rodriquez is the bartender at Mooring?"

"Yes. And I think he's the one who killed Fred."

"He's really dead?" Roxanne sucker-punch exhales.

Sherry shrugs then shakes her head in hopeful uncertainty. "Rodriquez says Fred is away on business. He's not. Mooring is Fred's business. He said when he bought it he was going to go legit. He wouldn't have left it in the hands of muscle like Rodriquez, and he wouldn't have left me behind."

"Because you're his woman?"

"Because I'm his wife."

"Yeah? When and where did you get married?" Tom pushes.

"January 5, 2015, at the Portland Courthouse."

"Roxanne, pull up Portland Records Department, see if there's a marriage license for Sherry and Fred."

"There is. I can order a copy online and have it sent registered mail. If the Abenaki is up and running soon, it should arrive before the inquest."

"Do it. We won't be able to put Sherry's testimony into the record unless we can prove she's his wife."

"Or his widow," Sherry tears.

Sand Castle

Dale is sitting on a chaise on the tiny porch rubbing his sore leg when Marin comes outside carrying two enormous mugs of coffee. "Are we working the night shift?"

"Nope. We're celebrating."

"And the beverage of choice is coffee? One of us must have taken a big blow to the cranium because I think it's customary to celebrate with champagne or wine, maybe," she shrugs.

"Close your eyes and maybe your mouth, too." He strikes a match. "Okay."

She opens her eyes.

He presents a honey-glazed donut with a lit birthday candle. "I'm sorry I missed it. I'm sorry you missed it."

She smiles wide. "LL said I liked honey-glazed," she reaches for the yummy, closes her eyes, makes a wish, and blows out the candle.

"Who's LL?"

"June. It's what I labeled her when I first got home."

He laughs, "Yeah, most of the shit at Jacobs Jolly is labeled, even the damned soap opera Connie watches. She gives a holler each day, 'Dale, it's time for GH.'"

"GH?"

"General Hospital," he groans. "She can be a PITA."

"PITA?" Marin shrugs.

"Pain In The Ass."

She spits her mouthful of coffee.

"Connie means well, but I'm a grown man who could use a lot less hovering."

She nods and takes a bite. "Mmmmm," she licks a finger.

"You've got a sweet deal with Sand Castle. You've got help nearby, but you've got your space."

"Mmmmm," she licks another finger then gets really still.

He notices. He figures she's pulling a memory-thread. He waits.

"Do you ride a Harley?"

His face gets all smiley, then all grumpy, "Used to," he raps his bum leg, "Maybe again one day, who knows?"

Marin rips a piece of the donut, "Here." She pops it into his mouth, takes the last bite, "Mmmmm. Oh, wow, that is good. Don't tell June that I like the honey-glazed."

"Why?"

"Not sure."

"Hey, why did you label her LL?"

"She thought I forgot what a lesbian is. I suggested it was a barnyard animal with a long neck, so—"

"You labeled her Lesbian Llama."

"Yeah."

He cracks the fuck up, "You know, this labeling thing could be mad fun."

"Yeah? What would you label me?"

He doesn't miss a beat, "MB."

"Those are my initials."

"Coincidence."

"No such thing."

"Just proved you wrong. MB is a total coincidence, and that's your new label."

"Why?"

He laughs and nudges, "You'll figure it out, and when you do, I'll show you something."

"A riddle and a prolonged period of suspense. Not sure my banged to shit brain can handle it, but I'm in."

He takes hold of her hand and squeezes it, "I'm in, too, Marin."

Week Two – Day Two
Friday, November 3
Waxing Gibbous – Illumination 99%

Tom pushes his ass from the recliner at the first waft of bacon. He sprints through the kitchen without word, heads for the bathroom, throws himself into the shower, dresses for the day, and heads back toward the smell of Nirvana. "Gotta say, Ms. Norman, you're earning your keep with all the cooking you're doing."

"I used to be a short-order cook at the Beach Bum. Haven't done much by way of grub-preparing for the past couple years, although King put Cook on an 'as needed basis' after Edward died, so I did a little cooking at the estate, recently. I'm enjoying it." She hands him a plate, "A Sunny-Runny Nesting, and four strips of bacon."

He examines it, grabs a fork and plows in. "A Sunnyside egg sitting in the center of a piece of toast, never had one. This is damned good. What's the spice on top?"

"Oregano."

"I like it. Have you seen Sherry this morning?"

"She was on the screen porch. I think she's in the backyard, now."

He pushes from the table, heads in that direction, and returns with Boarder Number 2. "Okay, some house rules. Primrose Priscilla is at the end of a cul-de-sac and surrounded by deep tree growth that offers a good amount of privacy, but with work, someone could get close enough to put eyes on the place."

The tree sprite speaks up, "How long can we stay here without someone finding us?"

"A couple weeks, maybe a month if we're all really careful. Sherry, I'll start working with you this morning. The Council will be reviewing Christie Anderson's case first. They planned on getting testimony from Fred, but—"

"He's most likely dead."

"Let's start there. Why do you think he's dead and not on the run or in hiding?"

"Fred's an opportunist, and he'll squeeze anyone at any time, his weapon of choice is using shit he gets on people to get what he wants. His last shakedown put him in danger. I knew it. He knew it."

"Tell me about it."

"Everything about Mooring is tied to Diggers."

"Start there."

"The night Christie Anderson went missing was my first night waitressing at the bar. Fred and I started a thing when I came to Whisper to visit my grandmother for the summer. One thing led to another and he offered me a job. I wanted to stay on Whisper so I took it. When the shit hit that a teenage girl went missing from his place, he knew he was gonna get screwed by WPD, so he tested the waters. 'Tossed a few buoys,' he said. The way he explained it to me was that he didn't know who Christie left Diggers with, but he knew who she was riding inside his joint, and that he might be able to make bank out of it. Next thing I knew, Fred said he had a buyer for Diggers and that we were heading out together."

"Max Trainor bought the place."

She shakes her head, "That's what Fred thought, too, but when he bought Mooring, the paperwork from the State Liquor Board listed two licenses under Fred's name. One for Diggers and one for Mooring."

"So Max Trainor is a front man for Diggers."

"Yes. Fred said that someone fronted Max the money and put phony selling and buying paperwork through, leaving Fred as the owner. He said he never would have been the wiser if he hadn't bought Mooring."

"Who bankrolled the supposed sale of Diggers?"

"The King of Whisper."

Ruby stops washing dishes, makes her way to the table, and plops her ass. "The person Fred saw Christie Anderson with the night she went missing, it was Heir Kingston, wasn't it?"

"Yes."

Ruby's hand finds her baby bump.

Sherry notices, "That's Heir's baby."

"Yes."

"You're screwed if The King of Whisper finds out."

"More like I'm dead when he figures it out, and he probably already figured it out."

Sand Castle

Marin marches through the living area, wakes a couch-sleeping Dale on her way past, "I'll be back. Put on a pot of coffee."

"Damn you're bossy and bitchy in the morning."

"Get used to it, cause you're moving in."

June is at the kitchen window looking at the ocean when she sees Marin round the corner of the pale pink shoreline cottage, "Enemy forces heading this way, General Baxter." Jenny and Esmé push for viewing space.

"Ay dios mío, what now?"

The Three Women are shoulder to shoulder when The Promise door opens and the first salvo is fired, "Dale bought me a birthday donut. He held my hand. He's moving into Sand Castle with me. We aren't sleeping together. Yet. His mother is a PITA. And I like his company." She turns and leaves.

The Three Women plop back against the counter in silence. June breaks it, "I wonder if it was a honey-glazed? It had to have been a honey-glazed. There's **no way** she'd have him move in if he brought her a plain donut."

"You're wondering about donuts, I'm wondering what a PITA is."

"Marin's labeling things, Esmé. And she's referring to someone's mother as a PITA, so figure it out," Jenny nudges.

The mother turns in time to see her daughter round the corner at the cottage, "Pain In The Ass."

"Yesss," Jenny and June unison.

The young woman slams the door behind her, flips her chestnut waves over her shoulder, and drills Dale with her hazel-blue eyes, "These are the terms. You're moving in. We'll take turns sleeping in the bed and on the couch. We're going to try a boyfriend-girlfriend thing, and when I'm ready, we're going to try sex. You've probably already tried it," she pauses for his response.

He laughs it, "Yeah."

"And you remember it?"

He laughs harder, "Yeah."

"So it must be pleasurable."

Still laughing, "Shit, yeah."

"Then one day you will be pleasuring me, Dale Jacobs."

He's pulled her chest to chest in a heartbeat, "You know I will!" He kisses her. R.e.a.l.l.y. kisses her.

When Marin can pull another breath she says the first thing that comes to mind, "Shit, yeah."

Echo

King is in his office watching a crew of men clear debris from the backend of his estate, and haul away the remains of Edward's mint-green and white catamaran. "Fuckin shame. All of it. Edward's death. The fuckin inquest. Ruby's baby. The Cat. Every fuckin thing is going to shit." He pulls a swig and pushes back, way back, "It's only going to shit if I let it. I might not be able to fully exonerate Heir, but I can lessen the stain of his actions. And who knows, if I find out Heir and Dale knew each other, I might be able to frame the asshole with a few of Heir's crimes. Might be easy now that Dale is barely functioning after the bullet to his back and the smash and crash on Stony Beach." He lifts a file from his desktop, "Dale Jacobs. You are now the focus of a Kingston investigation. Every fuckin rock you banged against on that ill-fated night is going to be looked under. If there's a single thread connecting you and Edward, I'm going to find it, loop it, and hang you with it. Even if you are my son, you aren't the one I want here beside me. And if I learn you are the reason Edward is dead, then right backatcha. And the next time I get you in my sights, my bullet will take you the fuck out."

Carmichael Corner

Roxanne answers her cell just before the call goes to voicemail, "Yeah. Tom. I'm here."

"When are you and the chief scheduled to talk again?"

"Today at two."

"Okay. Follow up on these three things.

- Ask him if he received a Medical Examiner's Report on Edward Kingston IV, and if he has, ask him who else has a copy. If he doesn't have one, ask him to chase it down.
- Feel him out on the owner of Diggers. Sherry just told me that Max Trainor is a front man and that Fred Fuller still owns the place. Ask Banks if he knows there was a bait and switch. Do not tell him about Sherry and Fred. I want him to know I'm pushing all-in on this, but I don't want to tip my hand on Sherry.
- Ask him what happened to Edward's Jag."

"Got it. I'll call you later."

"Roxanne, before you go, I saw Lan yesterday."

"He's a fuckin mess, right?"

"Yeah. I told him to hang on for another eight weeks. So we need to get this shit done in that time frame."

"Can we?"

"Yes."

"Okay."

"And Roxanne."

"Yeah."

"He asked how your place did in the storm. I'm glad you stuck by him all this time."

She hangs up so she can keep her emotions to herself.

Outer Banks

The Chief enters his place and goes directly to the wall safe, grabs hold of several files, and heads to his home office. He tosses the paperwork onto his desk, heads to the kitchen for a beer, and bangs his conversation with Roxanne Carmichael as he pops and pulls a swig…

"Has an ME report on Edward Kingston IV been released?"

"A preliminary one."

"And the findings?"

"Cause of death: drowning. Manner of death: suicide."

"Will an official report be released before the inquest?"

"It's slated to be, but the Council is willing to accept and enter the prelim. King is none too pleased with the suggestion Heir killed himself. He thinks it implies consciousness of guilt. He's not wrong. If the ME's report was introduced in a court of law, it would weigh in favor of the prosecution, but with the Council, who knows if King has pressured or paid for favorable results."

"Tom wants you to send him a copy."

"In the mail. What else?"

"The owner of Diggers."

"Max Trainor. What about him?"

"Tom was wondering how he financed the joint."

There's a pause. A good long pause. "I haven't a clue. That's a thread that needs pulling. Tell Tom I'm on it."

"Okay. Last item. Any idea what happened to Heir's Jag?"

"The car was last seen parked at The Claremont, the waterfront high-rise Heir lived in. It went missing from there a week or so before he washed up on the shore. I'll pull my files and get the information to Tom."

The chief rifles through a handful of files, "ME's report." He reads the name of the deceased, "Edward Kingston IV. That's wrong, that's so fucking wrong." He bangs his fist on his desk as his mind bangs against the last conversation he had with Kathleen Beckwith Kingston, the woman who left him for The King of Whisper a quarter century ago...

Vernon sat at Kathleen's bedside for more than an hour before she stirred.

"Vern. You came." **A tear slid her cheek.**

He wiped it with the pad of his thumb, "I'd follow you to the ends of the earth, Kathleen," **he said the words he used to say when they were a thing, all those years ago.**

"Not this time, Vern. You need to stay here and keep an eye on things .... On your son." **She waited for him to pull the thread.**

"Edward. He's my son, our son?"

"Yes. I'm so sorry, Vern. More sorry than you will ever know. I should have told you, I should have chosen you, Vernon."

He patted her hand, "You followed your heart, Kathleen."

"I followed the money." She teared, struggled to take his hand and weave her fingers with his, "Please ... please take care of our son."

The man who never found his way to another hangs his head in shame, "I didn't do a damned thing to care for our son, Kathleen. I let him be raised by that son of a bitch, and look where it's put our boy. In an early grave. Thank God you aren't here to learn the awful things about your Eddie. The worst thing, Kathleen, is every damned word that's being said is true. Your son was raised by a monster and he became a monster. And I stood by and let it happen. By the time I got my shit together, it was too late. The damage to Edward was done. The damage to Christie, Laire, Danielle, and Joe, was done. The stain of their blood is on my hands and I'll burden that crimson, but I won't burden it alone. As God is my judge—as you are my judge—the Kingston men will shoulder their sins. And if I die trying to right my wrongs, and if I am so blessed, I'll gladly follow you throughout all eternity, Kathleen."

Jacobs Jolly

A man known only as Paxton parked a borrowed Tacoma down the street from an adorable cape on the western side of Whisper. He pushed the driver's seat as far back as possible, stretched his legs, twisted the kink from his back, and did a fair amount of grousing. "As soon as the Abenaki is up and running, I'm bringing my own ride. Sitting in this fucker is gonna tie my back in knots." He shines his penlight onto the file Edward Kingston III gave him and bangs their recent conversation...

"That's a picture of Dale Jacobs. He lives in a little cape with his mother, Connie. I don't have a picture of her, but she used to look like June Cleaver. She's probably in her sixties now. Dale is recuperating from a gunshot wound to the back and a prolonged bang on a rocky shore during hightide. Word is he's getting better physically and mentally. Full disclosure, he's a cop out on injured duty. So don't discount his abilities."

"Just those two live in the cape?"

"That's what I'm paying you to find out."

Paxton walked out, "I'll be in touch."

Connie Jacobs has an unsettled feeling, she's had it all night. She walks the floors, makes several cups of tea, each of which goes cold on the end table, tries to lose herself in a book, and in a television program, and in an old photo album, but something keeps nudging and running her spine in a very uncomfortable way.

"I wish Dale was here." She shakes her head and smiles, "No I don't. I'm more than happy that he's with Marin. Being away from her all that time was such a source of pain and frustration for him. Just hearing her name got to him, hurt him, worried him. It's good they're together, and now that he and I aren't under the same roof, maybe he won't think I'm a pain in the posterior." She laughs—stopping cold when she gets a heebie-jeebie. She checks the doors and windows three times each before retiring upstairs, spends time in the bath, wraps her hair in a silky turban, moisturizes her face and hands, fluffs and puffs her pillow, then hunts for slumber. She never quite finds it—not the restful kind anyway.

Week Two – Day Three
Saturday, November 4
Full Moon – Illumination 100%

Roxanne Carmichael, the plucky reporter for WCWI news, has spent the day with a camera crew on the far end of the eastern side of the island, not too far from her bungalow. For the past hour, she's been busy putting up her rain slicker hood, then sliding it down, then pushing it back up again. All that time, she's had her back turned toward a windy whip of rain coming off the ocean and has been grousing that her ass is soaking wet. "Tim, make sure you don't film from my waist down. The audience will think I've pissed my pants."

"No problem, Roxi."

Roxanne and two others were dispatched to report on the unearthing of the hull of a ship that went missing a long, long time ago, most likely during a nor'easter similar to the one that hit Whisper a handful of days ago. Roxanne slides her hood off at the finger-countdown of her cameraman and begins.

"Good afternoon. For those Whisper Island residents with electricity, I appreciate your tuning in. I think you will be very happy you did because we have quite a story in the making."

She meanders toward the obvious shape of a ship's hull imbedded in wet sand.

"This, ladies and gentlemen, may be the remains of a cargo ship last seen in 1901 entering Casco Bay during a fall nor'easter—at least that's what Clarkston Bainbridge, a fifty-year resident of Whisper Island, and professor emeritus in marine biology and archaeology at Northeastern University thinks. Professor Bainbridge came upon the wreckage the day after our storm, did a bit of research, and concluded, preliminarily, of course, that this unearthed hull may be part of a missing vessel known as, *Darling*. The professor contacted Northeastern and asked a team of researchers to join him in a field study of this exciting find."

The cameraman does a panoramic swing while Roxanne continues.

"All across our island, there are reminders that humans are at the mercy of powerful and uncontrollable weather events. Our community members are in the process of cleaning up homes and property, and have ventured out to share stories of where they were during the two-day Halloween storm. Simply stated, our families and friends are sharing their personal histories. One day in the future, Professor Bainbridge and the team of experts at Northeastern will have concluded their work, and will be able to tell the story of this unearthed hull. That's when the people of Whisper Island will add *Darling*, or whomever this ship may be, to our personal histories. When my time comes to share this story, I'll begin by saying I had the privilege to stand a few feet from a historical find on the wonderful island of Whisper. On behalf of WCWI Channel 4, this is Roxanne Carmichael, thanking you for tuning in to the mystery of, The Whisper Island Shipwreck. Stay safe."

Primrose Priscilla

The shades and curtains are drawn in the front room of the yellow bungalow. There's a dying fire, and Ruby and Sherry are telling Tom about Roxanne's shipwreck report. The Boarders are very animated and maybe even a little starstruck by the T.V. reporter. Tom enjoys the back and forth a bit, then pushes into his investigation. "Sherry, tell me how Fred got the money to buy Mooring."

"He said he ran into Heir on the docks, told him he wanted to buy the place and that he was going to bankroll it for him."

"He blackmailed Edward Kingston IV with the Christie Anderson information."

"Yes."

"Because Edward was the guy Christie was riding in Diggers?"

"Yes."

"How big was the payout?"

"A million. He said Heir told him it was the last money he'd get, and the next time Fred tried to shakedown a Kingston, he'd be talking to The King, himself."

"When did the transaction take place?"

"The transfer of money happened at the beginning of July, maybe a few days after the Fourth. Fred became owner of Mooring by the end of July."

"When did Fred go missing?"

"September 27th."

Ruby pushes to her feet and begins pacing the living room, then heads out to the kitchen and back again, then does another turnabout for good measure.

"What's going on, Ruby?"

"A memory. Maybe. I spent half of my time at Echo listening at doors, or from around corners, or tucked into nearby nooks. I know more shit than I'd ever be able to tell you, but sometimes the stuff I heard didn't make sense. Like now." She puts her hand up, "Give me a minute ……. Okay, I overheard one of King's phone conversations. He was really pissed and probably lit to shit, so I didn't think he made any sense back then, but now ……. King said to whoever was on the other end of the phone that he wanted the guy taken care of."

"When was this?"

"After I moved back from the mainland, so sometime in August. I might have jotted it in the 2017 calendar I gave you. King said to make sure he suffered for every single dollar of the mill he shook down." Ruby tears when she sees Sherry's face, "I'm sorry. Maybe I shouldn't have said anything." She sits next to the tree sprite, wraps her arm around, and pulls her close.

Tom gets up, "You two should head upstairs. I have work to do." He waits for the women to leave, does a lock check, sets the alarm, and heads to his recliner. He checks the time, then makes the call. "Is it too late?"

"Nope."

"Are you busy tomorrow?"

"Nope."

"I need to check out Watch Ledge, see if there's any damage from the storm. I thought I'd check out Wind Ledge at the same time. Do you want to come along?"

"Yeah."

"And tell your wife I'll be calling her about a job."

"Okay, see ya. Hey, what time?"

"How's seven?"

"Sounds good."

Tom grabs hold of the journal he's been moving through, kicks back in his recliner and spends time with his beloved Miss Prissy. He finishes the second tome for 1982, grabs hold of the paper he's keeping a running list on, and jots down the song she chose as 'her song' for that year. "*Always on my Mind*, well ain't that the truth, Priscilla. You are always on my mind."

Sand Castle

Marin is nestled in the V of Dale's legs, sharing a chaise, a wool blanket, and the Full Hunter's Moon.

Dale pulls her close and just sort of relaxes into the moment. "When I got home from rehab, I was bored, angry, restless, and a whole lot of other stuff. There were times when my mother's twitching became too much, lots of times," he sort of growls.

She sort of laughs.

"I used my father's den to put some space and get some peace. In the beginning, I'd sit and read or try to pull some threads—that was before I found his records. Matt Jacobs amassed an amazing LP collection. I knew he loved music, he played it all the time when I visited, but I must have thought he listened to the radio or something. I was looking through his stuff, trying to get a framework for a memory-thread, and I looked behind a bifold door, and there they were, hundreds of LPs." He kisses her cheek, "LPs are vinyl records."

She laughs, "I know what LPs are, you jerk."

He laughs, "I spent hours, days really, listening to Dean Martin, Patsy Cline, Tony Bennett, Andy Williams, Connie Frances, you name it, he had all the greats. Then I found this separate section, it was stuff I never thought my father would listen to."

"Like?"

"Skynyrd, The Doobie Brothers, CCR, Jackson Browne, Bob Seger, Springsteen, Joe Cocker, Van Morrison, a really eclectic mix."

"And?"

"And I think we should have a song."

She giggles.

"Forget it."

"No. No. I've heard about couples having 'their song' but I imagine Marin before BB thought it was silly, though I can't say for certain."

"And now?"

"We can have a song, so long as it's not a stupid one."

"It's a Van Morrison song."

She sighs. "My father's favorite Morrison song was, *Into The Mystic*."

"Since you know Morrison's music, you probably figured out our song."

"Crazy Love."

He cracks up laughing. "No, but it could be. It's Moondance."

"Mmm. It's perfect."

"It will be perfect when I can dance with you," he taps his leg. "As soon as this is better, promise me we'll dance."

"Promise." She snuggles back against him and smiles wide. "I really like having organic memories, like now, remembering my father's favorite song. Some things come so easily. Like the other day I had an easy memory of you. I think. Maybe. Tell me if I'm wrong. The first time we met was when I was jogging Stony Beach toward the far bend. Esmé wanted me back before the storm came, so I did a swift turnabout and smacked full-body into you."

"Your ass thudded hard onto the sand."

"And I twisted my ankle."

"And I gave you a piggyback ride to Wind."

"So that really happened."

"Yeah."

He wraps his arms tight across her chest and kisses her cheek. "The first memory I had of you was from *that* day, but before everything went to shit. We'd been up really late the night before helping Esmé pack her artwork and stuff, so we sort of eased into the day. The weather was overcast and cold so we threw on jeans and sweatshirts, had coffee, I think on the veranda at Wind Ledge, and then went down to the beach. We watched people build stone temples and shit—"

"Stonehenge. Huh, I think that's a memory."

He kisses her cheek and continues, "And we did some jogging, and you went on and on about lunar phases and ocean tides."

She presses back against him, "I think you meant to say I impressed you with my knowledge about that beautiful satellite right there."

"The Hunter's Moon."

"Very good, Mr. Jacobs. It's late this year."

"Here we go. A dissertation by Marin Baxter on November's full moon."

"The Hunter's Moon follows the Harvest Moon in October. That full moon is closest to the autumnal equinox. I'm not sure what the date of the Harvest was this year, but November 4th is just about the latest possible date for a full Hunter's Moon?" She's quiet for a minute, "Well, I'm not sure where all that came from, but it was nice."

He wraps her tight again and smiles big. "I did a little reading on the Hunter's Moon and thought I'd impress you with some shit, but after that show off routine, I think—"

"No, no. Tell me."

"This year's Hunter's Moon is influenced by Neptune and Venus. It's said it will guide people to their sensitive, intuitive, emotional, and romantic sides."

She wraps his arms tighter, "Proof positive, wouldn't you say? We are all slaves to the moon."

He kisses her cheek. "Getting back to my memories of *that* day, after you impressed me with your lunar dissertation, we moved to the far end of the beach and stretched out on the sand."

She snuggles against him, drifts into a memory and talks herself through it. "I woke to raindrops hitting my face. Within a second I heard a gunshot. I panicked when you weren't next to me. I started for Wind, but I remembered you had your gun with you because you were my protection." She shifts quickly from an almost robotic recitation to an emotional one. "You said I should stay with you, but you left me." She begins crying – really crying and trembling.

Dale moves out from behind her and pulls her to her feet. "Come on, let's get inside and sit by the fire."

She waits while he tends to the dying embers, and when he joins her he sets the mandate, "Let's talk. Just talk. About nothing or something, but no memory talking."

"That's going to be really hard to do, Dale. Like, what if I wanted to tell you my favorite kid's book, or my favorite vacation, or pretty much anything. All of my stories depend on my memories."

"Okay. Good memories then." He stretches his sore leg the length of the sofa.

She lifts it and puts it onto her lap. "Okay, me first."

He nods.

Her smile spreads wide and her eyes light, "My favorite kid's book is, *I Love You, Stinky Face.*"

"Never heard of it. Why is it your favorite?"

"First of all, the illustration is wonderfully vivid with goofy, oversized characters. The pictures inspired me to try my hand at drawing, but the story is why I love it. It's about a little boy who wonders if there are boundaries to his mother's love, like would she love him if he smelled like a skunk, or looked like a big, scary ape. It basically reinforces the premise that a mother's love is unconditional." She's quiet for a minute then pushes in, "I actually remembered that, from a really warm place in my heart and head."

"I know. I could tell."

"It felt good."

He leans forward and slides his cell from his jeans pocket, "Speaking of mothers." He answers her call, "Kinda late, is everything okay?"

"Yes. I'm just tired. I didn't sleep well, but that's not why I'm calling. Are you coming to the house tomorrow for your therapy session?"

"Tomorrow's Sunday. I don't have a session tomorrow, and I scheduled Monday's appointment at the rehab center."

"Oh, okay. How are things with Marin?"

"Good. Things are good."

"I hope to meet her before I head off island. It won't be anytime soon, but when you want to sell Jacobs Jolly, I'll have to go home."

"We'll talk about it."

"Okay. Tell Marin hello, and I love you, Dale."

"Ah. Yeah. Mom, are you okay?"

"Yes. Yes. I'm fine. Goodnight."

Dale sits looking at his phone, "Well, that was weird."

"What?"

"I don't think I ever heard my mother say she loves me. She does, of course, she just never says those words. It's always been something like, 'you're my favorite person in the whole world' or 'my cup runneth over' – that kind of stuff."

"Do you think you should go home? Maybe stay the night?"

He checks the time on his cell, "It's almost midnight. I don't want to ask the Baxterettes for a lift."

"Ha! You call the lesbians the Baxterettes?"

"Yeah. I guess."

"That's hilarious."

She lifts his leg off her, crawls the length of him and stretches long. His response is of the l.o.n.g – h.a.r.d variety. She lifts her hips, "Oh."

"Yeah, oh. You should get up."
"Am I hurting you."
"Not in the way you think."

Week Two – Day Four
Sunday, November 5
Waning Gibbous – Illumination 96%

Marin tossed and turned, rolled to and fro, fluffed her pillow, then tossed and turned a bit more before heading to the shower. She rinsed, lathered, and repeated, twice, hoping the warm wet jets would help soothe and relax. She dried, moisturized, and flipped her head back and forth and side to side getting most of the wetness out before pulling on a tank top and pair of boy short bottoms. She slipped into bed and waited. It took the agitated young woman a very long time before sleep welcomed her, and when it did, it was fitful…

"Dale!" She pressed her sweatshirt to his back, saw movement from behind a boulder. "Shooter. Run."

~~MARIN~~
~~DANGER LURKS~~

"Dale. Help!" she calls out from her bedroom.

"Marin! Wake up! You're having a nightmare."

She pushes free from his embrace, "Can't. Breathe. Get him off of me! Oh, God. Please get him off!"

Dale watches her struggle for air and push angrily at the bedcovers and rip at her top.

He wraps her in his arms, "Marin."

She calms a bit.

"Good. That's good. Open your eyes. Please."

She does, then closes them right back up. "The shot. I heard it. The blood. I felt it. The man who shot you. He was there. Behind a rock. We should tell Tom."

"We will. Tomorrow."

"I need to see it."

"What?"

"The bullet hole."

"What?"

"I don't know why, but I need to see it."

He pulls his T-shirt over his head, and turns his back toward her. She traces along the scar. "I tried to stop the bleeding. I didn't want to leave you," she chokes on her sobs.

He turns and pulls her close. "It's alright now, Marin. I'm alright now. Sort of," he laughs.

She shakes her head and chants, "No. No. No. It's not alright. Laire said, 'Danger Lurks.' She is telling me that we won't be safe until we know who shot you and why? Someone put a bullet in your back and left you to die. Who did that? Why did he do that?"

Dale runs her words through his head, *'Laire said Danger Lurks, that we won't be safe until we know who shot you and why'* — *does Marin think a spirit talks to her?* Dale repositions himself on the bed, "You need to think about something else. Anything else." He puts his hand onto the back of her head, pulls her near and kisses her temple, runs his fingers through her recently shampooed, still damp hair, "Mmm. What's that smell?"

"Raspberry sorbet," she rolls her eyes, "I asked Jenny to get me something fruity. I hated the shampoo in rehab, it was awful."

He takes a deep inhale, "Well, this sure the hell isn't awful."

"Glad you like it cause it's the only shampoo I have."

"Speaking of showers."

"We weren't."

"I could use a cold shower right about now."

"You can use the hot water, Dale."

He laughs, "Yeah, but I think a cold shower is in order." He kisses her and heads inside the bathroom.

Marin notices the bulge in Dale's jeans as he walks away, hops off the bed and begins pacing – the bedroom – then the living area – then the kitchen – then back again. She steps out onto the porch, feels the rise of goosebumps from the cold November air, and stares at the Hunter's Moon. "Ah, the influencer of romance. I guess I can blame *this* on the moon." She hops back inside and storms to her bedroom, strips her clothes, opens the bathroom door, takes an eyeful of the guy in her shower and joins him. "I have absolutely no idea what to do now that I'm naked and you're naked."

Dale steps forward. Marin steps forward. Dale wraps his arm around her waist, "Are you sure about this?"

"No."

He steps away. "You should leave, really, please."

"I don't think I can. I really want this, I just don't know how."

He kisses her, runs his fingers slowly down her cheek, chin, neck. He stares into her eyes, her beautiful hazel-blue eyes, kisses her, slowly, haltingly. She leans in, presses hip to hip. He molds her breasts, teases her nipple with his fingers, his lips, smiles when it buds tight in his mouth. He moans and pulses with his need for her, almost loses himself when she touches him.

"Will it fit?"

He touches her mound, fingers her gently, feels her excitement build and her wetness welcome, "Yeah, it'll fit fine. Are you sure?"

"Yesssss." They laugh. "Hurry before Esmé gets too far into my head."

He backs her against the wall, spreads her for his entry then turns the shower dial to freezing-fucking-cold.

She screeches, "What the hell!"

"We need birth control. Come on, let's dry off."

She takes hold of his hand, "Are you mad?"

"Not at you." He pulls her close. "I'm mad I wasn't prepared. It felt good, really good, too good."

She kisses him, "I liked it so far."

He laughs, "Yeah, me too." He returns to the couch.

She returns to her bed and tosses and turns, rolls to and fro, fluffs her pillow, tosses and turns a bit more then heads for a shower—a cold one.

Marin is standing on the dock when Tom pulls onto the driveway. He waves and heads her way.

"What are you doing out here? It's freezing."

"I needed to think."

"And you can't think inside."

"Dale's still sleeping. I didn't want to wake him."

"Sleeping? Inside? Sand Castle? Dale?"

"On the couch. He's staying here for a while. I need him here. I want him here."

Tom puts his arm around her shoulder, "What are you thinking about?"

"The man who shot Dale. I saw him, you know."

"No. I did not know."

"He was crouched behind a boulder. Whoever he is, he's the man who put a bullet into Dale's back and left him to die."

"Does Dale know?"

"He knows that I saw a man. He said he was going to talk to you about it."

"Okay. I'm running an errand with June. It'll take about an hour. Tell Dale I'll be back. The three of us will have a talk in your cottage."

"I'll put a pot on."

"I'll bring a box of yummies."

"Yes, please."

June has no sooner parked her ass inside Tom's truck when he starts in, "Dale lives with Marin?"

"Uh huh."

"Are they? Have they? Jesus, what are they? Friends? More?"

"Not sure what they are today, but the other day he was the guy who brought her a birthday donut and held her hand."

"What's Esmé thinking about all this?"

"She likes Dale. We all like Dale, and we all sort of saw this coming, even before the shit fest at Stony. Marin was crushing on Dale, and if he felt the same, he hid it really well, but there was this underlying thing. Esmé thinks their age difference is concerning. I keep reminding her it's the same age difference as her and Joe."

"Things were different back then."

"That's her argument, a flawed one in my opinion."

"You always have an opinion."

"As I was saying, the age argument had merits when Marin was a minor, but she's eighteen now. She can do whatever with whomever. Shit, most girls have done the deed long before eighteen. The reason Marin is a virgin, or was a virgin, is because she had goals and ambitions—they were always way more important than boys and hormones. If those two get down to business, I suspect Marin will initiate it, and it won't be about twittery feelings, it will be a pragmatic decision or a damned science experiment."

"Jesus, things sure are different these days."

"Things are different and Marin is different. The only constant in all this is that she has a thing for Dale and he clearly feels something for her. My guess is if they aren't doing it already, they soon will be."

"So you're fine with all this?"

June looks out the window and quietly takes in the morning sun lifting over rolling eastern waters. When Tom turns onto Cliff Road she answers, "Marin and Dale were nearly killed on Stony. They want to heal together. Who cares if it's sexual healing."

Motormouth silences pretty quick when she sees the damage at Wind Ledge. While Tom assesses, she climbs over this and around that, and makes her way to the access ladder platform. "What the?" She shades her eyes with her hand, "Tom. Tom. **Tom!**"

"What?"

"There's a body on Stony."

He climbs over this, and around that, and joins her on the access ladder platform. "For Christ sake." Even from the distance and the height, he knows whose body washed ashore on Stony Beach. He steps away and places a call, "Roxanne, we're off the record. I'm at Wind. There's a body on the beach. I'm pretty sure it's Fred Fuller. I'm going to call it in. Before I do, I need you to go to Primrose and hang with The Boarders. I'm not sure how long I'll be. If the television station wants you to do the story, give me a call." He hangs up and calls Chief Banks, "Vern, there's a deceased male on Stony near the access ladder at Wind. I think it's Fred Fuller. There's a lot of damage at the Baxter place, a tree took out Joe's shed, so you'd better get a crew here to clear a path to bring the body up." He hangs up and calls Dale, "June and I ran into a problem at Wind. It'll be a while before I get there." He hangs up and addresses his cohort, "Hey, June."

"Yeah."

"I need you and Jenny to stop by Primrose tomorrow. I don't want Esmé, Marin, or Dale to know."

"Will we be finding any cadavers? Cause Jenny really isn't good with goosebump-raising events."

"No dead bodies." He looks out at Fred Fuller, "so far as I can say."

Echo

Paxton parks the Kingston Tacoma on the circular drive, walks into the estate, and heads to King's office. "Fuller's body washed ashore."

"Where?"

"Stony Beach."

King felt the punch of that.

Paxton planned it that way.

"Who found him?"

"Tom Martin. He was on scene until the body was removed."

"Fuckin no-good-do-gooder. I thought I'd be rid of him when he left WPD and became a widower, but he keeps coming around and around."

"Want him whacked?"

"Not yet. I want Dale Jacobs, first. Then Chief Banks."

"The chief is going to cost you big, King. And after that hit, I'll be out of commission for a while, so pick and choose the order of things and stick with it."

"The Jacobs kid first."

"He hasn't surfaced, yet. I've been parked near Jacobs Jolly since Friday, and the only one in and out and staying the night is Connie Jacobs. She leaves once a day to go visit Matt Jacobs at Pleasantvale. Other than that, she sticks close to home. The stuff I pulled on Dale confirms he's been getting at-home physical therapy on Mondays, Wednesdays, and Fridays, so I'll have my ass parked outside Jolly on Monday. Meanwhile, I found out Dale was in the process of selling his father's house to pay for the long-term care facility, and was in the process of buying Wind Ledge from Esmé Baxter. Both transactions are on hold pending his recuperation. Jacobs Jolly was actually on the market, but Wind Ledge never went up. It looks like it might have been a word-of-mouth deal handled by the real estate agent. I want to pull a few threads on this to see if Dale has a personal relationship with the Baxters."

"Esmé Baxter recently bought Jasper Crane's place on Main Street."

"Yeah, but it's on Main Street. The town is torn to shit. And there's absolutely no opportunity for surveillance."

"It's waterfront property. Take a damned boat from the marina. Anything on Ruby Norman?"

"Nothing, but Shaky is still a mess. Few people are out and about. You think that's where she'll go until the inquest?"

"If Ruby could get off island, she'd leave. So she's either long gone, or someone has her hidden, someone who could get her to the inquest."

"Vernon Banks?"

"Maybe."

"Tom Martin?"

King shakes his head some, "He would protect a witness, especially one against me, but how would Ruby get from Echo to Primrose?"

"Banks?"

King does another round of head shaking, "The chief and the former detective are at odds. Still, they might join forces to fuck me over. Figure this shit out and get out."

The Promise

Marin, Dale, Esmé, and Jenny, are waiting for Tom and June in the huge eat-in kitchen. Nibbling food and sodas are laid out, and every bit of it is being nibbled and sipped. It's after nine when June blows in, already in full-motormouth-mode, "Dead bodies. Everywhere you go on this island, there's a dead body. There – look over there – dead body. And there – look over there – dead body. I'm telling you, Marin nailed it when she renamed this place Murder Island. This time the dead dude washed ashore at Wind Ledge, but I'd be willing to bet if we traveled the shoreline, we'd find another carcass, maybe two," she pops a cheeseball, maybe two.

Tom parks his duff onto a high stool, grabs a beer, pulls a long swig, then balances out June's rant with some good old police talk. "The deceased male has been preliminarily identified as Fred Fuller, former owner of Diggers."

"Do you think the dead guy was dumped into the bay by the same guy who dumped Laire MacTavish?"

All Eyes Turn Toward Marin.

She reacts to the silent scrutiny. **"What?"**

"You remember that?" Tom's words drench with astonishment.

She looks past him and thinks a bit. "I'd already remembered that Laire was in Casco Bay, but I think this is the first time I actually remember seeing a man dump her in. Maybe." She. Goes. Quiet...

Marin climbed over the windowsill, moved quietly along the back of the cottage, slipped between a lush grouping of lilac bushes, and moved along the walking path, occasionally stealing a look at the waning gibbous moon reflecting off a gentle rolling sea. "Soooo pretty." She picked up her pace, found her space, leaned back and stared at Earth's only natural satellite. "Ninety-six percent illumination. Beautiful." Movement just outside the tail of light pulled Marin's attention toward the water. She silenced and leaned forward when a boat moved into the path of light, then watched the small craft lift and rock on slapping waves. "Adrift?" Her eyes locked onto the image of a crouched person. "A man? On his knees?" She began to get up, an instinct stopped her—she sat back down and crouched low, sure she caught the man's attention. Goosebumps ran her flesh and her heart began pounding erratically. She went flat onto the ground, watched the man stare in her direction. He waited until the boat bobbed beyond the lighted swath, bent low, took hold of something, "A body?" He dumped it overboard.

"He dumped it overboard ……. He dumped her overboard ……. Edward Kingston dumped Laire MacTavish overboard." She quiets while she pieces some stuff together, then admits, "I've been recovering memories of what happened on Stony. It took some time for me to assemble the pieces because there were two big things that happened there. There was the man in the boat who dumped a body into the bay, and then there was the man who tried to drown me. They were the same man, Edward Kingston. She tried to tell me all along that he killed her. She told me to save myself – that night during high tide – she told me to save myself."

Tom steps into Marin's circuitous path, "Who told you?"

"Laire MacTavish. I heard her voice. She told me to save myself."

Silence can be gilded.
It can be tarnished, too.

Marin searches the faces staring hard at her, "You don't believe me." She looks to Dale, "You don't believe me. Tell them. Tell them you heard her."

He steps her way. "Marin."

"No! Dale ... don't you dare suggest I'm confused, or remembering drug-induced shit. Don't you dare suggest that I'm diminished. I. HEARD. HER. And I saw someone behind the boulder. And I remember Edward Kingston on top of me, pulling me to sea. I remember it all— and I wish I didn't." She storms to the door, banging her injured wrist on the doorjamb.

By the time she gets to her cottage it is throbbing, and she's emotionally broken. She paces a circuitous route while she dissects the events. "Start with what you remember, the things the rest of them already know. Put the events in chronological order. I snuck out. I saw a man in a boat dump a body in the bay. I remember now that the man is Edward Kingston, he goes by the name Heir. The body he dumped was Laire MacTavish. Okay, no one at The Promise questions that stuff, so all of it must be true. Now for the day I almost died. I woke because of a gunshot ... no, no. I woke because I felt rain on my face, then I heard a shot, then I found Dale on the ground, bleeding from his back, then I saw a man behind a boulder, then I heard Laire tell me to save myself." She pauses, tries to grab hold of the memory-thread and finally succeeds. "I was at the cliff, trying to climb the ladder. My hands slipped and I fell onto the rocks. That's when she told me to save myself. From whom? Dale had been shot. Edward was in the ocean. Who was she warning me about? The man behind the boulder?" She plays the scene from when she sees Dale until she leaves him to get help. "If the man behind the boulder was a danger to me, he could have killed me when I was with Dale." She sits quietly on the couch for a few minutes, waiting, hoping the pieces will fall into place. "Go back. No one disputes that I saw Dale after he was shot. I'm not sure if they believe I saw a man behind a boulder, but they definitely Do Not believe I heard Laire's warning."

~~BEST TO HEED MY WARNINGS~~

Marin pushes from the couch. "*That* was not a hallucination."

Dale heads to The Castle long after Marin stormed out. He finds her standing on the dock nearly frozen solid. "If I wrapped my arms around you, would you push me in?"

"No."

"Would you start crying?"

"Yes."

"I'd rather you push me in, Marin. I hate seeing you upset."

"Then maybe you should leave."

"I'll leave, but you need to move inside, first."

"Afraid I'll jump?"

"Nope. Afraid you'll get pneumonia. It's fuckin brick out here."

She takes one last look at the moon and steps his way. "What's in the bag?"

"Dinner for two."

"I'm not hungry."

"Didn't think you would be, but Esmé asked that I try."

Marin looks toward The Promise, sees The Three Women staring in her direction, "Any of them call the whitecoats, yet?"

"No."

"I know what I know, Dale. And I know there's lots of stuff that doesn't make sense, but if the people who supposedly love me doubt everything I say, I'm going to stop saying things. Everyone encourages me to find my memories, so I do. And after the painful process of trying to understand them by myself, for myself, I share them. And if they aren't understood by others, I'm told they can't be my memories, that I'm wrong about them. What the hell am I supposed to do with that? Pretend the stuff inside my head isn't really there? Because if so, then what's the point? Why should I bother trying to find out who I was, and what I went through? Why don't I just start with a clean slate and move the fuck on?" She stares at the sky for a few minutes then turns and demands, "Are you struggling with any of this shit because it sure doesn't seem as though you are?"

He shrugs, "My head was full of whacky crap when I was in rehab. I couldn't distinguish between a real memory and a drug fantasy. When a memory-thread came, I pulled it. If it made sense, I relaxed with it, if it seemed too weird or disturbing, I tucked it away for future work or I abandoned it altogether. Now that I'm being introduced to myself through other people's experiences with me, and the memories from being a cop are shaking free, I'm getting context with that weird shit."

"Tell me."

He shakes his head, "It's hard to explain. It's like I was two people. Dale the guy who remembered tooling on his Harley, and spending time at the beach, and gazing at the moon with you. Then there was another Dale, one who felt dark, dangerous, secretive. Now that I'm reacquainting myself with Dale the cop, I'm thinking the dark, dangerous, secretive parts of my memories are tied to my work .... I have to tell you, Marin, some of the threads I pulled actually had me thinking I was a homicidal maniac. Your mother was the one who reminded me that I was one of the good guys, one of the ones who hunted homicidal maniacs. So yeah, I've had problems with memory recovery." He pulls her near, "I'm really glad I remember how I was beginning to feel about you." He wipes a tear or two that travel Marin's beautiful face, brushes back her wavy hair, and gets lost in her eyes for a minute, "Can we put what happened at The Promise aside and get back to what was happening with us? Please?"

She nods and follows him inside.

Week Two – Day Five
Monday, November 6
Waning Gibbous – Illumination 90%

The couple reconnect in the tiny cottage by the shore. They talk about the important and the trivial, hold hands, and do a bit of hip-chucking and shoulder nudging. Then, they spend long quiet moments with Marin in the V of Dale's legs, his arms wrapped tight, quietly looking at the moon over the bay. Sometime after midnight, they share one of the meals Esmé sent, tidy the place, and call it a night with a kiss and a separation at the bedroom door. Shortly before 2 AM, Marin crawls from bed, pitter-patters to the living area, sits on the coffee table, and runs her fingertips down Dale's arm.

He takes her hand in his, "Is everything okay?"

"Where did you go today? When you went for a walk."

"Peduzzi's."

"The drug store?"

"Yeah."

"Did you buy condoms?"

"Yeah."

"Can we try again?"

"Hell, yeah!"

They shower together, this time strictly for foreplay. She notices a tattoo below his hip for the first time, "A crescent moon." She remembers what he said the day he brought her the birthday donut, "MB. You said you labeled me that for a reason, and if I didn't figure the riddle by myself, you'd show me something. Is this it?"

"Yeah."

"First, what does MB mean?

"Moon Babe."

"A bit sexist, but I kinda like it. When did you get inked?"

"On my first trip into town after rehab."

She leaves the shower, wraps herself in a towel and heads to the bedroom. He follows, sans a towel. Her eyes travel his length as he moves about the room. Her breath hitches when he nears. She watches with some fascination when he puts the condom on, and she feels a heat build when he puts his hand to her cheek and kisses her. He loosens her towel, lifts her into his arms and places her onto the bed. He kneels between the V of her legs, and stares—he just stares, "You. Are. Beautiful." He leans over her, gently moves her wild, crinkle hair away from her face, then leaves a trail of kisses, until he finally finds her lips. He steadies himself over her, exploring every curve and swell, first with his hand and fingers then with his lips and tongue. Her mews and moans harden his want, and when he lies on top and slides in he has to work not to lose himself. "Marin," he groans when he feels a tiny tightening and pulse around him. "Marin," he lets himself go.

She starts giggling.

He falls flat to his back, takes care of business, and finishes with a groan, "What's so funny?"

"Not funny. Interesting. That was *interesting*," she singsongs.

"Interesting," he groans.

"Can we do it again?"

"Goodnight, Marin."

Marin joins him in the kitchen late morning. He takes one look and laughs big, "Gee, Marin, did you get laid last night because everything about you screams that you did, and that you might have found it interesting."

"It was interesting." She does a little twirl, slaps her hands onto his thighs, nestles between when they spread, and kisses him. "Mmm. Is that powdered sugar? Did you get donuts? Where? When?"

"The box is in the micro and hours ago."

She grabs the box, opens it, does an eyeball search and deflates, "No honey-glaze? After last night, I figure I deserve a honey-glaze."

He joins her at the counter, pulls her close, opens the cupboard above her head, and takes a plate that has two honey-glaze sitting upon it, "After last night, you deserve two."

His kiss is interrupted by a knock.

"Come in," Marin hollers.

The Three Women bottleneck the doorway. They take one look before Marin confirms their suspicions. "Dale and I had sex together."

Esmé leaves.

Jenny leaves.

June cracks the fuck up and leaves.

Dale planned to hitch a ride to therapy from one of The Three Women, but under the circumstances, he opts to trolly it, even though his leg is feeling the pain of his bed-romping with Marin. Before heading back to Sand Castle after his workout with Conan the Crusher, he heads to Jacobs Jolly.

"Hey, Mom!" he calls upon entering.

The woman in starched dress, hose and pumps, descends the stairs, moves lithely through the living room and into the kitchen before offering a greeting, "Dale. What a wonderful surprise. You look ..." she touches his cheek and assesses ... "You look *different*." She hugs him tight.

"Must be the therapy with Conan. He worked my ass today."

"Dale, language."

He smiles, leaves the kitchen, and walks the length of the living room a few times. He heads back to the kitchen, "The Tacoma parked across the street, whose is it?"

"What Tacoma?" She steps toward the living room.

"Don't look out the window, Mom. It's a small, dark blue truck."

"Oh, that. It's been parked there on and off for days. I think the man inside is appraising damage from the storm."

"Why?"

"It looks like he does computer and paperwork, then he leaves for a while and comes back again."

"What time does the truck leave for the day?"

"Oh, I don't know. After I go to bed, I suppose."

"It's there until after dark?"

She tilts her head in thought, "It was there very late on Friday night. That's the night I didn't sleep a wink. I'm not sure about other days."

"I'll be right back. Don't go anywhere near that window."

Dale steps onto the screened porch and makes a call, "Hey, Tom. Any chance you can drive past Jacobs Jolly? There's a Tacoma parked across the street and down a bit from the cape. My mother says some guy's been parked in that spot since Friday. She thinks he might be doing storm appraisals, but he was parked on the street late into the night Friday. I'm thinking he's been waiting for me. If that's the case, he's gonna follow me when I head out."

"On my way."

Dale heads back inside and sits for the lunch he neither asked for nor really wants. "What've you been up to?"

"Well, we kept power, so I've been keeping the place up, and I've been able to watch my programs. You've missed *General Hospital*. I could catch you up."

"I'm good, thanks. What else?"

"I spend time with your father. Did I tell you he spoke?"

"Really?"

"The night of the nor'easter. I was visiting and was in a bit of a memory-mood, you know, talking about things from way back, and when I was done, I told Matt I was spending the night at the care center because it was too dangerous to drive. He said, 'good' – that's it, one word, but it sure was good to hear."

Dale smiles wide, grabs his ringing cell and heads outside, "Hey, Tom."

"I recognize the truck. It belongs to the work crew at Echo."

"Huh. Thoughts?"

"Whoever's inside was hired by King, and there's no way he's doing storm appraisals. Any idea why The King of Whisper wants you tailed?"

"Haven't a clue." Dale gets a nudge – it causes a bit of intestinal turmoil. "Huh."

"Huh, what?"

"Trying to grab a memory-thread. Maybe it'll come around, again. Any chance the surveillance has something to do with the inquest? Am I on a witness list or something? Because I was a cop?" Dale gets another nudge. "Could the snoop be about the rogue investigation the chief said you and I were doing?"

"Not sure."

"The investigation, it was about Lan MacTavish, right?"

"Partly. Look, Dale, I've already been notified about testifying at the inquest. I'll check to see if you're gonna be called as a witness, but if you haven't heard by now, I doubt you'll be expected to show. How long will you be at Jolly?"

"I was gonna hop the 2 PM trolly, but I don't want the snoop following me to Sand Castle."

"I'll swing by in an hour. Be waiting outside. Make sure Tacoma Guy knows you see him when you come out. I'll take a look when I drive by. If he stays where he is right now, he'll have to bang a U-turn to follow us."

"Right."

"He won't, but he'll mark us and let us know he did."

"Okay, I'll be outside in an hour."

Connie is reading a two-day old paper when Dale returns, "It says here that someone gave the nor'easter a name."

"This should be good."

"Hallows' Tide. The name is really quiet clever. Instead of All Hallows' Eve, they put reference on the ocean." She chuckles. "I love clever people." She quiets a bit and reads a bit. "It says here that Halloween is a three-day observance that's actually called All Hallowtide. It represents the time in the liturgical year dedicated to remembering the dead, including saints, martyrs, and all of the faithful departed. Well, I never knew that. Did you, Dale?"

"Nope."

"There's an announcement here that Whisper Trick or Treating will be rescheduled to Saturday evening." She crumples the paper in her lap, "Oh, for Heaven's sake, I'll have to buy more candy. I already worked my way through the first batch. Ooo. Ooo. I saved you one of your favorites bars." She slides open the kitchen drawer and hands him a Mounds, kisses his head, and clears the table.

He takes a walk or two past the window, sees the truck across the street, goes back to the kitchen, and gives his mother a kiss on her cheek. "Do me a favor, do not look out at the truck. Just ignore it. And if you go visit dad, or whatever, just pretend you don't see it. If you get home late and it's still there, call me. Okay."

"Okay."

"Promise."

"If you promise something in return."

"What?"

"That you'll bring Marin by before I leave."

"Promise."

"My cup runneth over, Dale."

Mooring

Rodriquez answers Paxton's call and heads to the backroom. "Yeah?"

"Fred Fuller's body showed up on Whisper."

Rodriquez says nothing about that or about the woman he was supposed to be watching—the one who skipped out on him. He figures he'll take care of Sherry as soon as the Abenaki is running again. "Is that why you called?"

"If anyone shows up at Mooring asking questions about Fred, I want to know about it. Immediately."

Rodriquez says nothing about the badge-wearing, Glock-totting guy that already paid him a visit. He figures he'll take care of that guy as soon as the Abenaki is running again. "Yeah, I'll call."

The Promise

Marin finds her mother in the gallery, "Where's the J-Team?"

"Not sure. They said they had an errand.

"Can we talk?"

"Is it about sex?"

"Sort of."

"Come on." Esmé leads her daughter into her bedroom suite next to the gallery. They kick off their shoes, sit cross-legged in the center of the bed, and hold hands. It's something they've done since Marin was little.

"I told Dale about my favorite book."

"*I Love You, Stinky Face*," the mother smiles wide. "I love that book."

Marin squeezes her mother's hands, "It's about a mother's unconditional love."

"It is."

"And about a boy who tests that love by being a nudge."

"Yesss."

"Mom, I know I've tested you … life has tested you a lot lately."

She nods.

"And this whole sex thing is another test."

She nods.

"And you have feelings about this."

She scoffs, "Yesss, mija, I have lots of feelings, and questions, and concerns, and fears, and—"

Marin laughs. "My thing with Dale isn't about feeling things, it's about doing things. I've been so bottled up by memory loss, and physical injuries, and mental confusion, that I just want to act. I don't want to think, you know?"

Esmé smiles, "I know."

"I'm tied in knots that I won't remember who I was, or worse, that I will remember and I won't like who I was. It's all pretty confusing, and isolating. Having sex with Dale is about fun and feeling free, and now I'm feeling bad about it, like I should apologize because you are upset about him and me, but I really don't want to. I want to be happy about being Marin and doing what I want."

"Okay."

"Okay?"

"You should be happy about it, Marin. If you are without reservations or second-thoughts after having sex, then it means the experience was right for you."

A nudge pushes and a shiver runs.

"Mija, what just happened?"

"I'm not sure. I think I just felt a sense of dread."

"Ay dios mío. ¿Mija, esto realmente está sucediendo ahora?"

Primrose Priscilla

The Boarders are in Sherry's bedroom, their backs pressed tightly against the wall, occasionally looking out at a truck parked on Tom's street. "How long has it been there?"

Sherry laughs, "Two minutes longer than the last time you asked."

"So forty-two minutes."

"Yes."

"Should we call Tom?"

"Yes, but we don't have our cell phones."

"Right. We need to tell him when he gets back that we need an emergency cell phone."

Sherry nudges Ruby, "The guy's leaving."

"Good, I need to sit."

"Go ahead. I'll keep a lookout." She's still at the window an hour later when Tom's truck parks in front of the house.

When he walks into the bungalow, he feels a drift of danger. He runs upstairs, first to Ruby's room, then to Sherry's. "What's wrong? What happened?"

"A guy in a truck was parked on the street staring at your house."

"For how long?"

"Forty-two minutes," Ruby informs.

"He left an hour ago."

"We wanted to call you, but we don't have a phone."

"Yeah. That's not good. I'll get a burner, but you need to promise me you won't call anyone but me or Roxanne."

"We promise," they unison.

"Okay. Let's go downstairs. We need to talk about something."

Sherry nudges Ruby, "It's bad news. I can tell."

Ruby doubles over and starts gasping for air. Tom and Sherry help her back to the bed. She grabs hold of Tom's hand, "The truck. I think that truck might be from Echo."

He nods.

"Oh. My. God. Does King know I'm here?"

"No. The guy in the truck wanted to send me a message. He had someone else under surveillance earlier today. He planned on following the person, but I prevented him from doing that. He was on my street to send a message, that he knows who I am."

"Why did he leave before you got home?"

"Something must have come up."

Ruby pulls a few cleansing breaths and calms a bit. "Okay. I'm okay. I just got scared. The thing you want to tell us, is it about me?"

"No."

The tree sprite boarder stiffens her spine, "It's about me, about Fred, he's dead."

Tom takes her hand and pats it, "Yes."

"You're sure?"

"I found his body."

Sherry is quiet for a few minutes, "You found him yesterday. That's why Roxanne came and spent the day with us."

"There's no pulling the wool on you, Sherry."

She chuckles, "Fred used to say that."

Ruby inches across the bed, wraps her arms around her fellow boarder, "Do you want to sleep here tonight?"

"Sure. That'd be nice." She gets up and heads toward the door, "I think I'll have a good cry in the shower, first."

Her pain fills Primrose Priscilla.

Week Two – Day Six
Tuesday, November 7
Waning Gibbous – Illumination 82%

Edward Kingston III

Christie Anderson

King is behind closed office doors. His credenza is covered with documents, both side chairs are stacked with files, and he's working his way through a legal pad. The documented information chronicles the events that led to the violent death of a teenage girl and that of her killer.

- Teen went missing from Diggers, Sunday, July 24, 2014. Girl was last seen getting off a trolly on cliff side.
- Heir confessed to me on September 5, 2014 that he killed her and dumped her body into Casco Bay.
- On Saturday, September 6, 2014, I pulled Danielle Rayburn's marina logs for the night of July 24th to see if anyone was on the waters when Heir was dumping the body of Christie

Anderson. There were no boaters, and since Heir used a private boat from our home, there is no record of him being on the waters.

- Met with Vernon Banks on Friday, September 12, 2014 and told him about the death and dumping.
- Met with Vernon Banks on Monday, October 6, 2014. He provided a review of the case and detailed the pushback he was getting from Detective Tom Martin about naming Lachlan MacTavish a Person of Interest.
- Received a call from Fred Fuller, owner of Diggers on Wednesday, October 8, 2014, saying he saw Heir with Christie the night she went missing and planned on notifying the cops. This was the beginning of his shakedown. He said there were rumblings that the Town Council was going to petition the State Liquor Board to conduct an investigation into underage drinking and possibly pulling his license. He 'suggested' I buy the joint.
- On Wednesday, October 15, 2014, my front man, Max Trainor told Fred Fuller he was going to buy Diggers.
- Max Trainor received $250,000.00 to handle shell purchase of Diggers. He was handed a check for $750,000.00 for full purchase price of Diggers, on Sunday, November 30, 2014.
- Max Trainor and Fred Fuller signed doctored Purchase and Sale Agreement on Monday, December 1, 2014.

"Fred Fuller is dead and can't testify about seeing Heir with Christie Anderson. There are no records of anyone being on the waters that night, so there's little chance anyone saw him dump her body. Heir confessed to me about the murder, and I told Vernon, but if he testifies to that, it'll be his word against mine, and it proves criminal misconduct, and tarnishes his testimony. The $250,000.00 payment to Max Trainor for acting as a front man was way-way-way off the books. The $750,000.00 financing came from private investors. The doctored legal documents could be problematic down the line, but without Fred Fuller to testify about the transaction or my involvement in the purchase and sale, it will be a slow slog through the legal system. Now for the dangling thread: Sherry Flynn, the slut waitress who married Fuller. She's under the watchful eye of Paxton's associate. If she becomes a problem, he'll handle it."

The King of Whisper pushes away from his desk and paces his office. "Now for potential problems. The Council plans to present the cases in chronological order. I could object, but there's no reason based on my review and assessment of the Christie Anderson case. No one can put Edward with Christie unless there's a surprise witness. I've got a couple people on the Council who will let me know if there's an addition to the witness list, so Sherry Flynn shouldn't be an issue. The Christie Anderson case is scheduled to last a week beginning Monday, November 13th. The Laire MacTavish case begins Monday, November 20th. The Danielle Rayburn case begins Monday, November 27th. King packs the Anderson files into a briefcase, stacks the other two on his credenza, and heads to the marina.

Chief Vernon Banks

Christie Anderson

The chief is in his neat-as-a-pin home office, there's a file open on his desk, and he's reading information he's recorded on a legal pad. "Don't need to push through all of this again. The evidence is what it is. Unless there's a surprise witness, Heir isn't going to get charged with anything related to Christie Anderson."

He pulls another legal pad and reads the title, **Edward Kingston IV timeline**. "I know he was responsible for Christie and Laire, but establishing that for the Council will be a crapshoot. Now for what I don't know: where was Edward during the Danielle Rayburn murder and the Joseph Baxter cliff incident? I need to dig into this shit."

He puts the pad aside and grabs a file labeled, **Dale Jacobs shooting**. "This is the case I should be working and would be working if not for the inquest." He flips the file open and reads the ballistics report, "Victim shot with .38 snubnose revolver." The chief scoffs, "Throw a stone at any guy on this island, and he'll turn and shoot you with a .38 snub. Of course, there's only one man coward enough to shoot a man in the back." He rips a page from a legal pad and writes two words:

- Who?
- Why?

"There's a story here, but damned if I'll ever have the time to dig into it."

Retired Detective Tom Martin

Christie Anderson

The detective is in his den, kicked back in his big-ass recliner, a beer on the end table, and soft music in the background. He has several pocket notebooks tossed onto the four-poster bed, and on his lap there's a yellow legal pad with several pages of notes. There's a question at the top of the page:

How To Prove Edward Kingston IV murdered Christie Anderson?

It is answered with a name:

- Sherry Flynn.

Week Two Comes To An End
Wednesday, November 8
Waning Gibbous – Illumination 72%

Chief Banks gets to work.

Claremont Luxury Waterfront Condos
"Henri, Vernon Banks here."

"Oui, Chief Banks, I thought I'd be hearing from you. The inquest is forthcoming, oui?"

"Testimony begins Monday, November 13th. I'm calling about the video for the month of July."

"Oui, I have it on a USB ready for registered mail, arriving on the very first postal run. I'm holding it in my office until the ferry service is back online. Any date on that, Chief?"

"Casco Bay Ferry Lines will be up and running Friday, the 10th."

"Merveilleux. I will get it to the pier first thing."

State of Maine Liquor License
"Thank you for calling State Licensing. How may I direct your call?"

"Director of liquor licensing, please."

"One moment."

"Stella Crenshaw, how may I assist you?"

"Director Crenshaw, this is Chief Vernon Banks on Whisper."

"Yes, Chief. I'm glad to hear your island is getting back online. You sure took a wallop from the storm."

"We did and I'm afraid it has caused a delay in my preparing for an inquest scheduled for Monday."

"The Kingston inquest."

"Yes."

"How can I help?"

"I need paperwork on Fred Fuller. He owns Diggers on the island and Mooring on the mainland and holds liquor licenses for both establishments. I'm in need of certified documentation." He listens to rapid keystrokes.

"Yes. Your information is accurate."

"Any chance I could trouble you for a certified copy of that?"

"No trouble, but I'm not sure you'll have it by Monday. I think the postal ferry is still down."

"It is, but the passenger ferry, Abenaki, will be up again Friday morning. I wouldn't normally ask, but nothing is normal right now on Whisper."

"I'll ready this as registered mail and get it to the docks first thing Friday morning."

"Thank you, Director."

"You're welcome, Chief."

South Portland PD

"Chief Banks calling for Detective Warren." ....
"Mohamed, it's Vernon."

"I was gonna give you a call, make sure you survived the storm."

"We took a hit to property and infrastructure, but happily, all of our islanders survived and are picking up the pieces."

"Good. Good. So this can't be a social call."

"It's not. I need a favor, off the books."

"Got 'ya."

"A blue Jag, VIN 77492Z92554G722 was recently registered to Robert Dunlevy—hang on let me give you the date .... August 30th. I have Dunlevy as the owner of—"

"Bob's Boat Trader, over on Mile Road."

"Yeah."

"What year's the Jag?"

"Twenty-fifteen, fully loaded, and fucking beautiful."

"No way Bob Dunlevy could afford that ride."

"Between you, me, and the rocks on Stony Beach, the Jag used to belong to Edward Kingston IV. I'm pretty sure Heir traded it for a boat, probably the Cat75 that was found crashed on one of the uninhabited islands near Little Diamond."

"Yeah, heard about that. The Cat supposedly became untethered from the marina here. I think it belonged to Dunlevy. Hang on, let me check something ……. yeah, it was registered to Bob's Boat Trader."

"Mohamed, I'm stuck on Whisper. I need some information for the inquest. Can you swing by and have a little talk with Dunlevy? I don't think he's in the wrong on anything, but I need to know when Edward Kingston showed up at his place, what his demeanor was, whether there was a Bill of Sale or some transfer paperwork. I also need pictures of the Jag, the VIN, and Edward's plates and registration if Dunlevy has them."

"Will do. I'll call you tomorrow."

"Thanks, Mohamed."

When his calls are finished, the chief types Colt 1911 For Sale into a search engine and waits. "Let's see if anyone bought one recently." He scrolls through the Sold page, "Paydirt. A Colt 1911 was purchased on July 23, 2017, two days after the shooting on Stony Beach. That sure looks like the gun King pulled on me when he suggested I start wearing Kevlar." He leans back in his chair, kicks his feet onto his desk, puts his hands behind his head and stares at the ceiling.

He asks himself a few questions: "Would a father purchase a gun online two days after he learned his son was dead? If the father is Edward Kingston III, the answer is yes." He stares a bit more, thinks a bit more. "Fred Fuller is lying on a cold slab at the ME's office. Mr. Fuller sure would have caused an uproar if he testified in Kingston Re: Anderson. Further, if

King found out about a possible shakedown of Heir by Fuller, he'd absolutely put a bullet into the man's back, and if he used his .38 snub, he'd have to get rid of it which would necessitate his need for a new weapon." Vernon grabs his phone, hits speed dial and waits for the ME's office to answer. "Doc, it's Vern."

"You want a COD on Fred Fuller."

"Yeah."

"What's left of him is pretty beat up, but there's a bullet hole in his back, so manner of death will be homicide."

"How long has he been dead?"

"Hard to say at this point. The bullet killed Fred Fuller, but he could have succumbed to other injuries, and he was in the ocean so that's another issue, Chief."

"Ballistics?"

"Entrance is consistent with a .32 or .38."

"If you could send a report before the inquest on Monday, I'd appreciate it."

"Won't be final."

"No problem." Vernon hangs up sure about one thing, "King has a .38 snubnose S&W 442, at least he had one."

The chief walks past Donna, "I'll be back." He heads to Outer Banks, opens his safe and takes out the ballistics report from Dale Jacobs' shooting. He knows what the report says—he's not sure what the report means.

.38 snubnose revolver.

He returns the report and heads downstairs when he sees Detective Warren's name on caller ID. "Thanks for calling back, Mohamed."

"No problem. I got a complete rundown from Bob Dunlevy on the transaction between him and Edward Kingston III."

"Let me grab a pad and pen. Okay, what've you got?"

"On Monday, July 17, 2017, a man, later ID'd as Edward Kingston IV entered Bob Dunlevy's office saying he wanted to make a trade — his 2015 F-type convertible Jag for a 2012 Cat75. Bob asked what the catch was. He was given a couple stipulations: Bob needed to get the Cat into the water that night under Bob's name, and he wasn't allowed to drive the Jag until August. Bob agreed. He said Heir Kingston handed a scribbled Bill of Sale and the Jag's registration, then followed Bob to the marina, grabbed a brown paper bag from the Jag, handed off the keys, got into the Cat and left."

Sand Castle

Marin bundles up, grabs her camera, and shouts, "I'll be back."

Dale steps out of the shower, wraps a towel, and shouts, "Where are you going?" He's dressed and on the porch for ten minutes before Marin answers that question with a wave his way. "The beach? It's fuckin brick out here." He heads inside, grabs a cup of coffee and a blanket, then stretches out on a chaise. "Pictures. She's taking pictures." He heads inside.

The photographer pops a squat on the sand, flips through thirty shots, deletes half, then chooses one, "The starfish. Definitely the starfish." She raises her hand to shade her eyes at the sound of a motorboat nearing. "Kinda cold for a joy ride," she gets back to her work, stops when the engine cuts and the boat takes to bobbing. She turns back to watch. "A man in a boat. Watching me?" A shiver runs up – down – and back up again when the man starts looking in the direction of Sand Castle. "Dale? Is someone looking for Dale? The shooter?" She grabs her cell.

"Marin? Are you still on the beach?"

"Do not come outside. There's a guy in a boat with binoculars and I think he's looking into Sand Castle. I think he's looking for you or maybe at you. He was watching me for a few minutes, but he's been watching The Castle for a whole lot longer."

"Come home."

Primrose Priscilla

Tom is in the backyard saying a silent goodbye to Bessie and explaining things to Priscilla. "She just can't be saved, dear." At the first sound of saws, Tom heads inside to the denroom, the combo name The Boarders gave his converted den/bedroom. "Fuckin tired of death, dying, and destruction." He plops his ass, takes Miss Prissy's journal and gets lost for a few minutes—in her words, in their lives.

> Tom and I made love last night. I woke to my period this morning. Somewhere very deep inside, I know we will be one of those childless couples. At some point, friends and family will stop asking when we will start a family, and take to questioning, in hush tones, whether Mr. and Mrs. Martin can become a family. We are a family, though I ache to hold a Little One in my arms, but my embrace is already full with the love I have for Tom, my handsome, loving, strong, passionate, Tom. I am already so blessed, that if I am never to have a child, I will still rejoice in having Tom. (1983)

He puts the journal down and picks up the legal pad of notes and questions, "Time for a review. King has two pregnancy test strips. One belongs to Ruby Norman. One probably belonged to Laire MacTavish. Chief Banks knows about the rogue investigation Dale and I were doing. How does he know? When did he find out?" He reopens the envelope he received from Banks and pulls the prelim ME report on Edward Kingston IV. Then he does a little brain dump on things he needs to know. "Okay, the cause of death is drowning, the manner of death is suicide. Shortly before Edward went off the deep end, he brought Quinn Hughes home and introduced her as his yearlong girlfriend. Was she his girlfriend? Is she on the inquest list? Shortly after Fred Fuller bought Mooring, he disappeared. A thug set up shop inside the joint to keep eyes on Sherry. No question as to why, but who hired him? And the Tacoma. The guy inside is surveilling Dale from inside an Echo work truck. The truck showed on my street – to send me a message or was he looking for Ruby?" Tom's review ends with the thud of Bessie. Unable to look, he pulls his ass up, heads upstairs, knocks on Ruby's door, and enters when he's called in.

"Good, you're both here. I need to leave. The tree guys will be here a good portion of the day. You should stay up here until they leave." He hands off a small cooler, "Soda. Juice. Water. Apples. Grapes." He hands off a bag, "Figgie cookies. Granola bars. Chips. Crackers. If you absolutely have to go downstairs, and you should not go downstairs, keep the shades drawn, do your business, and get back up here." He hands each boarder a burner phone. "My number is on speed dial. Press 5 and you'll reach me. Do Not—"

"Call anyone else!" they unison.

Echo

King is reviewing information Paxton put together on Dale Jacobs. He's got a page of information on a legal pad, all background info, some worth noting:

- DOB: November 20, 1992.
  Born: Whisper General.
  Birth parents: Constance Monroe Jacobs;
  Matthew James Jacobs.

Elementary school: Columbus Park, South Portland, Maine.
High school: South High, South Portland, Maine.
College: University of New England.
BS: Environmental Science, Summa Cum Laude.
State of Maine Police Academy: 2013.

"He's smart and driven. And if he's part of the fuckin mess in Edward's life, he's ruthless." He laughs, "Maybe Dale Jacobs is my son."

- Applied to WPD: January, 2014.
  Hired: August, 2014.
  Island residency: Jacobs Jolly.
  Friendships/relationships: None noted.
  Vehicle: 2015 Harley Softail Breakout.
  Financials: Pending.
  Addendum: Real estate transaction to buy Wind Ledge put on hold after shooting and hospitalization.

"Jacobs was on Whisper for seven months before he filled some hours with police work. Question is, what did he do with his time before that, and who did he spend his time with?" King rifles through a stack of files on his credenza, smiles when he finds what he seeks, "Edward's 2014 calendar. I need to look at what Heir was doing during those seven months and if I find something interesting, I'll pull every fucking file apart looking for a thread that leads from Edward to Dale."

Boardwalk

Tom calls Dale from the hole-in-the-wall donut shop, "I'm across the street."

"Good. We need to talk."

"Here?"

"Yeah."

Dale passes Marin who's camped out on the couch, her sketchbook resting on bent legs, her camera in hand, her face doing a series of contortions most of which show displeasure. He watches a minute—her brow furrows, her lip curls then gets pulled between her teeth, all the while her fingers dreamily twirl a strand of hair.

She realizes she's under scrutiny, "What?"

"Your kinda cute when you're in contemplation. What are you doing, anyway?"

"Research."

"On?"

"Do you have someplace else you could be?"

"Ouch." He laughs, "Actually, I'm heading out to meet Tom."

"Where?"

"Boardwalk."

"Bring back—"

"Yummies. Got it."

As soon as Dale gets to Main Street, Marin grabs her backpack, stuffs it with what she needs, and hoofs it past the backside of The Promise toward Shaky. She hops the first trolly heading cliff side. Within minutes a memory lifts…

Marin packed a beach bag with towels, sunscreen, and a Frisbee, for a day on the sandy side of Whisper. She and her father hopped the first trolly that passed by, the one that headed past Watch Ledge. She noticed a man sitting on the front stoop.

"Who's that?"

"Who?"

"The man who waved?"

"I didn't see anyone."

"Back there. At Watch Ledge."

"Huh. Didn't see anyone. I must have been daydreaming."

"Really? Because it looked like you leaned forward so the guy couldn't see me. Who is that guy? Do you think he has something to do with that girl's disappearance?"

"You saw Lachlan MacTavish."

"The missing girl's brother?"

"Yes."

"That's him?"

"Why?"

She shrugged. "He's young. You should let him know you didn't see him wave, or he'll think you're rude."

"Not sure you should be counseling me on what I should and shouldn't be doing, Marin."

The sting of that memory is just the beginning...

The father nudged his daughter's shoulder, "You should come clean, Marin."

"About?"

"Whatever it is you know, or think you know, or saw, or heard, or all of the above. I already know you snuck out of the cottage, and I'm pretty sure you only did it so you could sketch the moon, but I also know you were out of the house at the same time a teenage girl went missing. If you found yourself in the wrong place at the wrong time, and if you saw something that could put you in danger, you really need to tell me."

He was met with silence. Lots and lots of silence.

Joe nudged again, "When you're ready to talk, I'm ready to listen. For now, I need you to listen, really listen. Okay?"

"Okay."

"Your mother and I have been married almost eighteen years and in all that time I haven't lied to her or kept secrets from her. Not once, Marin. And now, every word that comes out of my mouth is a lie. I hate what I'm doing and I will pay dearly when all of this comes to light. So while you're stewing about whether to tell me or not to tell me what you know, make sure you consider the collateral damage being caused on this end."

Marin pushed from the sand, grabbed and rolled her towel, stuffed her things into the beach bag and marched away, "I want to go home."

Joe followed her to the trolly stand, arriving in plenty of time to see Lachlan MacTavish being escorted into Town Hall.

Marin didn't miss a beat, "Hey, isn't that him?"

"Yes."

"And isn't the police station inside Town Hall?"

"The police station and the county court."

"Do you think they found his sister?"

"Don't know what to think, Marin."

The trolly driver's call pulls Marin from her thoughts. She gathers her backpack and detrollies at the access path to Cliff Dunes. She does a respectable impersonation of a Billy Goat hopping down the steep trail, then does a perfect 10.0 gymnast landing. "Stuck it," she announces when her feet go ankle deep in soft, dune sands. She trudges easterly through tall grass and splendors in a part of the island she's yet to explore. "I *like* this side." A memory of the other side tries to push and settle, but she bats it away. "Nope. Not interested in the rocky side and what happened there." When she rounds the bend, she passes an adorable shack, "Carmichael Corner. Huh. I wonder if that's the reporter's place?"

She continues past a few well-spaced properties until she comes to her destination, "Well hello, *Darling!*" She circles the yellow-taped perimeter of the unearthed shipwreck, marveling in its appearance, "This is amazing." A thought pushes, "I bet I would have studied this kind of stuff at WHO-ee. Huh. A memory. Without any work." A push of regret hits, "I didn't get to go. I'll never get to go." She files the disappointment, drops her pack, rummages for the newspaper article on the shipwreck, reads it again, and proclaims, "Wow. It's soooo much more amazing in person." She grabs her camera and starts taking pictures. Thoughts fill her head – time becomes irrelevant —— until the motorboat appears off shore.

Boardwalk

The waitress tops off the men's cups, and the men get right back to their conversation when she leaves. "So Tacoma Guy followed me, then headed to your place to send a message."

"Yeah."

"Why? I know you predicted this, but what's the point? What's the message?"

"Not entirely sure, and I don't think we'll figure it out until we figure out why King has you under surveillance."

Dale laughs, "This is where you tell me, right? Cause if you're waiting for me to remember shit or figure shit out, it's gonna be a long wait, Tom."

The former detective pulls a sip. "Does the name Quinn Hughes mean anything?"

"Nope."

"She might have been Heir's girlfriend at the time of his death."

"And?"

"She's a thread. Maybe. When the chief stopped by and told you he knew about our rogue investigation, did he give any indication how he knew?"

"Nope. I probably would have asked, but I was trying to figure out how long it would take to get inside Jolly for a piss."

Tom chuckles and takes a sip of brew, "By the way, I got my hands on the ME's report on Heir."

"And?"

"COD was drowning. MOD was suicide."

"Fucking dead asshole almost drowned Marin. Speaking of which, Marin was on the beach taking pictures earlier. She called and said there was a guy in a boat with binoculars watching her, then he turned his attention to Sand Castle. I told her to come home. She and I stayed inside and out of view until the boat left."

"Looks like King's surveillance guy is thinking you might be involved with the Baxter women."

"Yeah, getting near The Promise by truck is too obvious."

"So he's surveilling from the bay. I don't like it—" He pulls his ringing phone from his jacket, "I need to take this" ……. "Something wrong?"

"Marin Baxter walked past my place a while ago."

"Headed where?"

"Toward the shipwreck."

"Shit. And?"

"There's a guy in a boat—"

"Don't take your eyes off that boat. ETA to your place, five minutes." Tom tosses a five onto the table, "Come on, Dale. Marin could be in trouble."

The nomad-photographer who knows she's under surveillance by the guy in the boat distracts herself with a few more pictures, then makes her way up a dune, parks her ass behind a tall grassy section, and pretends to get lost in the splendor of the late afternoon. "I need to keep my eyes on the man in that boat. Fucking men in fucking boats. It's like my cross in life." She leans back and focuses on darkening eastern waters. She moves her fingers around in the sand and feels a pinch of discomfort. "Should have worn the brace." She knows there's a set of binoculars trained on her, "Watch all you want jackass. So long as you're watching me, you aren't watching Dale." A gripping fear bangs her from head to toe. "Is that man the one who shot Dale? Does he have a gun? Will he shoot me?" She grabs her backpack, thinks about going up the very steep incline, then thinks better of it. "I'm going to have to move out the way I moved in. Here's the plan, get to Carmichael Corner. If no one's home, get behind the shack and wait. Someone will notice I'm missing ……. but no one knows where I am. Shit." She is so lost in thought that she doesn't notice the man in the boat is trolling her as she trudges toward the corner. "New plan, go to the first shack you see."

Paxton moves slowly toward the bend.
He lowers his binoculars, then speeds away.

Tom Martin ignores Boat Man because Dale is at Roxanne's watching every move the boater makes through a pair of binoculars. The detective marches toward Marin, takes her by the elbow and awkwardly sand-marches her toward Roxanne's. "I suppose there's a good reason why you are alone on a beach, without your cell, and without having told anyone where you were heading, but I don't want to hear it, Marin."

"But—"

"Save it."

He lets her pass him into Roxanne's.

She points a finger at Dale, "Don't you even dare." She spins toward Tom, "And don't you ever treat me like a .... like I am diminished. I took a damned trolly to the beach because I felt like it. I spent time by myself because I felt like it." She falls apart, "And I was scared shitless by some guy in a fucking boat. Everywhere I go there's a guy in a boat watching me."

Dale makes a move toward her. "Don't! You woke up this morning and decided what you'd do today, and when **he** called you, off you went without clearing it with anyone. Why? Because you're a guy? Because you're a former cop? Or is it because you're capable and people know you are?" She realizes Roxanne is in the room. "Hi. You do a good job with the news. Can you give me a ride home? I'm Marin Baxter, by the way." She storms outside and stands next to a bright yellow Jeep Wrangler.

As soon as the Jeep is out of sight, Tom asks Dale about the boater.

"He was definitely watching Marin through binoculars until you stormed the beach."

"Description?"

"Caucasian. Maybe in his forties. Short, dark hair. Dark jacket. And he's the same guy from earlier today – at least it's the same boat."

"We need to find out why King has all of us under surveillance. Hang on." He answers his ringing phone. "What?"

"Tom, it's Ruby. That guy in the Tacoma is back, and he's walking your property, talking to the tree guys."

"Get upstairs. Lock the door. I'm on my way. Dale, you need to hang here. We can't lock the place, and I don't feel comfortable leaving it open. See if Roxanne can give you a ride to wherever you're headed next."

"Doubt it'll be The Castle."

Primrose Priscilla

Tacoma Guy and the tree service guys are gone by the time Tom arrives home. He checks on The Boarders then places a call, "Hey, Mike.

Sorry I didn't get back before you left. Thanks for handling Bessie."

"Yeah, no problem. We cut most of her back to firewood. It's stacked by the shed. We'll finish her off tomorrow."

"Good. Thanks. Any chance the insurance appraiser showed while you were here?"

"When we were packing up. He did a cursory look and said he'd be back tomorrow."

"Did he check inside the screen porch?"

"Yeah, and he moved along the windows."

"Good to know. Will you be back tomorrow to haul the stuff off the driveway?"

"We'll be chipping most, hauling the rest."

"Do me a favor. If the appraiser shows while I'm not home, tell him to come back. I really want to walk the place with him. I'll give the company a call and arrange a time, but in case he doesn't get the message."

"Sure, Tom. I'll let him know."

"Thanks."

Sand Castle

Marin is on the porch under a blanket when Roxanne drops Dale off. He notices she's wearing her wrist brace, "Hurt yourself from all the bitch slapping you did?"

She laughs. "About that. Any chance you'd be willing to write it off as post-TBI anger?"

"Nope." He parks his ass on the nearby chaise, grabs a corner of the blanket and kicks back. "I'd like you to keep quiet. I need to address your earlier accusations, and I don't feel like a back and forth. I didn't dictate my day, I planned it around some dude in a boat surveilling us. I made sure you and I weren't seen by Boat Man. I met with Tom because he needed to talk about something. I told you where I was going. I took my cell." He waits until she looks his way. "You need to listen to this. I do not think you are diminished. I do not think you are incapable. I did not know where you were and if you were safe, and I did not like feeling the way I did."

"I know. I was wrong."

"What?"

"About all of it, but mostly about raging at you for caring about me."

"Look, Marin, I'm falling pretty hard for you. I want to protect you because I," he pushes up before finishing his sentence. "Do you feel like grilled cheese?"

"If it comes with tomato soup."

"Give me ten, then head in."

Marin stares at the rising moon and whispers,
"Because he what?"

Week Three – Day One
Thursday, November 9
Waning Gibbous – Illumination 62%

Paxton is waiting in King's office when he comes downstairs.

"What the fuck are you doing here? How the fuck did you bypass the alarm?"

The man laughs.

King does not. "What's happening on my island?"

"I think Dale Jacobs is shacking up with Marin Baxter at Sand Castle." The man waits a beat or two, "What's your interest in Jacobs? He's out of commission from WPD, isn't well enough to testify at the inquest, and was a rookie detective when the Edward shit started hitting the fan. Why are you having me sit on him when I could be hunting Ruby Norman, or doing some witness intimidation, or whacking a target?"

"For what I'm paying you, you should be doing all of it."

"I'm doing what you want, in the order you want it, but I'd be more effective if I knew your angle on Jacobs." Paxton ends his lean against the wall. "The Abenaki goes online tomorrow. I'll be heading to Portland to ferry my ride here. Too many people have seen the Tacoma around town."

"Yeah? Who?"

"Tom Martin. Dale Jacobs. Maybe the Carmichael babe. The three of them have been intersecting."

"What about Banks?"

"He's moving between WPD and Outer Banks, so I've probably crossed his path a few times. The chief's been putting long hours at both places."

"He's gunning for Heir. He might get him for the MacTavish whore, but he won't be able to put Heir inside Diggers with Christie Anderson unless Fred Fuller comes back from the dead."

"Or his whore shows up to testify."

"Sherry Flynn. She could be a problem. I'm amending your workload. Take care of Sherry before you do anything else."

"I'll handle her tomorrow on the mainland. Too bad, cause she's fuck worthy."

"Then fuck her before you whack her."

Boardwalk

Dale grabs a seat at the window. From where he sits, he can see Marin on the docks at Sand Castle, her legs over the side, kicking to and fro. He turns when someone approaches, and he doesn't hide his disappointment, "Chief."

Banks laughs, "Can't tell you how often that's the greeting I get."

"What do you want?"

The chief takes a seat.

"Oh, fuck."

"You do remember I'm still your boss, right?"

"What I remember could be stored in a thimble."

"Any chance you remember who shot you?"

"Nope."

"Any chance you remember the events leading to the shooting?"

"I was messing around on the beach with Marin Baxter. We took a square of sand to rest, and I..."

Dale was woken by a shout. He bolted to his feet, eyed the beach in both directions, then checked Marin who was fast asleep. "Shit, what time is it?" He started to slide his cell out, heard someone yell from around the bend at Stony. When he got onto the stretch he headed toward Echo, heard a scream, saw a man raise a gun to his head. "Hey, you!" The man turned in his direction.

Chief Banks waits for something to indicate Dale is back from wherever the hell he just went. "What happened? Did you have a flashback?"

Dale pushes from the table, "Someone put a bullet in my back. Figure out who."

The chief stands, "I think I know who shot you, Dale. I think you know, too. The question is why would he want to."

Dale starts to walk away. He turns and asks, "Did you get the ballistic report?"

"Thirty-eight snub."

"Shit, Chief. Stand in the middle of Main Street and ask who has a snub, and you'll find it's the gun of choice by most islanders."

"You remember that?"

"I guess I do."

Sand Castle

Marin hairy-eyeballs Dale, "Where are the yummies?"

"Sorry." He heads to the fireplace and spends a few minutes tending to something that really doesn't need tending.

"What happened?"

"Nothing."

The hairy-eyeball pays another visit.

"I ran into Chief Banks."

"And he took my donuts?"

Dale laughs, "No, he pushed a bruise."

"Looks like it caused some pain."

"He wants to know who shot me."

She scoffs, "Who doesn't?"

He drops his duff onto the couch, puts his elbows onto his thighs, hangs his head, and stares at the floor.

She waits until she can wait no longer, "Did you have a memory? Do you know who shot you?" she crawls across the sectional. "Dale?"

He shakes his head, "I had a memory, and recovered stuff from after we stretched out on the sand." He gets silent for a few. "I was woken by a shout, I think. I got to my feet and scanned the beach for the source of the sound, then thought I might have dreamt it because you were still sound asleep on the sand. I heard something from around the bend and when I got onto the stretch toward Echo, I heard a scream and saw a man with a gun. I yelled to him and he turned."

She waits. And waits. And waits.

He struggles to find the thread. "I know I saw the shooter. I just can't get to the memory."

"Then you aren't ready. Let it go."

He pushes to his feet. "This isn't like trying to remember my favorite candy bar, Marin. Someone put a bullet in my back. Not only do I not know who, but I don't have any clue why someone would shoot me and leave me for dead."

"Did you tell the chief you had a partial memory?"

"No. I told him to find the fuckin shooter." He heads to the door, "I need to do something. I'll be back."

"Bring yummies!"

He reaches in his pocket, "Catch."

The red wrapped projectile bangs off her brace and skips across the floor. "A Mounds bar?" she asks when it ends its travel.

"My favorite candy bar. I stopped to see my mother, and she gave me the last one. She's heading out for a few more bags for the trick-or-treaters."

"I think I already like your mother."

"Why?"

"Because she eats all the Halloween candy and has to get more. It's what my mother and I do, and it drives my father crazy. It drove my father crazy." She swallows her tears, then rips into the wrapper, pops half of the gooey coconut treat in and chomps loudly, "I'll save you half. Don't forget the yummies."

He laughs when the door slams. "Damn girl's got me wrapped."

It's a long while before he returns and when he does, Marin rushes them out the door to The Promise for dinner with The Three Women. When they arrive, Esmé hands her daughter a brown paper bag. "What's this?" The mother shrugs. The daughter peeks. The daughter folds the top over a few times, and tosses it onto her jacket.

"What's inside," he asks. In two seconds he'll wished he hadn't.

"Condoms."

He groans long and low. "You have no idea how much I want those five seconds back." He gives his head a good shake, and gives another long and low growl, "Jesus, this day's sucked big time."

June is up and pushing, "Why? What happened? Is there another body? Spill."

"I had a partial memory."

"And he's desperate to pull the thread," Marin offers.

"Let the memory-thread dangle, Dale."

"I am, Esmé. It's tough though. It's about the shooter. I get to the point when he turns toward me, but the memory ends without my seeing his face."

"Lo siento, mijo, you've been through a lot."

June hands him a beer, "You could use this."

"I could use two," they clink their bottles.

After dinner, dessert, and a spirited game of Uno, Dale calls an abrupt end to the evening, "Come on," he pulls Marin to the door, helps her with her coat, and practically pushes her outside.

"Is this some sort of weird foreplay?"

"No. Come on. Hustle."

After several, "Where are we goings?" and even more, "Slow down, Dale, your legs are longer than mine," the couple ends their sprint at the dock. He silences. She marvels.

"Oh, look, the Abenaki is decorated in lights. It's so pretty. Thank you for bringing me to see her."

Dale wraps his arm around and walks her up the boarding plank, "The ferry is doing a

celebratory Moonlight Run. We are joining her."
He hands their tickets to the captain.

"Oh My God, this is the absolute best thing
you could have ever planned." They step onto
the ferry with a fever pitch of excitement. She
heads to her most favored spot, takes hold of the
blue rail and waits for their night of romance to
set sail.

Marin and Dale stay at her spot until the
ferry turns and heads back toward Whisper.
They sit on a bench for two at the bow, his arm
draped around her shoulder. Marin is so quiet,
her breathing so rhythmic, Dale wonders if she's
drifted off. She hasn't.

"Dale."

"Yeah."

"Did you know that once every nineteen
years, the month of February goes without a full
moon?"

He laughs, "How the hell would I know that
and how the hell do you remember that?"

"Don't know and don't know. It's during
those years that there is an assured Blue Moon
in either January or March."

Silence.

"You do know what a Blue Moon is, right?"

"It's a Belgian Ale usually served with a
slice of orange."

"Nope. Well, maybe, though I've no
personal knowledge. I'm referring to the
phenomenon when there are two full moons
during the same month."

"That's cool."

"Mmm. Though the moonless month of February is far more thrilling, don't you think?"

"Yeah." He kisses the top of her head, "Marin."

"Mmm."

"Are you about to tell me this coming February will be moonless?"

"I am. And I want you to promise me that we will do something really big to celebrate it."

"Promise."

The Three Women are at the window when the lovebirds return from their date at sea. "He's good for her," Esmé sighs.

"He's good to her," Jenny sighs.

"He's still six years older than her," June reminds.

Two of The Three Woman groan and head for bed.

Week Three – Day Two
Friday, November 10
Last Quarter – Illumination 50%

Islanders stand shoulder to shoulder on Whisper docks awaiting the return of the Abenaki from her first post-nor'easter run. Some have tickets in hand for their trip to Portland, a certain number are dockside to mark the return of normal island life, and two well-known island men are on the dock to conduct business. Tom makes his way to his former boss, "Chief Banks."

"Detective."

"Retired."

Banks nods, "I remember. Are you setting sail?"

"Nope. Awaiting a Special Delivery. And you?"

"Awaiting a Special Delivery or two."

"You and I need to meet."

"WPD lower level conference room, Saturday night. The squad will be out in force for the trick-or-treaters."

"Ten?"

"Ten."

The men shake hands. Tom discretely pockets the handed-off key that will open a side door at his old stomping grounds.

Paxton waits in line to board the Abenaki. While he waits, he watches the lawmen chit-chat. "A chance meeting?" He lingers until the last minute, gets at the end of the boarding line, finds a place at the bow rail, and waits while the men approach a postmaster and conduct their business. "Special Delivery envelopes. Must be something important for the chief and the detective to retrieve them from the dock rather waiting for home deliveries."

Portland

Rodriquez keeps to the shadowed alleys while others get in line to board the arriving Abenaki. "Got my ticket. Got my gun. Got to make sure I don't know anyone setting sail." He takes a hand drawn map from his pocket and reviews it – for the umpteenth time. "Abenaki will dock on the sandy side of the island. Western end is where Kingston marina and the Kingston estate is located. Eastern end has a section known as Shaky Town. That's where Diggers is located, and it's where Sherry Flynn lived with her grandmother. Up around the eastern bend is where former detective Tom Martin lives." He traces his finger along a red line he drew that travels from a private beach upward to a deep grove of trees. "The detective's house can be accessed through this heavy tree line and is located at the end of a very secluded cul-de-sac." He folds the paper and considers his plan one more time, "I don't have much of a choice. I need to silence that bitch. Better to tell Paxton I made an executive decision and whacked her than to tell him she slipped me and might be spilling her guts to fuckin Tom Martin." Rodriquez nearly shits when he sees Paxton standing at the bow of the docking ship. The thug steps deep into the darkness and waits for his boss to get off the boat.

After the passengers disembark, the captain welcomes the harbor master onboard. "Good to see you, Al."

"Welcome to the mainland, Pat. How was the trip?"

"Smooth sailing," he smiles then hands off a piece of paper, "Updated schedule. The Abenaki will be operating nearly non-stop for the next two weeks, then we'll scale back to the winter schedule."

"Good to know." Al hitches his head to the boarding line, "Good number of people heading to the island."

The captain nods, welcomes his travelers aboard, then reopens the boarding gate for a passenger jogging his way, "Almost missed the crossing."

Rodriquez smiles wide, "Been waiting for days to get to the island. Sure glad you're getting a late push off, otherwise I might have missed her sail." He takes a seat near the stern and watches Paxton enter Mooring. "He's gonna flip his shit when he figures things out."

The contract killer unlocks and enters the dockside bar. It becomes immediately obvious that something's up. He walks the place turning on lights as he goes, steps behind the bar, finds the cash register open and empty, heads to the inner office, finds the safe open and empty, then finds a set of keys on top of a note that reads, **Explain later.**

Paxton whips the keys across the room, "Fuck you, Rodriquez. I don't have time now, but when I do, I'm gonna hunt your fuckin ass, turn it to chum, and dump it into Casco." He pulls himself together piece by piece and begins backtracking. He checks his cell, "Last time the thug and I talked was on … Monday, November 6th." He runs the conversation…

"Fred Fuller's body showed up on Whisper. If anyone shows up at Mooring asking questions about Fred, I want to know about it. Immediately."

"Yeah, I'll call."

"That fucker could have already been gone during that call." He checks Mooring's security system, "Working." He downloads the footage onto a USB, pockets the device, and heads out. "Plan. Get my Benz, swing past Rodriquez's place, see if it looks like he's long gone. He could be off doing a side job – either way he's a dead man. After that bullshit, I'll head to Sherry Flynn's hole—the one where she lives and the one between her legs."

He's already hard when he pulls to the curb at Sherry's place. He loses his boner when there's no sign of life inside. He bangs out of his Benz, walks the perimeter of the tiny rowhouse, then leaves in a huff when he realizes she's not there. He checks his watch. "Eight-thirty. It's too early for her to be up and out." A sour churn hits his gut, "Did she leave? Is that why Rodriquez is gone? Does she know Fred's dead. She wouldn't have left Portland unless she knew he wasn't coming back." He gets into his ride and cruises while he thinks, "Where would the bitch go? How would she get there? She's piss poor without Fred. Unless Rodriquez gave her some money, and if he did he's dead. Okay, let's assume she has money, where would she go? Probably to her family. She met Fred on Whisper when she was visiting her grandmother. Could she be on the island? How could she get to the island? Fuck, did she just board the Abenaki?" His boner returns. "Sherry Flynn, if you're on Whisper I'm gonna fuck the life out of you."

Sand Castle

Marin is home from a doctor's appointment and working through some unsettled feelings about the evaluation. The overall assessment was positive, but being back in that world was awful for her. She's puttering and muttering as she moves about the space. "Another evaluation scheduled for December." She gets a bit reflective .... "If we hadn't gone to Stony that day, if Heir Kingston hadn't tried to drown me, if I hadn't banged the shit out of my head on rocks and boulders on that godforsaken strip of land, I'd be getting ready for WHO-ee in December. I'd be spending Christmas and New Year on Murder Island, and then I'd be leaving. Instead, I'm stuck here." She pulls back a bit, "It isn't all that bad. I'm with Dale. We wouldn't be together now if all that shit hadn't happened." A memory lifts. She can tell it's going to be a pleasant one, so she happily waits…

Marin got off the back of Dale's Harley, unclipped her helmet, and handed it off with an enthusiastic, "That. Was. Awesome!" She ran her fingers along the big-ass machine, "She's a Harley, but what kind?"

"She?"

"Antiquated labeling, I know, but this machine is .... sexy. Woman sexy."

He laughed. "Yeah. This 'machine' is sexy." He stepped off and eyed his ride. "She's a 2015 Harley Softail Breakout custom cruiser, V2, four-stroke, with 6-speed gearbox, 75.1 HP, and 95.9 ft. lbs. of torque."

It was Marin's turn to laugh, "Boys and their toys."

Another memory surfaces…

June dropped Dale and Marin at Wind, "I'll be back to get you and your first load by four. Work on getting the small stuff to the driveway. Anything big, the five of us can schlepp tomorrow."

Marin nudged Dale, "Do you think this crap will ever end?"

"The packing and moving crap?"

"The getting dropped off so no one knows you hang with us crap."

"Yeah, it'll end, pretty soon I think, but I have to tell you, riding in a Mercedes is pretty sweet."

"Riding a Harley is a lot sweeter."

"Yeah, that bike is tits."

She laughed.

He apologized, "Sorry for the slip. I've been working overtime on keeping my language PG."

"Ha! So there is a bad boy under the squeaky-clean Boy Cop routine."

He. Laughed. Big. "You have no idea how bad."

A memory from their time in bed the night before, raises a blush and a desire. When he walks through the door a few minutes later, she presses him against it and kisses him.

He r.e.s.p.o.n.d.s. "What was that for?"

"The mood struck."

He brushes away her mass of waves, "Any chance my sudden mood can strike?"

"Sorry, no time for that kind of striking."

"That's not what I meant."

"What?"

He kisses her. "I'm all-in, Marin. I'm in love with you. I'm pretty sure anyone who sees us together knows how I feel about you, so I thought you should know."

She puts her hands to his face, pulls him close and kisses him. "Should I be saying those words to you?"

"Not if you don't feel them."

"I'm not sure what I feel. Is that okay?"

He kisses her. "More than okay." He kisses her again, "Are you hungry?"

"Starved."

"Let's go out."

"Where?"

"The Beach Bum. It's open for business."

"Perfect!"

"We're walking, so put on warm clothes."

"Have you seen my thumbhole sweatshirt?"

"Kitchen stool."

She finds it and zips it.

He stops her when she flits by. He unzips the sweatshirt, starts getting down to business – a kiss here – a touch there. She wriggles from his hold, "Not now. I'm starved."

He growls low, "Me too."

She giggles when he kisses her neck, "Not that kind of starved. Come on, I need a Beach Bum burger."

He steps back, waiting for a bit of loosening in his jeans.

She ignores the deflation process and jumps into a conversation she's been wanting to have, "I had a thought earlier. I understand that you want to protect me and keep me safe. I feel that way about you. That's why we need to find out who—"

He kisses her, "Not tonight, okay? Let's just take tonight off. No thinking about the past or the future. Let's just be Marin and Dale grabbing some grub and having some fun."

"Deal."

Main Street

Rodriquez ordered a coffee and muffin at a place called Boardwalk then sat his ass at a window table with direct view of the Abenaki dock. "Paxton will either be on the last ferry in or he'll stay on the mainland overnight—I'll either be able to do some surveillance work around the eastern bend tomorrow morning or I'll have to lay low for a few days." By the time Rodriquez finishes his second cup of Joe, he has his answer. "Paxton's back and he brought his ride with him." The thug slips out a back door near the bathroom, hoofs his way through a connecting line of alleyways, and sprints along the far end of Main Street toward Shakyside, a hole-in-the-wall motel on the outskirts of Shaky Town. He heads to his 'parking lot view' room, turns on the tube and waits it out. "If Paxton's Benz shows up, I move to another dive." He sets his alarm for hourly reminders to check the parking lot, then throws himself into the shower. He thinks about the tree sprite woman he's about to whack and gets hard, r.e.a.l.l.y. hard. "If there's any chance to ram that bitch before her bullet ..." He leans against the shower wall, pulls his pud awhile, then lets it spray. "Yeah. She's gonna feel the pain of *this* before she gets a bullet."

Echo

King spends the day raging from one end of the estate to the other: first about Dale Jacobs, then about Ruby Norman. The drunker he gets, the more desperate he becomes, "I need to find that bitch, get her ass back here, get that baby, and make it an orphan. As far as the world knows, that kid is a Kingston. It needs to be raised under my roof." He heads to his office, puts the whisky bottle he's been embracing onto the cocktail bar, sits behind his desk and opens the center drawer. He rummages wildly. "Where the fuck?" He opens the side drawers, trying to think, think, think. "Where the fuck are the pregnancy tests?" The bottom falls out of his gut. "Gone. They're gone. Who's been in this office? Paxton," he growls. "That son of a bitch." A push of concern. "Could'a been the bitch who used to ride my dick. She might have taken them when she left. How did she leave? Who took her? Where the fuck did she go? Probably back to Shaky." He slams the drawers, grabs his jacket and a set of keys, and heads out.

Beach Bum

The place is wall to wall with very happy customers, half of whom greet Dale with friendly smacks to the shoulder, and handshakes. After every single one, Marin raises her brow. He smiles wide and answers her unasked question, "Recognize some faces, can't place the names." They find a seat by the window, attack their food with a vengeance, play footsie under the table, and enjoy being Marin and Dale out on a date.

She runs a French fry through a puddle of ketchup, leans close and asks, "We don't have to hide our relationship anymore?"

"We've already been made by whoever is following us. He knows I'm living at Sand Castle, so we might as well be ourselves. I figure it's better that we stick close, and when we're hungry we feed ourselves."

"We can feed ourselves here every day of the week if you want," she takes a bite of her burger – he wipes the juice that runs her chin.

"I like you, Marin."

"Uh oh. I've been demoted already? An hour ago you loved me, and now you only like me?"

He joins her laugh, "Nope, I still love you, but I like you, too. You're fun, easy, brilliant, challenging, and sometimes an all-around pain in the ass, but I like all of it."

"I like you, too, Dale."

The speed of a Tacoma past the window sends a chill up Dale's spine. "Finish up. I want to get back to The Castle."

Ten minutes later they're hoofing it back. The Tacoma speeds past in the opposite direction. "Shit. He looped around."

"Who?"

Dale grabs Marin's hand, checks over his shoulder a few times, watches the Tacoma pull into and out of the Beach Bum parking lot and fly toward them. Dale waits – waits – waits, then grabs Marin around the waist and hurtles them off the road into a ditch. She lands hard on top of him, taking a major blow to her already injured, unbraced wrist. He moves out from under, long after the truck is gone from sight. He helps her to her feet, moves her into the tree line and makes a call. "Tom, someone in a Tacoma just tried to hit Marin and me. We've taken shelter in the woods between Beach Bum and Diggers."

"I'm on my way."

Echo

King parks the Tacoma at the end of the circular drive, nearly falls out of the vehicle and onto the front stairs. He steadies himself by leaning against a big-ass porch column, slurs a few words about the fucking cop and the mental midget, then bangs through the front door.

Paxton steps from the shadows as soon as The King of Whisper makes it inside. The contract killer plays the cell phone video, gives a good laugh, "Perfect recording of the truck cutting across the lawn, and King's drunk-tumble from the truck, and drunk-stumble to the front door, and the slurred words of admission. This will bring bank." He waits several minutes, makes his way back around the estate, steps inside the office and gets back to the work he was doing before the Tacoma incident. "Why did King put me on Dale Jacobs? What does the cop have on Edward Kingston III?" When Paxton finds the file folder labeled, Brother, and the legal pad full of notes and questions, he knows. "Okay. Things are making some sense. Heir must have found out Dale Jacobs is King's illegitimate son. Then what? King got pissed that Edward knew and shot Dale Jacobs on Stony Beach? Could be, but there has to be more to the story. It could explain the call to action I got…"

"You need to come to Whisper."

"I told you never to contact me."

"Look Paxton, you did a job, it went south, and you did some time in prison. I paid you a pretty penny for a job you fucked up and to keep your mouth shut, so you owe me."

"Fuck you."

"Five million."

"For what?"

"Three hits."

"Who?"

"I haven't decided yet, but they're all local."

"....... Tough break about Heir." **He purposefully pushed the bruise.**

"Shut up. Get your ass to the island. I need you to get rid of a piece."

"Why not dump it yourself?"

"Every eye on this island is on me. Even if I could get far enough out to sea, there'd be followers. I want this done today."

"Add another 25Gs."

Paxton paces. While he paces he pieces some shit together. "King must have used the snubnose to shoot Dale Jacobs." Paxton flips through the Brother file, page by interesting page, taking cell pics of each. "I don't have time to figure this paternity shit out. I need to cover my ass. First up is making sure King doesn't find out I didn't dump his gun. I need to make sure he doesn't find out I gave it to Rodriquez to use on Fred Fuller." He takes a hip on King's desk and pulls a few threads – lands at the logical conclusion – "It's just a matter of time before ballistics ties those two shootings together. Chief Banks is gonna be all over this shit when he pulls the investigative threads and they twist around The Fucking King of Whisper. It's time I bow out of this shit fest. Tomorrow, I'm getting off Whisper and I'm putting a shitload of distance between me and Edward Kingston III."

Outer Banks

Vernon pulls open his front door, "Tom."

"Don't bother telling me I shouldn't be here."

"What's going on?"

"The driver of the Tacoma that's been trailing Dale Jacobs made a move. He tried to run Dale and Marin down. Fucking almost succeeded based on evidence at the scene."

"Dale and Marin, are they hurt?"

"Bumped and bruised."

"Did you call it in?"

"No. I'm guessing the hitman is going to get off island for a while, so you and I are gonna get him before he does."

"Do you know who he is?"

"Nope, but we know every resident on this island. The Abenaki is scheduled to run tomorrow at 7 AM, we'll be on board long before to spring a trap."

The Promise

Marin and Dale did the whole question and answer thing with Tom, then did another round of Q&A with The Three Women, who got a watered down version of events. The couple is now behind closed doors in Marin's upstairs bedroom, all showered and changed into warm, comfortable sweats. She's got her face pressed to her telescope, her injured wrist braced and hanging at her side. He's stretched out on the bed, rubbing the outer thigh of his injured leg. She turns when he groans, "Your leg?"

"Yeah. I fucked it up some. How's your wrist?"

"I fucked it up some, but at least you protected my skull. Maybe I should start wearing my head gear, at least until we catch whoever's after you."

He laughs big, "Bet that's a sweet look."

She closes the French doors and joins him on the bed. "I bet it's your wit."

"What's my wit?"

"The reason someone wants you dead."

He pulls her near.

She pushes away. "What *did* you do to make someone want to kill you?"

"No clue. I'm thinking I must have learned something when Tom and I were investigating, or maybe I learned something about another case."

"It must be the other case, otherwise the shooter would want Tom dead, too. Right?"

"Mmm. Maybe." He kisses her head, "I was thinking—"

"You're not moving home, Dale. You are staying with me, so we can keep each other safe, right?"

"Right. But."

"No, buts, Dale. Now, stop talking, I'm tired."

"Good God, you're a bossy one."

"Having second thoughts?"

"Nope."

"By the way," she swirls her good hand in the air, "this is off limits."

"Because we're under your mother's roof?"

"Because I have my period."

Shakyside

Rodriquez watches Paxton pull onto the parking lot and head inside. He checks the time, "A little after 2 AM. Okay, here's the plan, get some shuteye and figure shit out in the morning." He sets his alarm for seven and hits sleep hard. At six-thirty, he hops from bed at the sound of Paxton's voice. He watches as the contract killer and another guy head to parked cars. He eases open his window for a better hear.

"Where was the near-hit-and-run?"

"Right on this main road, between a boho eatery called Beach Bum and a popular bar called Diggers."

"Did the cops get the guy?"

"Nope, but witnesses say the driver was in a Tacoma."

"Good thing I'm leaving the island. Wouldn't want my ride hit by some jackass."

Rodriquez watches Paxton toss his gear into his Benz and leave the seaside dive.

Week Three – Day Three
Saturday, November 11
Waning Crescent – Illumination 39%

The lawmen boarded the Abenaki a few minutes before 6 AM. Harbor ferry master, Jim Kay, approved the plan the night before and became part of it acting as ticket sales rep at the dockside box office. A couple dozen passengers move to the walk-on docking platform just before seven, and fifteen vehicles, one of which does not have a WI resident sticker on the windshield, wait at the vehicle drop plank at the ship's stern. At a few minutes before seven, the ferry master leads the boarders up the plank, makes his way to the hull, hands a slip of paper to Chief Banks, and continues to the vehicle entrance ramp. While he begins the docking procedure, the chief reads the note.

"Black Mercedes SUV. Lone passenger. Male. Forties."

"Good thing it's Saturday, otherwise this hull would be full. Any changes to the plan?"

"Nope. Jim blocked the entrance to the stern stairway, so anyone who wants to go to the deck will have to use the bow entrance."

"Our guy's not gonna go deck side."

"Nope. We'll wait until the hull is empty and approach his vehicle from two points."

Tom nods.

The seasoned lawmen called the scenario to the letter. Paxton pulls into the hull, parks his Benz as close to the back as possible, watches passengers leave their cars and make their way up the open bow staircase. He slides his seat back and readies himself for a sit in the hull.

At twenty-two past seven Paxton wonders why the ferry is still docked. At twenty-seven past seven he learns why.

Chief Banks steps from behind a big-ass steel column and trains his gun on the semi-reclined man, "Put your hands onto the ceiling of your car. If you move a muscle, I'll assume you're going for your piece."

Tom makes his way to the driver's side door and opens it, "Put your hands on your head, lock your fingers, and step out of the vehicle."

"What are the charges?"

"Sloppy parking. You're outside designated lanes."

Banks laughs.

Paxton steps out, automatically turns, bellies against the Benz, puts his hands behind his back, and waits for Tom to slap on the cuffs.

"Cuff him in front, Detective."

"What are the charges?" the thug asks again.

"Attempted hit and run, times two, for starters."

"Wasn't me behind the wheel of the Tacoma."

Silence.

"I want a lawyer."

"I bet you do," Vernon starts. "And you're gonna need one," Vernon finishes.

The Abenaki was delayed three hours before setting sail. It took that long for a tow truck to get the Benz out of the hull and brought to the lot behind Town Hall. When the chief walks Paxton down the ferry plank, there's nothing to suggest the man is under arrest – his cuffed hands are hidden under a jacket and he's chatting up the chief.

"You and I should have a sit down, Chief Banks."

Silence.

"I have enough evidence in my Benz to put Edward Kingston III away for life. I'll give you what I have, if you'll get me the fuck off this island without charges."

"Still want a lawyer?"

"Nope."

"Well you're gonna get one." He addresses Tom, "Why don't you ask Ms. Stuart to join Mr. Paxton and me in the conference room at Town Hall."

"Chief, Ms. Stuart is—"

"Going to join us."

The Promise

Tom is welcomed in by Esmé, walks past with a grunt, takes hold of Jenny's arm, "A minute of your time, Counselor. Where can we get some privacy?"

"Upstairs in my office."

"Let's go."

"Chief Banks wants you to sit in on something ...."

"Illegal?"

"Questionable. Possible. Probable. I'm not sure."

"Tell me."

"There's a guy at WPD, in a conference room, **not** under arrest, though that was the intent when the chief and I set a trap for him this morning. We thought he was the driver of the hit and run attempt on Dale and Marin. I don't think that anymore, and I don't think the chief does either. The guy wants off Whisper in a very big way. He's offered to turn over evidence against Edward Kingston III. He said the stuff he has could put King away for life. I'm pretty sure the chief wants you to find a way for both parties to get what they want."

"If the guy remains a non-prisoner, he's free to give you whatever he wants to give you."

"That's it?"

She shrugs. "It's certainly a starting point in negotiations."

"Are you in?"

"I'll listen."

"Let's go."

The detective and the lawyer exit through the front door of Promise bypassing four inquisitive minds that want to know what the early morning hubbub is all about.

WPD

Chief Banks introduces Eugene Paxton to Attorney Stuart.

"Mr. Paxton. Are you under arrest?"

"No."

"Why are you in the police conference room?"

"I parked my Mercedes between lanes on the Abenaki."

The men laugh-grunt.

She smiles. "And?"

"The chief and the detective thought I might be responsible for an attempted hit and run, but I explained that I wasn't behind the wheel at the time of the incident."

"Uh huh."

"Should I continue?"

"Please."

"I'm in a hurry to get off Whisper, and since there aren't any charges against me, I thought I would leave today."

"In return for?"

"Nothing."

Silence.

"But I'm in need of a favor."

"Continue."

"You and I should speak in private."

The lawmen leave.

"I'd like to retain your services."

"Do you have a dollar bill on you?"

"In my pocket. Should I get it?"

"Yes."

"You're representing me?"

"For one hour."

"I've done prison time. I have two warrants out for my arrest in the great state of New Jersey. If The King of Whisper finds out I'm being held and questioned, he'll know I'm giving him up, and it'll be a matter of time before I'm dead. My demise might not happen on this lovely island, but it will happen. I have evidence in my Mercedes that will implicate Edward Kingston III in several federal and state crimes. Additionally, my records contain the name of a Kingston associate who helped carry out certain gun-related crimes, including the murder of a former Whisper resident. I want to offload the information and get the fuck off this island."

"The chief won't let you walk without knowing what you have."

"I'll tell him one thing, a show of good faith. The rest he can learn thirty days from now."

"Why thirty days?"

"It will take that long for me to get out of the States and dig a hole deep enough that I won't be found."

Silence.

"I'll turn over everything to you, USB drives, my cell phone with conversational and picture texts, some that show documents that no one knows I found, and several pictures of a gun used in a crime or two and dumped in Casco Bay. There's a financial journal in my handwriting, my computer, and some other shit. Anything in that vehicle is the chief's—"

"This seems extreme, Mr. Paxton."

"Edward Kingston III is a broken man. He's staying this side of life for one purpose— revenge. He has a hit list, and he's going to work through that list with the aid of a contract killer, or by himself. This visit to WPD just put me onto that list, Ms. Stuart."

"I'll be back." She meets the men in the hall. "He retained me as his lawyer for one hour. He is willing to turn over, to me, his computer, USB drives, a financial journal, and his cell phone. He said the information he's accumulated will implicate Edward Kingston III and a Kingston associate in certain gun-related crimes, including the murder of a former Whisper Island resident. He said there are cell phone pictures of a gun that was used in a crime or two and dumped in Casco Bay. There's a catch. Mr. Paxton wants a thirty day lag time before the information is transferred to you for review."

"Why?"

"He wants to get out of the States. He's done time in prison, and he says there are two outstanding warrants for his arrest in New Jersey. More to the point, he said Edward Kingston III has a hit list and Mr. Paxton doesn't want to be added to it. He said he would give you information on one topic to show good faith."

"What topic?"

"He didn't say."

"Let's go find out."

"I explained things to the chief and the detective, Mr. Paxton. They are willing to consider your proposal, but they need you to give them information on the 'show of faith' offer before making a final decision."

Paxton eyes the chief. Waits for The Nod. Smiles when he gets it. "I have information on the attempted hit and run on Marin Baxter and Dale Jacobs."

The chief pushes in, "You already said you weren't driving."

"I'm willing to show you a date and time stamped video recording of the person who *was* driving the Tacoma. You'll want to see the video, and you will, *after* I get an agreement in writing. The contract needs to include your assurances that no law enforcement agencies, located elsewhere in the United States, will be tipped as to my whereabouts."

"Show the video to your attorney. If she suggests we proceed with this arrangement, we will."

The men leave.

Jenny watches the video.

The men return.

"It is my professional opinion that you will want to see that video. At face value, it looks like an easy charge and conviction of a DUI.

However, the voice recording evidences a purposeful hit and run attempt on two individuals labeled by the person talking as a fucking cop and a mental midget."

Tom seethes.

Vernon decides. "Please draw up the agreement, Attorney Stuart."

The men leave.

"Mr. Paxton, my retainer for one month's legal service is $100. Are you able to pay at this time?"

"Yes. May I reach in my pocket?"

"Yes."

Eugene Paxton hands her the money.

"Thank you."

"Thank you, Attorney Stuart."

A chill runs her spine. She leaves the room.

An hour later a chief, a detective, a lawyer, and a thug watch a video of Edward Kingston III stumble and slur his way to a future arrest warrant.

The Promise

Tom and Jenny stop on the driveway, take a lean-to against his truck, and watch Chief Banks stand sentry at the Abenaki dock. They laugh when Paxton sends a wave their way from the bow of the departing ferry. "Good work, Attorney," Tom nudges.

"Was it?"

"Essential work, Attorney," he amends.

"I can accept that."

Esmé's had time to stew about the early morning invasion of her home and abduction of her lawyer-friend. Concern and frustration are more than evident when Tom and Jenny enter the kitchen. "Was last night a contracted hit and run on Marin and Dale?"

"I can't—"

She gets all up in Tom's face, "Dime toda la verdad. Don't you dare hold back information."

"Everything suggests they were targeted."

"Everything?" the mother pushes.

Dale and Marin enter the kitchen and the conversation, "Someone has been following us," they unison.

Esmé and June hairy-eyeball Tom.

"The pieces just fell into place, and the chief is on it."

"Is there a POI?" Dale asks.

"I'll know more later. Sure hope the five of you are staying put tonight."

Silence hangs heavy. All eyes turn Esmé's way. God only knows where her mind is.

Marin moves toward her contemplative mother, wraps her arm, "Mom? We're all staying in tonight. Right?"

"Yesss. Of course. The trick-or-treaters will be visiting The Promise, and I can't wait to see the costumes. I need a happy distraction."

"Do we have candy?"

"Yesss."

"Because she restocked," June offers.

Mother and daughter laugh at part of their history emerging freely.

Tom edges in, "Patrols will be out until 10 PM. Make sure you lock your doors before then. Dale and Marin, I'd appreciate it if you'd stay at The Promise tonight."

They nod.

Esmé sighs, "That's it? That's all it took? A pleasant request and these two concede. What's your trick?"

"Or treat?" Tom laughs, then catches a pained look that travels Marin's face, "Are you alright?"

"Sore."

"Your wrist?"

"Very sore." She turns and heads for the stairs, "I'm gonna go lie down."

The room quiets until she leaves. Tom heads for the door, "Dale, grab your coat." At the F-150, the detective says it straight, "You need to be carrying. Someone is gunning for you. Your proximity to Marin puts her in the crosshairs."

"I told her I should leave."

"Too late for that. You need to stay with her, and you need to be armed."

"I haven't used a piece since the Stony shit."

"Riding a bike, Dale. Until I know more than I know now, I want you carrying. We'll swing by Jacobs Jolly for your piece, then grab some food. I want to catch you up on a few things."

Wind Ledge

Tom and Dale set their breakfast grinders and juices on the coffee table in the living room and dig in. All conversation ceases until the last bite is swallowed, "Why'd you want to come to Wind?"

"I wanted some privacy."

"Is your place bugged or something?"

"I have houseguests."

Dale shrugs.

Tom laughs, "You aren't interested in who's staying at my place?"

"Should I be?"

"Nope." Tom points to something between the cushions of the couch, "What's that?"

Dale grabs hold, then whips it across the room, "Fucking big-ass spider is what it is."

The men wait for the big-ass arachnid to scurry away. It just lies there. Dale makes a move on the eight-legged creature, taps it with the toe of his shitkicker, then picks it up. "Plastic." A memory-thread loosens…

Dale pretended not to notice the women scurrying to and fro hiding things all over the home he'd soon buy. Esmé hid tea bags, Jenny and June hid Boardwalk coupons, and Marin went old school and hid an entire package of black plastic spiders in shoes, on cabinet shelves, tucked between sheets and towels, between couch cushions, on top of doorjambs, inside potted plants, drawers, and closets. "Payback will be a bitch," he quietly promised.

Dale makes a little showing as he heads to the window, takes hold of a spider from the dirt of a long-ago deceased potted plant and tosses it at Tom, runs his hand across the top of a doorjamb, takes hold of a spider and tosses it at Tom, shakes a pair of running shoes, takes hold of a spider and tosses at Tom. "Marin hid these and a hundred others the night before ……." He silences and sort of disappears into himself…

A yell woke him. He bounded to his feet and scanned the beach. Something on the water caught his eye. It lifted and lowered at the mercy of the tide. "What the fuck? Is that Edward?" He heard the yell of a man.

Tom moves near Dale who is miles away in some sort of fugue state. He waits for the tiniest hint that he's working his way back, "Dale. Where'd you go?"
"To Stony. I saw Edward Kingston IV bobbing in the water. His body was moving toward the shore. Then I heard a yell." He tries to grab the memory; he shakes his head as though in pain. "It's there. Right there, but I can't grab hold of the image."

Tom places his hand on Dale's shoulder. "Don't push it. You might lose it altogether. We should go."

"You wanted to talk about something."

"It can wait."

Primrose Priscilla

Tom brings The Boarders a box of Boardwalk yummies then gets the hell out of the way.

"Dibs if there's anything chocolate," the pregger yells.

"Dibs if there's anything cream filled," the sprite yells.

"Save me one, don't care what kind," he yells on a laugh and an exit. He shuts the denroom door, "I'm taking a nap." He plops his ass on his recliner, kicks it back, ruminates on the morning's events, then tries to clear his head with a Prissy journal. "Nineteen-eighty-three. Four plus years into our marriage, our childless marriage. That's the year I surprised her with a trip to Hawaii for Christmas."

Tom and I are buckled in for our flight to the islands. When he gave me this trip as a Christmas gift I reminded him that we live on an island. He reminded me that Whisper is not Hawaii, and Casco Bay is not the Pacific Ocean. I am so excited, I can hardly bear it. In case I forget, there are two things at the top of my Hawaiian To-Do list: have Tom take a picture of me getting my welcoming lei at the airport, and a picture of me picking my very own pineapple. My man, a very busy detective, patiently listened when I told him it takes 20 months for a plant to produce its first pineapple, and another 15 months for it to produce it's second, and that after the second harvest, the plant is

knocked back, and the growing process starts all over again. His response, "I don't like pineapple, dear." My response, "You'll like Hawaiian pineapple when I feed it to you in bed." His response, "I'll gladly eat the whole damned thing, dear." I love this man. (1983)

Tom falls asleep with memories of Priscilla wearing nothing but a lei in bed that first night in Hawaii. He wakes a few hours later with his first-ever craving for pineapple. "God, I loved that woman."

Echo

Banks rings the doorbell, six times, then steps away from the door when the tow truck appears on the circular drive. He follows the truck and instructs the driver, then starts back toward the house.

King storms outside, "Get the fuck off my property!"

"Mr. Kingston. This vehicle was involved in a road incident last evening in Shaky. Were you behind the wheel of the Tacoma between the hours between 6 PM and midnight or do you know who was?"

Silence.

"This truck is being impounded pending an investigation."

King grabs his cell and punches a number. He leaves a directive, "Call me!" He points to Banks, "Wait outside." He storms through the front door, begins pacing a circuitous route around the massive foyer as fragments lift through his sobering brain...

"Where the fuck?" He rummaged his desk for the pregnancy tests, open and slammed drawers. "Where the fuck are the tests?" He grabbed a set of keys – drove Main Street – raced through Shaky Town – saw the lying bastard – revved the engine – slammed his hands when they hurtled themselves into a ditch.

Fully sober now and fully aware of why Vernon Banks is on his property, he laments his failure from the night before. "I missed the lying bastard and his mental-midget whore." He ignores the knock at the door.

"Mr. Kingston, open the door and sign the impound paperwork." Another knock, "Mr. Kingston, you are ordered to open this door. If you do not, forceable entry will be made."

King opens the door, signs the paperwork, and tries to slam the door. The chief stops it with his hand, steps close and talks low, "Paxton left the island. Before he set sail, he gave me the goods. All of the goods. On all of it. You are going down. And when you're spending the last miserable days of your life in jail, remember this." He moves closer. "The **father** of Kathleen Beckwith's son is the one who beat your ass and put it behind bars." He removes his hand and walks to the WPD Rover. "Have a nice day, Mr. Kingston."

The King of Whisper loses his shit. Then he surrenders his mind to Kathleen...

"Look Eddie, Daddy's home."

He took the baby boy and handed her a piece of paper. He watched her as her eyes filled.

"Edward is Vernon's—"

"Edward is **MY** son. You will never tell Vernon, and you will never tell Heir otherwise." He left her in tears, on that day and every day for more than two years.

Kathleen was on the bottom stair waiting for King to arrive home from one of his weekend 'business' trips. When he stumbled in, he brought with him the scent of another and the look of a man who'd been pleasured. "I'm leaving you, King."

"You won't be taking my son."

She hands him a document, "Daddy drew up papers. Vernon will be served with them tomorrow. He will know the truth, and he will come for **his** son. If you want the façade of a happy home to continue, you will stop dicking around, and you will treat me the way Vernon would have treated me. If you choose to battle things out, you will lose. The world will know that the Heir to the Kingston fortune is another man's. The court will rule in the true father's favor, and the man who still loves me will accept me with open arms. Make your decision, Edward, and tell me in the morning."

The man who would be King made his decision before she took one step away. "You are my wife and he is my son." He took her hand and led her upstairs.

~

Vernon was standing outside Kathleen's hospital room when King exited. The King had lost his queen.

Vernon stepped close, "Kathleen told me."

"What are you going to do?"

"Whatever I want to do you goddamn son of a bitch." He started walking away, turned and finished his piece, "I should tell Edward. I should take him, but he just lost his mother, and though he'd be well rid of you, he would pay an emotional price. Be forewarned, you selfish bastard, I'll be watching."

King huffs upstairs to his master. He forces himself to remember the day he died inside...

"Mr. Kingston, your son is dead on Stony Beach."

Hours after the tide receded from Stony, the body of Edward Kingston IV was strapped to a rescue basket, carried around the bend, and brought to Echo. It was placed on the lawn near the rattans until the medical examiner's team arrived. King listened to Doc Schuster's words, but his eyes never left his son's body —— until his son's real father arrived. Edward Kingston III walked past Vernon Banks and nearly spat his words,

"He's all yours."

A Private Beach

Rodriquez walks east along the shoreline from the motel toward a sweet little beach cove. He recognizes the place from his research. "This is the area behind Tom Martin's place." He takes several pictures of the little inlet, moves further up the bend and takes a few pics of the properties that abut the area. He pops a squat and looks out at bay waters, making sure anyone watching thinks he's just a guy out and about. When he's finished with his work, he backtracks and heads to the Beach Bum for takeout. He continues the whole visitor-façade by eating on a jetty near the motel. "Okay, up-close surveillance of Primrose Priscilla is possible. Tomorrow I head out for a trek up the dune and through the wooded area." He makes a mental note to check his surveillance gear. "Tonight, I'll kill some time at the home of Sherry's grandmother. Maybe I'll get lucky and she'll be visiting the old lady, but in order for me to get my hands on her, I'll most likely be paying a visit to Martin's place. Bottom-fucking-line, it doesn't matter where the bitch is hiding, I'll find her, fuck her, and whack her."

Town Hall

Tom enters the building through the side entrance and heads to the lower level conference room. The chief is waiting. Tom shuts the door behind him, "We should cordon this room and process it as a crime scene because whatever the fuck happened here was straight up criminal."

The chief chuckles. "It's been a fuckin day. I'm goddamn beat, but I wanted to spend time discussing Christie Anderson."

"No need. I'm more than prepared," the detective holds back on telling the chief about his surprise witness.

"Good. We might not get Heir for Christie, but the following week when we bring evidence on the Laire MacTavish case, I think we'll get a finding of homicide, times two."

"You know Laire's dead." It wasn't a question — it should have been.

He nods.

"Since when?"

"Since the night it happened."

"Heir?"

"At the order of King."

"Why!?"

"This isn't the time to get into what I think, but soon."

Tom pushes a few thoughts until he settles on one. "So Laire was pregnant."

"You suspected it?"

"Yeah during my rogue investigation, then figured it was a foregone conclusion when Ruby Norman said King has two pregnancy tests—"

"Had."

"You pilfered them."

"Yes."

"Have you run them for DNA?"

"Not yet."

"Does King know they're gone?"

"Probably."

"He'll think Ruby took them. His motivation for finding her just went through the roof."

"Any problems with her being at Primrose?"

"An Echo Tacoma was parked on my street the other day. At the time, I didn't know who was inside casing my place, but now I know it was Paxton. My sense is that he was there to send a message. He'd been surveilling Jacobs Jolly for days and when Dale showed up there, I kept Paxton from tailing him to Sand Castle. The thug headed to my place to fuck with me. He showed up a few days later pretending to be an insurance claims adjuster. The only thing he saw inside my place was my alarm system."

"Once the inquest starts, things could get dicey for Ms. Norman."

"She's gonna need 24/7 protection from the second she steps out of my house."

"Ideas?"

"A few."

"Tell me when we get there. Okay, I'm fried. I'm heading home."

"Yeah. See you at the inquest. If you need anything, contact Roxanne."

Tom leaves.

Rodriquez watches the detective's truck pull onto Main Street. "Fuckin prick caused me some pain and aggravation. Backatcha asshole."

The Promise

Dale wakes alone in bed. He sits and leans against the headboard, watches Marin at her telescope, then gets in on the moon-gazing. "Waning crescent?"

"At 39%, I think."

"Want some company?" When she turns his way, he sees the wrist brace and the pain etched on her face "You're in pain? Is that why you can't sleep?"

She pulls the French door closed, "I need to have it checked. I just don't want to."

He bounds off the bed, gently taking her hand in his. "Your fingers are bruised and swollen, Marin. Why didn't you say how badly you hurt yourself?"

She starts to cry, "I'm just so tired of sliding backwards. It was so hard to get here, and I really like where I am, where we are." She raises her braced hand to her chest, supports her elbow with her other hand, and walks into his embrace.

He kisses the top of her head, "God, you're little. What are you, like 5'4"?"

"Yes, but what does that have to do with my wrist?"

"Nothing. Do you think you need to go to Emergency tonight?"

"No, but I need to call my doctor tomorrow, first thing."

"Okay."

"I wish I could sleep in the recliner at The Castle."

"Come on."

"Tom said to sleep here."

"That was before I started carrying again."

He walks to the nightstand, tucks his gun into the waistband of his jeans, moves them to the door, and leads her out. They creep the hall, careful not to wake the J-Team, but by the time they get to Esmé's bedroom suite, the whole house is awake. After an explanation and an examination of the pained wrist, The Three Women give their blessing, then put a pot on. They watch Dale and Marin round the corner at Sand Castle in silence then the mouthy one does a reporter-esque voiceover.

"Come to Whisper Island where you, too, can find dead bodies and sleepless nights." June laughs at her own funny, "Maybe I'll try my hand at writing slogans."

Esmé and Jenny groan in unison.

Week Three – Day Four
Sunday, November 12
Waning Crescent – Illumination 29%

Tom wakes with a nudge—it is deep and unrelenting. He drags his ass off the recliner, walks the house, checks the windows and doors, the alarm, puts the flood lights on in the backyard, watches the area a bit, then returns to his recliner—only to get up and do it all over again, two more times. When The Boarders wake, he grunts his greeting, has breakfast with them, calls Roxanne and suggests she stop by sometime that day, then he parks his ass back in his recliner with a few Miss Prissy journals.

Several hours later, Sherry knocks on his doorjamb, "Roxanne is about to do another piece on the shipwreck, *Darling*."

"Ms. Flynn, I think it's way too soon in our relationship for you to call me, *Darling*," he teases.

She laughs and scurries to tell Ruby the joke Tom made.

"Hello, Whisper Island residents. This is Roxanne Carmichael, and I am on the eastern bend of Whisper with an update on the unearthed shipwreck found after our recent nor'easter. Preliminary analysis by experts at Northeastern University suggests that this is, indeed, *Darling*, a cargo ship that went down off the coast of Portland in 1801."

The cameraman does a long, slow pan of the barely exposed hull.

"Wood analysis confirms construction of the ship's hull predates the American Revolution which began in colonial North America in 1765. Professor Emeritus, Clarkston Bainbridge, has traced *Darling's* last voyage from the North Shore of Massachusetts to ports along the coast, tragically ending in our very own Casco Bay. The professor and his team have reviewed newspaper accounts from ports along the Eastern Seaboard that include 'quotes of concern' by shipmen's next of kin. Professor Bainbridge said there is a very strong historical thread to be pulled. As reported in today's *Whisper Telegram*, the professor is quoted as saying 'Beginning in 1902, Marblehead, Massachusetts, home to many of the lost sailors, began holding an annual commemorative service at a garden near the dock where *Darling* set sail. A bell tolls once for each man lost at sea, and a woman in period clothing stands atop the widow's walk at Town Hall symbolizing the long, lonely wait for her husband's return. When news broke that this shipwreck may very well be *Darling*, many relatives and friends of the lost have been in touch. They are eager to know for sure if the last chapter in the story of *Darling* will finally be told.' The professor went on to say that there are many more things to learn about *Darling*, the most important of which is who will excavate her and where her final resting place will be. Until those decisions are made, researchers will begin a construction project tomorrow to erect a structure to keep her protected during the upcoming winter months. On behalf of WCWI Channel 4, this is Roxanne Carmichael, thanking you for tuning in to the mystery of, The Whisper Island Shipwreck. Stay safe."

Tom watched the program with Ruby and Sherry, and though he seemed to enjoy their banter and carefree moments he could not ignore the burn of concern in his gut. "Ladies, I'd like you to pack the cooler," his code for getting things ready for a prolonged stay upstairs. The women take to the kitchen, make sandwiches, grab snacks, waters, and juices, make sure they have their burners and head upstairs. Tom belts his gun, grabs his jacket and heads outside. He tidies up some branches that fell after the tree service did their thing, coils and stores a garden hose, seals a hole in the storage shed, and through it all he takes casual looks in the tree line. And when Preacher Paulson stops by unannounced, Tom considers the churchman just might be the source of uneasiness he's been carrying. The man is resisting the pull down the religious rabbit hole when Roxanne parks her Jeep on the driveway. "Divine intervention," Tom whispers. He taps the preacher's shoulder, "Terribly sorry I can't invite you in, Reverend, but I have a meeting with Ms. Carmichael." He joins Roxanne at her Jeep, takes her by the elbow and moves her toward the back of Primrose.

The holy man and the reporter say a passing hello, then to Tom he reminds, "Sundays are for prayer. I'm sure I'll be seeing you perched on a pew next week."

"God willing," Tom hollers as they round the corner. "I could kiss you, Roxanne."

"Or you could say, 'Praise the Lord, Roxanne Carmichael has great timing.'"

"Praise the Lord, Roxanne Carmichael has great timing."

The kitchen lights flicker.
Tom smiles at his beloved's admonishment
from on high.

Outer Banks

Vernon makes himself get out of bed after his all-nighter. "I need to get ready for the inquest." He heads to the kitchen, scrambles an egg, microwaves a couple pieces of pre-cooked bacon, pops bread into the toaster, slathers it with butter and seedless strawberry jam, pours a cup of coffee, and sits in the same chair he's used for a quarter of a century. "Sunday morning breakfast." He checks the time. "Sunday afternoon breakfast. Every damned Sunday for as long as I can remember, I've had this breakfast." He chews on that and his food for a few minutes. "It's what you prepared for me after our first night together, Kathleen, and every week after that. A month of Sundays, that's how we promised we'd measure our relationship. Four months of Sundays later, you crawled out of my bed and into his, and you took my unborn son with you. I should hate you for it, but I would never, could never, hate you for anything." He takes his uneaten portion to the sink and dumps it into the disposal, "But him. I hate him with every fiber of my being. And I'm gonna grind that asshole." The chief heads to his safe, takes out a few files, "I'm gonna make **our** son take ownership for his actions, Kathleen, then I'm going after those who played a part in the deaths of Christie Anderson, Laire MacTavish, Danielle Rayburn, and Joseph Baxter. Mark my words, Kathleen Beckwith, if it's the last thing I do, I'm bringing everyone involved in this shit fest down. Even me."

Shakyside

Rodriquez pulls his ass from bed after his all-nighter. "I'll get back to surveilling Gladys Flynn later. I don't want the rental seen during daylight hours. Good fuckin thing I got the ride when I did. Last car available, shit comfort, but I shouldn't be on the island too long. That reminds me, I need to get a copy of the updated Abenaki schedule." He throws himself into the shower, into some clothes, and grabs his surveillance bag. "Okay, I need to get into the tree line behind Tom Martin's place. It's the weekend, so the eastern side might have a few looky-loos near the shipwreck and maybe some beach-strollers along the shoreline. If it looks like I'll call attention by hanging near the dune wall, I'll scrap the attempt and try tomorrow. Maybe do some nighttime snooping when the detective is at the inquest."

Echo

King screams into his cell, "Paxton! Call me the fuck back!" He slams the phone onto his desk. Within minutes, shit starts filling his headspace

– where's Ruby – did she take the test strips – did Vernon take her – has he had her this whole time? He ratchets himself down and talks things through. "Ruby had to have left Echo with Vernon, or someone who works for him. Who else would have been on the streets the day after a two day nor'easter? So assume Vernon took her and stashed her somewhere. Why? To get information, that's why. And she has the goods. That bitch lived under my roof for years. She knows things about the Kingston men. She'll be a valuable witness at the inquest. Vernon needs to keep her safe. Who better to keep her safe than a retired detective. Tom fuckin Martin has my bitch under his roof. I need a replacement for Paxton." King picks up the phone and calls Mooring, "What's the fuckin guy's name that runs the place now?" The phone rings. And rings. And rings. "Sunday afternoon, the joint should be open." He slams the phone down, pushes from his seat, grabs a bottle, and heads upstairs to Edward's room. He ties one on and passes the fuck out.

Whisper Rehab Center

The Three Women wait in the parking lot for Marin and Dale. Esmé's nose is a bit bent out of shape, "Is this the way it's going to be? Dale will do all these things with her now?"

"Yes," J&J unison.

"And is he going to be around All. Of. The. Time?"

"Yesss," they tease in unison.

"And should I be bothered by this?"

Silence.

She exhales, "¡Pero qué puta mierda! No, I shouldn't be upset by this. What is wrong with me?"

"Sounds like you're jealous," June answers from the seat in the far back.

"I miss her. I miss Joe. I miss talking about her with Joe."

"Yeah, I miss Joe, too," June admits.

"Me, too," Jenny adds on.

"This will be the second holiday season without him," the widow tears.

"It'll be our first Thanksgiving and Christmas on the island."

"Yesss," she sighs.

"You brought all of your decorations. You could start a new tradition, use some of the old, and add something new. They must sell decorations and stuff on the island," Jenny goes upbeat.

Esmé's smile takes all available space on her beautiful face, "I don't need to buy a thing, and I'll still make it new."

"How?"

"It's a surprise." Her smile drops when she sees the bright blue cast on Marin's wrist, and Dale is back using his cane. The Three Women resist the urge to get out to help, then resist the urge to ask questions.

"I've refractured my wrist. And his therapist wanted to brace his leg, but relented when Dale said he'd use his cane."

"My leg's bruised to shit, but it doesn't hurt any more than it did before the ditch-diving event. I'm using the cane because there's no sense arguing with Conan the Crusher."

Marin laughs, "God, that man is huge."

"Yeah, and he's had my ass in a gym and on a massage table three times a week for the past three months. God, I hate that man."

June leans over the back seat, "You guys up for a trip to Beach Bum?"

"Can we do takeout? I want to get back onto the recliner at The Castle and do some sketching. Thank God, I draw with my non-busted hand."

June nods, "Take out is fine. I'll write orders, so shout them out."

"Veggie pocket."

"Times two."

"Toasted meatball grinder with American."

"Times two."

.... "Okay, got it. Be quiet while I call it in."

When June is finished, Esmé pipes up. "We're having Thanksgiving and Christmas at The Promise. Dale, please invite your mother, and when she asks what to bring, tell her anything she'd like, and I'll invite Tom, and we'll divvy the food prep."

"Tom will bring Figgie cookies," Marin laughs, "so tell your mother she can't bring that," she nudges her guy.

Esmé pushes back in, "Not finished. And we're blending our old Christmas traditions with new ones, so if there's something you want added to our festivities, Marin, let me know. And Dale if there's something you'd like added, don't be shy, speak up."

The young couple laughs.

Esmé twists in her seat, "What?"

"Dale, shy? Not a shy bone in his body."

"And if there was, it would have been broken on Stony."

Marin cracks up.

He stares her down.

"Oh, that wasn't supposed to be funny?"

"No, you weirdo."

"Well, it was."

He puts his arm around, pulls her near, and kisses her head.

Esmé turns back around in her seat and relaxes into her new place in her daughter's life.

Week Three – Day Five
Monday, November 13
Waning Crescent – Illumination 20%

Sherry is a nervous wreck. Tom and Ruby give her a wide berth and do little to try to calm her. Right before he readies to leave for the inquest, he gives some instructions, "Ruby, pack a cooler, go upstairs, and stay upstairs. Make sure you have your burner on you. Pick a room and lock yourself in. Don't do anything that would suggest there's someone in this house."

"Okay, Tom."

He goes and sits on the coffee table in front of Sherry. "You're going to do fine. Just tell the truth. You can't hurt Fred by repeating what he did to turn a buck. Fred is gone, and you have everything we need to make sure the people who killed him are brought to justice."

"I know. That's not what's bothering me."

Silence.

"My grandmother doesn't even know I'm on Whisper. Tomorrow morning, she's going to read the *Whisper Telegram* and know what I've been up to."

"And she's going to know that you helped solve the Christie Anderson case. And when all this settles, she's going to know that Fred

Fuller's widow is the sole beneficiary to his belongings, which includes transfer ownership of Diggers and Mooring."

"Really?"

"Really. You ready?"

"Yes."

They wait until Ruby is upstairs before heading to the F-150. "We have a stop to make before we head to Town Hall."

"Where?"

"Outer Banks."

The chief is heading to his Rover when Tom blocks him in. "We need to talk, Vernon. Inside."

The chief takes a look at the passenger in Tom's truck, "Who's that?"

"A surprise witness."

"Jesus to shit, Tom. I don't like surprises, and the Council won't add a witness this late."

"They will."

"Come on." The trio take their positions, the chief on one side, Tom and the surprise witness on the other. "Who is she?"

"A witness who can testify that Lan MacTavish wasn't with Christie Anderson inside Diggers."

"Can she put Christie with Edward Kingston IV?"

"Not with a positive ID."

"Then—"

"Vernon, I should properly introduce the two of you. This is Sherry Flynn, she was a waitress at Diggers on the night of July 24, 2014. She was given the job by her then boyfriend, Fred Fuller. Since then, Sherry became Fuller's wife. She has information about the supposed sale of Diggers, the shakedown of Edward Kingston IV for the purchase of Mooring, and the disappearance of Mr. Fuller on September 27, 2017. She has suspicions about who helped with or handled Fred's subsequent murder."

"She needs protection going into Town Hall, while she's in, and coming out."

"Yeah."

"And I can't guarantee the Council will let her testify."

"Don't you worry about that. Roxanne Carmichael is ready to shine a spotlight on this witness and anyone who stands in the way of getting her onto the witness stand."

Vernon laughs, "I'm starting to like that young woman."

"Did you see her report on the shipwreck?" Sherry asks.

Tom gives a chuckle and a nudge, "Sherry's completely intrigued by *Darling*."

"I didn't see Ms. Carmichael's report, but I'll tell you this, Ms. Flynn, if we get you on the stand and back to Tom's in one piece, I'll sit my ass down and watch a rebroadcast with you. Come on, let's get this shit fest going."

Inquest
Whisper Island, Maine

Edward Kingston IV –
Re: Christie Anderson

Homicide

Monday, November 13, 2017

Opening Statement:
Norman Collins, Chairman, Town Council

"Before we gavel in for tonight's proceedings, I want to address the members of the press. The Council encourages fair and accurate reporting of these proceedings. The use of telephones and laptops are prohibited inside the chambers and anywhere else in Town Hall this evening, Monday, November 13, 2017. Further entered into record is the reminder that it is a criminal offense to take photographs of the three guest panelists, or witnesses, including those from the Medical Examiner's Office, the Whisper Police Department, and members of the Town Council and Board of Inquest. Sound recordings are permitted by members of the press who sought and received Council approval. The recordings can be used for accuracy; they are not to be used in broadcast programming of any kind. A final note: anything said in the absence of the panel will not be published or reported on, in any fashion, until after a decision has been rendered on any and all of the cases presented to this Council." He moves away his script and begins, "Members of this chamber, please stand."

They stand while members of Christie Anderson's family enter and take seats. The crowd sits, and the chairman continues. "Madam Secretary, please call and swear in the first witness."

"The Council in the matter of Kingston Re: Anderson calls Retired Detective, Thomas Alan Martin." Tom is sworn in, handed a sheet of paper, and directed to a platformed seat.

The chairman begins, "Detective Martin, the paper you are holding, is that your case summary in the disappearance of Christie Anderson? Please read the entire page before answering."

Tom reads. Tom answers, "It is."

"Is there any mention in that statement that Edward Kingston IV was interviewed in connection with the disappearance of Christie Anderson."

"There is not."

"Let the record show that Edward Kingston IV was not interviewed, or mentioned as being a patron of Diggers the evening of July 24, 2014. Absence of any new evidence or testimony, this case summary will stand as permanent record. A copy of it will be provided to the press after a decision has been rendered in this matter. That is all, Detective, you may step down."

He remains seated. "That's it? No questions?"

"No questions. You may step down, and Madam Secretary, you may call and swear in the next witness."

"The Council in the matter of Kingston Re: Anderson calls Chief of Police, Vernon Charles Banks." Vernon is sworn in, handed a sheet of paper, and directed to a seat.

The chairman begins, "Chief Banks, the paper you are holding, is that the case summary Detective Martin submitted in the disappearance of Christie Anderson? Please read the entire page before answering."

Vernon reads. Vernon answers, "It is."

"After the retirement of Detective Martin, did any new witnesses step forth, or was there any new evidence presented in the matter of Christie Anderson?"

"Nothing credible."

"Objection."

"Council Member Cranston Willis, please state your objection."

"If new witnesses came forth and gave statements, then the Inquest Board should hear the statements and determine credibility."

Edward Kingston III smiles wide. He shits his pants when Vernon Banks and Tom Martin smile even wider.

"Very well, Councilman Willis, the Council will accept new witnesses to these proceedings." He turns to Chief Banks, "Who are the two witnesses?"

"Whoever provided you the number of witness was off by one, Chairman Collins, there are three witnesses who have provided new statements. Max Trainor, the supposed owner of Diggers, who is really a front man; Camilla Stephian, the supposed witness to a meeting between Lachlan MacTavish and Christie Anderson; and Sherry Flynn, the widow of Fred Fuller. Ms. Flynn is here this evening to testify on behalf of her husband since he is unable." The chief raises his voice a bit, "As you know, the body of Mr. Fuller washed ashore on Stony Beach after taking a bullet to his back."

PANDEMONIUM ERRUPTS
IN THE CHAMBERS.

The chairman empties the room, "Chief Banks, council men and women, and members of the press, please remain in chambers." He addresses Vernon Banks. "You can't add a witness during the inquest."

"You just opened the door by allowing new witness statements through my testimony," the former attorney pushes in.

"I allowed the testimony because neither Max Trainor nor Camilla Stephian are here this evening."

"Councilman Collins, you just went on record, as a representative of this Council, that testimony from all pertinent parties should be heard. There isn't a person more pertinent to these proceedings than Sherry Flynn, widow of Fred Fuller, and an eyewitness to events inside Diggers that night. I'm sure Whisper residents will want to know why you deny Ms. Flynn her say, if that is your intent."

Roxanne shoves a recording device in the chairman's face. "You're on the record, Chairman Collins."

The chairman reads the room.
"Sherry Flynn will be heard."

The members take their seats, and the chairman addresses the madam secretary, "Let's get the room filled, and swear in Sherry Flynn."

The chamber fills. A palpable silence lowers then hovers. Several people jump at the rap of the chairman's gavel.

"Madam Secretary, please call and swear in the next witness."

"The Council in the matter of Kingston Re: Anderson calls Sherry Flynn." Sherry is sworn in and directed to the platformed seat.

Tom sends her a wink when she searches him out.

"Ms. Flynn, do you have documentation that proves you are the widow of Fred Fuller?"

"Yes." She hands an unopened Special Delivery package from the City of Portland records department to the secretary.

The chairman has it marked into evidence and opened by the secretary. She hands the contents to the chairman who reviews and reports. "This is a certified copy of a marriage certificate for Sherry Flynn and Fred Fuller, showing the marriage took place on January 5, 2015 at the Portland Courthouse." He addresses Sherry, "Is that the date and place of your marriage ceremony?"

"Yes."

The chairman gavels for silence. "I'm calling for a recess. Chief Banks, please stay in chambers to explain what this witness can and will testify to."

Edward Kingston III
storms from the room.

The Inquest Board votes 7 to 2 that Chief Vernon Banks will question Sherry Flynn. By all appearances, The King of Whisper thought the vote would go 7-2 in the opposite direction. He soooo wants to get up and leave, but he wants the traitors to feel the weight of the decisions being made in that room.

Vernon walks to the stand and positions himself directly in front of Sherry so she can't see Edward Kingston III. "Ms. Flynn, were you in Diggers on the night of July 24, 2014, the night Christie Anderson went missing?"

"Yes."

"What were the circumstances for your being there that evening?"

"I was recently hired as a waitress and I was working my shift."

"Are you from Whisper Island?"

"No."

"But you took a job at an island establishment?"

"I was visiting my grandmother, Gladys Flynn, and she said I could stay with her as long as I wanted, but I would need employment. I began a romantic relationship with Fred Fuller when I first came to the island. He gave me a job, and I decided to stay."

"Given that you were new to the island, would you say you knew many residents on the night in question?"

"I knew very few."

"Did you know Christie Anderson?"

"Only by reputation."

"Please explain."

Sherry squirms a bit, "It was pretty well-known that Diggers allowed underage patrons in. On my first night, Fred pointed Christie out and mentioned she was underage and that he was watering her drinks."

"Did you know Lachlan MacTavish?"

"By name only."

"Please explain."

"There was a young guy sitting at the bar that night who had a Scottish brogue. I asked Fred about him, and he said the guy's name was

Lan MacTavish and that he was new to Whisper."

"Did you see Mr. MacTavish with Ms. Anderson at any point during that night."

"No, he was alone when he came in, remained alone the entire time he was at the bar, and he left alone, which was long before Christie left."

"How long before?"

"At least an hour."

"What did Ms. Anderson do during that hours' time?"

"She spent it with the man she'd been with all evening."

"Do you know who the other man was?"

"I do not."

"Can you describe him?"

"Only the back of him. His table wasn't in my section, so I only know he had Christie on his lap, and he wore a ballcap."

"Was there another waitress working that night."

"Yes."

"And her name?"

"I only met her once, so I might be off on this, but I think her name was Sandy or Cindy."

"It was Cindy. According to a summary written by Detective Martin and submitted into evidence for this inquest, the waitress named Cindy Gallagher said she didn't see the patron with Christie Anderson that evening. Does that make sense to you?"

"If Ms. Gallagher said she didn't know him or recognize him, that might make sense, but she had to have seen him. He was her customer. So unless she took his drink order, delivered his drinks, and collected his money with her eyes closed, she had to have seen him."

Banks addresses the Council, "Are there any questions for this witness on this subject?"

Silence.

"Okay, moving on. Who is the current owner of Diggers?"

"I think I might be."

"Please explain."

"On December 1, 2014, Fred Fuller signed a Purchase and Sale Agreement, and other legal documents transferring ownership of Diggers to Max Trainor. In July of this year, Fred applied for a liquor license from the State of Maine for Mooring, a tavern he purchased in Portland. When the paperwork came back, it listed Fred as the current owner of Diggers and holder of the liquor license for Diggers. He did some investigating and learned that he still owned the place."

"Did he have a suggestion as to how that could be?"

"He said the people who worked the sale must have put Max Trainor in place as a front man."

"Did he say who the people behind the scenes were?"

Silence.

Squirming.

Silence.

"Ms. Flynn, please answer the question. .... Ms. Flynn, did Fred Fuller name anyone who may have been involved in the sale of Diggers, regardless of whether the sale was legitimate?"

"Yes."

"We're waiting, Ms. Flynn."

She checks Tom. He nods and winks.

"He said it was Edward Kingston III."

PANDEMONIUM ERRUPTS
IN THE CHAMBERS.

The chairman breaks his gavel in two trying to regain control of his chambers. He stands, "That's it. Quiet or I will clear this room and postpone the remainder of tonight's hearing."

It takes some time, but the room silences.

The chief continues. "Did Mr. Fuller use proceeds from the supposed sale of Diggers to purchase Mooring."

"No."

"Do you know how he financed that purchase."

"Yes."

"Please explain."

"He said he blackmailed Edward Kingston IV for a million dollars."

A uproar fills the chambers. The chairman bangs his hand, "Silence!"

"When did this alleged transaction take place?"

"Early July of this year."

"When did Fred Fuller become owner of Mooring?"

"Late July of this year."

"Ms. Flynn, do you know the whereabouts of your husband?"

"I assume he's in the morgue at the Medical Examiner's building."

The chairman doesn't bother smacking his hand, "Silence! I want silence!"

The chief addresses Chairman Collins, "I'd like the opportunity to ask Ms. Flynn questions after the next witness."

"Who is the next witness?"

"The Medical Examiner, Doctor Simon Schuster."

"Madam Secretary, please call and swear in the witness."

"The Council in the matter of Kingston Re: Anderson calls Simon Schuster, Medical Examiner, Whisper Island." The doctor is sworn in.

The chief sets the perimeter, "Doctor Schuster, we expect to have your sworn testimony on several matters and will pose questions pertinent to each case. The case we are currently discussing is Christie Anderson. If there is crossover information or evidence, feel free to offer it, but please be prepared to be called to the witness stand when the other matters are before the Council."

The doctor nods.

The chief gets down to business. "Did you examine remains belonging to Christie Anderson?"

"Yes."

"When?"

"On July 31, 2016, I was called to the Kingston estate known as Echo to retrieve a bone that had washed ashore. I processed the female tibia that night and over the course of the next few days."

"Was the bone identified as belonging to Ms. Anderson?"

"It was."

"When?"

"Preliminary identification was made on August 5, 2016. Final identification was made on August 21, 2016. Next of kin were notified on both dates of the findings."

"On Christie Anderson's death record, what is the cause of death?"

"Undetermined."

The chairman shouts, "Silence!"

"On Christie Anderson's death record, what is the manner of death?"

"Undetermined."

The chairman shouts, "Silence!"

The room silences seconds before King has a chance to stop his lunatic-laughing. All eyes turn his way. He no longer gives a fuck.

"You may step down Doctor Schuster." He turns to the Council members, "I would like subpoenas drawn for Max Trainor and Camilla

Stephian to testify, and subpoenas for their financial records for the years 2014, 2015, 2016, and 2017. I'd like to recess this hearing until Wednesday, November 15, 2017, at which time Mr. Trainor and Ms. Stephian will be sworn in for testimony."

Chairman Collins stands and recesses the inquest.

Primrose Priscilla

Ruby's spent hours upstairs, and has talked herself into and out of going downstairs to retrieve the book she's reading. On the twelfth go around, she unlocks her bedroom door, creeps the length of hallway, pads down the stairs, and into the living room. She stands and scans, "Where is it? I know I brought it down, maybe the kitchen? .... Nope." When she heads back to the living room, she sees it on the T.V. console, scurries to retrieve it then back upstairs.

"Well hello, Ruby Norman!" Rodriquez delights from the tree line. "I was just about to give up for the night. I thought I might find Sherry Flynn at this bungalow, but I'm so glad you made an appearance. It would have been nice if you smiled for the camera, but these pictures will do just fine. I ought to get a fuckin great payout from The King of Whisper when I tell him I know where his baby mama is—if that's his baby. I don't give one good goddamn who the demonic offspring belongs to. All I want are the Benjamins I'll get for whacking you."

As Rodriquez packs his gear a thought occurs, "Paxton left Whisper. Normally, King would hire him for a hit or a kidnapping. I'm not sure King even knows Paxton farmed out work. The asshole Paxton probably took credit for Fred Fuller's whack when I'm the one who handled it. But Paxton's gone. I doubt King knows his Number One booked it out of here, but that might play to my favor. Maybe King will put me into action. I think I'll swing by Town Hall and see if things are still hopping. If they are I'll swing by Echo and leave a note. Low fuckin tech, but it's the only way for me to get in touch with Edward Kingston III."

Echo

King drags his pissed-off ass from his car to the front door, pushes inside, and kicks a piece of paper across the foyer. He grabs hold of it and reads, "I know where Ruby Norman is. It will cost you big. You have 24 hours to call." He storms to his office, grabs a bottle of whisky and drops his ass into a club chair. "If that bitch shows up to testify against Heir, it's bad. If she testifies against me, it's all over. Ruby was under this roof way too long. God only knows what she's heard and what she found during her snooping." He reads the note again, "But what if this is a setup?" He checks the time 11 PM. "The clock starts ticking right now. I need to decide about

Ruby by tomorrow night." He puts the bottle back without having taken a pull and heads upstairs. He goes to his safe, spins left and right, left and right, and clicks it open. He takes his big-ass Colt from inside and makes a vow. "Vernon Banks, someday soon, very soon, you will take a bullet. And when I pull the trigger this time, I'll hang around to make sure I fired a death bullet."

Week Three – Day Six
Tuesday, November 14
Waning Crescent – Illumination 12%

Marin has been sketching all morning, and there are countless crumpled pieces of paper strewn all across the living area to prove it. Dale laughs when he enters, bends to grab the trash, and pays a price. "Don't touch those!" She bounds from the recliner, hip chucks him out of the way, gathers the papers and throws them into the fireplace. "Do not look at my drawings, ever, especially the ones I've judged as crap."

"Okay. Okay. Geez, you're a challenge, Marin."

"Yeah, yeah, I'm a tough one. I think it took about a minute before I joined you in the shower."

He. Laughs. Big. "Speaking of shower…"

She kisses, then dismisses. "Later. I'm working on something."

"Wow."

"What?"

"There isn't a single thing on this earth that would keep me from jumping your bones."

"So I've got the upper hand."

"Yes, Marin."

"Really good to know. Now, if you don't mind, I'd like you to leave."

"The cottage?"

"Preferably, but minimally, the living area."

He grabs his coat, "I'll be at Jacobs Jolly."

"Okay. Make sure you mention Thanksgiving to your mother. Esmé likes things taken care of as soon as she mentions them."

"So that's where you get your impatience."

"Is that a complaint, Dale?"

"Nope." He taps on the window when he passes by.

She pulls her sketchpad close, "No peeking!"

Primrose Priscilla

Sherry sleeps in.

Ruby pushes in, "She told them everything?"

"She answered every question fully. There's some other stuff she'll be able to help clarify, but other testimony needs to be put into the record first. Two witnesses are being subpoenaed to offer testimony. If they do, Sherry will be asked to tell what she knows about them. I'm pretty sure the witnesses will be no-shows, and Sherry will be done with this case on Wednesday."

Ruby heads to the kitchen counter and wipes it down, straightens a few canisters, and arranges the decorative what-nots. She repeats the process, twice for good measure. Tom hopes she'll broach the subject she's mulling. It takes a long time before she's ready. "King was there?"

"He was."

"And?"

"He was smug, then he was pissed."

"Why?"

"Sherry dropped a bombshell."

"She did? What?"

"I'll let her fill you in, but after the dust settled, there were a few 'if looks could kill' moments from King. Most were directed at Vernon Banks."

"There's a lot of hatred between those two."

Tom nods. "Miss Prissy used to say that enemies shouldn't get into bed with each other, but if they did, they shouldn't complain when they find themselves dead. Then she'd laugh and admit that the dead can't talk."

The kitchen lights flicker.

"King would kill Vernon in a heartbeat, and the chief lives for the day he sees King in jail."

Tom nods, "Pretty astute, Ruby."

She shrugs a shoulder, then turns and leans against the counter, "I heard things. Lots of things at Echo, Tom." She pauses and places her hand on her baby bump. "Too many things. As soon as King finds me, he's going to kill me to keep me from talking. I should tell you everything I know before that happens." A shiver runs, and she goes very pale.

He gets up and approaches her, "What's going on?"

"I feel it."

"What?"

"Danger. Real danger."

"Did something set you off?"

"Nothing specific, but last night, it felt like I was being watched. I thought for sure I would be kidnapped or killed before you got home."

"Did you stay upstairs?"

There's a pause.

Tom's hackles raise, "Ruby?"

"I came down for a minute, just to grab the book I've been reading."

He thinks a minute. "Okay, Sherry and I have to go to Town Hall Wednesday night. I'll have someone here to guard you."

She throws her arms around his neck, "I'd appreciate that, Tom." She jumps away and starts giggling, takes his hand and puts it to her belly, "It's the Little One. Wait, just wait." She giggles again when the baby kicks.

"Well, I'll be. That's wonderful. Any idea what you're having?"

"I think it's a girl. I hope it's a girl."

"No Edward Kingston V?"

"God, no." A memory pushes and she goes with it. "King accused the chief of having a thing for Kathleen Kingston."

"Kathleen was a beautiful woman. I'm sure there were lots of men who had a thing for her."

She shakes her ponytailed head, "It was more than that. King accused him of pining over her, and the way he said the words, they were all grunty and gruff. The chief was equally angry. He told King he stopped pining twenty-five damned years ago, and that he was glad she wasn't around to see what a colossal mess King did raising her son."

"When was this?"

"I'm not sure exactly. I might have jotted it in my calendar, but they had that exchange, then sometime later, I saw King take Kathleen's portrait off the wall in the foyer and walk away with it. That happened after another heated visit by Chief Banks, an unwelcome visit." She quiets, clearly working at the memory. "It was July 3rd. King and I were on the rattans having drinks and Banks stormed around the corner and said, 'Your office now.' Shortly after that Heir docked his Cat, and I told him that the chief paid an unexpected visit and the men were in King's office. Edward must have done some eavesdropping because when I made it upstairs, I heard him on the phone telling someone about the heated exchange between King and the chief."

"Tell me."

She lets the memory take its place, and talks her way through it. "If Tom finds it, the chief will make it look like Lan stole it from Echo. You need to stay away from Watch Ledge .... Okay, I've got to shower and head into town. I'm getting my girlfriend from the Abenaki."

The second she stops talking, Tom starts asking, "Who was Edward talking to?"

"No clue, but it felt like he was a spy and he was telling his partner some inside scoop. To be honest, I was more interested in the girlfriend stuff. That's the night Edward brought Quinn Hughes to Echo for the first time."

The detective heads to his denroom and shuts the door, stands still for many minutes banging some shit in his head, then takes a seat. He doesn't kickback; he leans forward, rests his arms on his thighs, and pulls some threads. "Edward was definitely talking about the missing earring. The same thing Lan was pressing in on when Dale visited him in prison..."

"There's something else, Tom, when I met with Lan he said he's been thinking about the missing earring. He's pretty sure the chief found both earrings in Laire's room during his search, then planted one in Lan's bedroom. He said you'd understand some of this."

Tom nodded, "Lan told me during one of our earliest discussions that he directed the chief to Laire's room the night he came to do a search, but he was sure the chief moved about his bedroom before coming downstairs. Lan's suggestion that the chief planted evidence in his room is a strong accusation, Dale."

"That's exactly what I said."

"And?"

"He said he was sitting his ass in prison for a crime he didn't do."

Tom talks himself through some mental organizing, "Edward was overheard telling someone to stay away from Watch Ledge." He ruminates a bit, "Who the hell was he talking to? Someone from Whisper? Someone from the mainland? Ruby said the 'spy conversation' happened on July 3rd. That was a week or so after Danielle Rayburn was murdered in Shaky Town, and on that night, Lan swore he was in bed with Danielle when Watch Ledge was broken into and trashed. Long after Lan was sent to prison, Marin confirmed Lan's story by admitting she saw someone trashing Lan's place." He pulls that memory…

Tom arrived at Wind Ledge right on time carrying the pastries he promised to bring. Marin greeted him at the door then stepped onto the porch. "I've decided to tell you what I know." She raised her hand when he started to say something. "I don't know if Mr. MacTavish committed any crimes, but I do know he was not the person who trashed Watch Ledge the night Danielle Rayburn was murdered, though I'm not really sure how I know that since the man wore a black ski mask."

"How'd you see the man in Lan's house?"

"Through my telescope on the widow's walk. I zoomed in on a figure that was moving quickly in and out of view. I got scared and stopped looking after a minute or so."

Tom pushes angrily from his chair, "Goddammit, could Heir Kingston have hired someone to frame Lan MacTavish?" Before he pulls that thread, he answers a knock on the back door, "Dale, is something wrong?"

"Marin asked me to leave Sand Castle."

"That didn't take long."

Dale laughs, "Not permanently, though she swings hot and cold, so I might be kicked to the curb someday. Right now, she's working on a top secret sketch, so I've been banished. I went to see Connie at the Jolly, but she's visiting dad at the care center. I ran out of places to go." He looks beyond Tom at women who appear around a corner then disappear in an instant. "Is that Ruby Norman?"

"Yeah." He steps back, "Come on in. We need to talk."

The Promise

The Three Women have been staring out the kitchen window for more than an hour, that's because Marin has been pacing the shoreline for more than an hour. "She must be freezing," the mom concerns.

"She must be working up a sweat with the pacing," the lawyer counters.

"She must be looking for a memory-thread, or she's hoping it will unravel or detangle or untwist or do whatever it's supposed to do," the perceptive one suggests.

"Do you think I should—"

"Nope," The J-Team unisons.

"But—"

Jenny wraps her arm around Esmé and leads her away from the window, "Let her work through it on her own."

"I'll keep an eye on her while you two start dinner prep," June says as she hops onto the counter.

Marin asks herself the questions she's asked countless times since the memory-thread loosened hours ago, "Where is the letter? Is there a letter?" She paces and replays the memory that floated when she was inside sketching…

It was 3 AM when Marin pulled her ass out of bed and began searching for her sketchpad, the one her father hid when he learned she'd been sneaking out at night to sketch the moon. "The sketchpad started this whole fucking mess." She talked herself through her search plan as she opened this and moved that, "My bedroom. My parents' bedroom. The living room. The kitchen. The first-floor bath. The pantry. The front porch. My mother's second-floor art studio. The second-floor guest room. The second-floor bath. The linen closet. The stairway and hallway leading to the widow's walk. I think that's it for inside the bungalow, then there's ……." Marin was on her hands and knees peeking under the foot of her bed when she saw a tie tape art portfolio. She slid it across the floor causing several dust bunnies to hop about, batted them away and placed the hidden treasure onto her bed. She pulled the end of the tie, lifted the top flap, and slid out one of her mother's works. She gasped when she read the title, *Girl on a Rock*, and teared when she saw her painted self perched upon 'her rock' looking out at Casco Bay. Marin was overcome with emotion, talking haltingly through sobs, "We … were so … happy then." She put it and the portfolio onto the bed, and an amber-colored envelope slid from within. The name Joseph and the words 'I Love You' were written in her mother's calligraphy. "Mom did this piece for Dad."

"Maybe that's the letter. Maybe I just think I wrote one and hid one." She paces some more, "Come on. Come on. Find the thread and pull it." Tired of her shoreline trek, she walks to the end of the dock, pops a squat and stares at the rolling surf, accepting the memory that rolls in with it…

June 25, 2017

Dear Daddy, The decision is final and reservations for four have been made for a trip on the Abenaki. Mom and I are returning to Murder Island this Thursday with Jenny and June.

"I did write a letter. I knew it. I need to find it." She wants to pull the thread on when it was that she last saw it, instead, the contents of the letter push through…

I begged Mom to let me stay here, but you know Esmé, when she makes a decision, it is final. I don't know why she wants me to return to Whisper, but I do know why

I shouldn't go. I saw a man dump a body into Casco Bay the night Laire MacTavish went missing. I know she is dead, I know where her remains are, and I think the killer knows I saw him. If I return, I'm afraid he will find me and kill me.

Dale walks the dock, interrupting her thread pulling. "What are you doing?"

"Thinking."

"You're hunting a memory."

Silence.

"You don't need to tell me, but it might help."

She pulls a few long breaths before starting, "I wrote a letter right before we left Oxford to come back to Whisper, and I know I put it into my backpack and brought it with me, but I can't remember what I did with it once I got to the island."

"Who'd you write the letter to?"

"My dead father."

"So it's an important letter."

"And I need to find it."

"Where do you think it is?"

"At Wind Ledge. I'm certain it's at the bungalow, I just don't know where exactly."

"Okay, so you don't know where the letter is, but do you know what was in it?"

"Bits and pieces."

"Why don't you write them down. Maybe after a while you'll have enough written that it won't matter if you find the original."

She raises her good hand, "Hoist me." She throws her arms around his neck, buzzes his cheek and runs to The Castle. "Genius! By the way, we're having dinner at The Promise. Esmé is serving Mexican lasagna."

He follows along, "Well, this ought to be good." He shuts the door behind him and takes a quick look for Marin, "Where are you?"

"Heading to the shower, I need to thaw."

"Make sure you wrap your cast. And is there room for me?"

"Nope, this shower is for defrosting, not reheating."

The Three Women agreed they absolutely, positively would not press Marin for details about the mid-November stroll along the shoreline. They make it through dinner and are enjoying dessert when Esmé breaks, "What was the sand pacing all about?"

"I was trying to follow a memory-thread."

"About?"

"A letter I wrote to Daddy before we left Oxford."

The Three Women suspend their flan-filled spoons mid-air, leaving their waiting mouths agape.

"The letter was sort of a ramble about why I felt Whisper was a dangerous place for me, you know, because I saw one guy dump a body in the bay, and I saw the other guy toss Lan MacTavish's place."

Dale joins in on the suspend-a-spoon, wide-mouth gape, except his pause includes a memory…

WPD officer, Dale Jacobs, started his patrol and was nearly through the bohemian village when he recognized several vehicles, "Lan MacTavish's black Beemer is parked at the Rayburn shack," and a little farther up the road, "Edward Kingston's navy Jag is parked at the Beach Bum." Dale listened to dispatch, then made his way out of Shaky.

June taps his foot under the table, "Are you alright?"

"Yeah. A thread is trying to loosen. Did I miss anything?"

Marin nudges, yes, but I'll repeat. "I said I think I remembered the body-dumping guy was Heir Kingston and he killed Laire and dumped her," she pauses, "if I'm not making sense, it's because the process of remembering and the sequencing of remembering is getting confusing." She does a bit of thinking, "Do we know why he did that? I mean I don't think I know, but do you guys why Heir killed Laire?"

The Three Women look at Dale.

"Why are you looking at me?"

"You were a cop."

"I took a bullet to the back and a boulder or two to the head."

Marin pushes in, "We should ask Tom." She nudges Dale, "We should stop by Primrose Priscilla on our way back from Wind Ledge tomorrow."

Three Women and a Man drop their spoons.

"Wind Ledge?" Esmé croaks.

"You want to go to Wind Ledge?" Jenny stammers.

"Are you out of your fucking mind?" Guess Who pushes in.

"I'm with them," Dale scoffs.

"What? I'm not going to the beach, I'm just going to look around the bungalow."

"Speaking of the bungalow," Dale nudges Marin, "Tom and I stopped by the other day and I found some black plastic spiders tucked here and there. Any idea how they got here and there?"

"Nope, but it sounds like something I might do as a prank."

"Yeah. Well payback is usually a bitch, Marin."

"And that threat is becoming your mantra, Dale."

He wraps his arm around his girl and kisses her cheek. "You're right, but when I get some payback, don't say I didn't warn you…"

"Miss Baxter's demise is necessary and imminent."

Dale shakes that memory, angrily pushes from the table and storms outside.

A stunned Marin remains seated, then gets up and watches Dale make his way to The Castle. She joins the others back at the table, "This memory-recall process sucks."

Shakyside

At 10:59 PM, Rodriquez answers his cell. "Just under the wire, Mr. Kingston."

"Who is this?"

"I'm the man who knows where Ruby Norman is. The man who knows Paxton skipped Whisper. The man who knows the snubnose I used on Fred Fuller belonged to you. The man who knows Chief Banks will match ballistics on a couple of very interesting Whisper crimes. Bottom line, Mr. Kingston, I'm the man who has you by the balls."

"Is Ruby still on the island?"

Rodriquez laughs big. "Ruby is in my crosshairs. You want her taken care of, put $500Gs into a duffle, set it on your front stoop on your way to the inquest tomorrow. Stay inside Town Hall and visible at all times. That's when the hit will take place."

King laughs. "So Ruby is on the island, otherwise you wouldn't be able to get the money **and** do the hit."

"It means I'm not working alone, asshole."

"How will I know it's done?"

"I'll text you a picture of the dead bitch by midnight. I'll be dumping my phone into the depths as soon as I hit send, so don't bother replying or calling."

"What if I want to use your services again?"

"You will. I'll be in contact with you a week from now. And Mr. Kingston, if the money isn't left on the stoop, or you stick around to see who retrieves it, the medical examiner will list your cause of death as a gunshot wound and the manner of death as homicide."

Week Three Comes To An End
Wednesday, November 15
Waning Crescent – Illumination 6%

The most recognizable reporter on Whisper Island started her day on-air and finds she's still in front of the camera an hour before Part Two of the Anderson Inquest is set to begin.

"At this late hour, it appears subpoenas for Max Trainor and Camilla Stephian remain undelivered. A spokesperson for WPD said Mr. Trainor was last seen boarding the Abenaki, Sunday, the day before the inquest began and remains off-island, and Ms. Stephian hasn't returned to the Wheelock Campus in Massachusetts after her weekend away. Unless something dramatic happens, it appears the two scheduled witnesses will be no-shows. This is Roxanne Carmichael for WCWI Channel 4 thanking you for tuning in and reminding you to stay safe."

Dale shuts off the countertop television and joins Marin in the living area. "You ready?"

"Explain again why I can't stay here."

"I'm not sure how late I'll be, and I don't want you here alone." He moves into her line of view.

She lowers her pencil and her eyes. "I haven't seen your thigh holster and gun since the night we were on the widow's walk at Wind."

He nods.

"Are you sure you're ready for this?"

He takes a seat and her hand. "I won't be able to chase anyone, but I know how to use my weapon, and I'll be staying inside Primrose the whole time. Try not to worry."

"The Three Women are going to bug the crap out of me wanting to know what's going on."

"Tell them. They know how to keep secrets, and they know how high the stakes are."

"Hmmm. Tell them. I never would have thought of that."

"Grab your coat, Tom will be here any minute."

A distracted Marin heads inside The Promise as Dale continues to Tom's truck. Marin calls out as she bounds back down the stairs and runs to the F-150, "Wait, I didn't kiss you goodbye." Dale opens his arms. Marin runs past him and plants a loud wet one on Tom's cheek.

He laughs big—then bigger when Marin walks past Dale and smacks him on the shoulder, "See, ya."

"Love you, too," he calls after her.

"Still haven't made my declaration of love, Mr. Jacobs."

"Right," he gets into the truck and slams the door. "Women. Can't live with them—"

"Suffer without them," Tom finishes.

Main Street

King parks his Lexus NX 200t in the municipal beach parking lot across from Town Hall at the same time Chief Banks pulls his Rover to the curb. The man who just left $500,000 in a duffle for an unnamed paid assassin smiles with the knowledge Ruby Norman will be dead before the night ends. A run of doubt – or dread – bangs hard. "She'd better be dead. And as for you, Chief Banks," he opens his glove box, smiling when he sees Edward's snubnose sitting there. "No better gun to use when I put a bullet in the man who fathered **my** son."

Rodriquez gets caught in traffic on his way from Echo to Shakyside. He patiently waits it out on Main Street, taking in the sights, "Sherry Flynn, Tom Martin, and Vernon Banks. Wouldn't surprise me if the next hit ordered by King will be one of those three. Speaking of King..." Rodriquez stops his rental at the outstretched hand of a WPD patrol officer and watches The King of Whisper march across the street and into Town Hall. A run of doubt – or dread – bangs hard. "What happens if I can't get to Ruby?" He glances at the docks, "I need to check the Abenaki schedule, make sure there haven't been any changes. I'll drop the money off at Shakyside, call the ferry service, and book a ticket on the last trip to Portland. Just in case."

Inquest
Whisper Island, Maine

Edward Kingston IV –
Re: Christie Anderson

Homicide

Wednesday, November 15, 2017

Opening Statement:
Norman Collins, Chairman, Town Council

"Before we gavel in," he raises a brand new gavel to the amusement of the attendees, "I remind the press and public at large of the rules of this Council in this chamber. Madam Secretary, please call and swear in the first witness."

"The Council in the matter of Kingston Re: Anderson calls Max Trainor to the stand."

The crowd waits. As it waits it does a bit of stirring and a bit of whispering.

The chairman gavels. "Madam Secretary, please update the Council."

"A sworn affidavit was submitted at 4 PM today by Chief Vernon Banks of the Whisper Police Department stating subpoena delivery to Max Trainor was unsuccessful. The affidavit also states that financial records for Max Trainor have been released by Whisper Bank and Trust.

The chain of custody of the records was the vice president of the bank to the chief of police, to me, secretary of Whisper Council." She hands a sealed envelope to the chairman.

"Thank you. Madam Secretary, please call and swear in the next witness."

"The Council in the matter of Kingston Re: Anderson calls Camilla Stephian to the stand."

The crowd waits. As it waits it does a bit of stirring and a bit of whispering.

The chairman gavels. "Madam Secretary, please update the Council."

"A sworn affidavit was submitted at 4 PM today by Chief Vernon Banks of the Whisper Police Department stating subpoena delivery to Camilla Stephian was unsuccessful. The affidavit also states that no attempt was made for financial records for Ms. Stephian."

"Very well. Madam Secretary, please call and swear in the next witness."

"The Council in the matter of Kingston Re: Anderson calls Edward Kingston III to the stand." The King of Whisper is sworn in.

A hush falls over the chambers.

The chairman begins, "Mr. Kingston, you own and operate Kingston Marina, is that correct?"

"It is."

"And someone at the marina is responsible for maintaining a log that records watercraft, particularly night time watercraft within one-half-mile of the island."

"Yes."

"To your knowledge, was there watercraft on the water after 11 PM the evening of July 24, 2014, the night Christie Anderson went missing?"

"To my knowledge there was not."

"How do you know that, Mr. Kingston?"

"Whisper Island ordinance requires private watercraft be docked at the marina from midnight to 6 AM. Very few islanders have docking privileges at their properties, and those who do are required to notify the marina if they are on the waters after midnight. Watercraft rented from the Kingston marina must be returned by 11 PM. According to our logs, no one was on the water that night."

"Do you have records supporting that statement?"

"Yes."

"Did you bring the records?"

King hands an envelope to the chairman, "Yes."

"Thank you." The chairman shuffles a few papers, "Now, for the matter of establishing an alibi for Edward Kingston IV for the evening of July 24, 2014, are you prepared to do so under oath?"

"I am. I was with my son all evening. We had dinner at our family estate, spent an hour or two in my office discussing an expansion project for Kingston Marina, then spent another hour or so sitting at the water's edge just shooting the breeze and enjoying a belt or two of whisky."

The room laughs.

The chairman gavels, "Is it your testimony that Edward Kingston IV never left the estate known as Echo at any time during the evening in question?"

"Heir was home from 6 PM until he left for work the next morning around 8 AM."

"Thank you, Mr. Kingston. You may step down. Madam Secretary, please call and swear in the next witness."

"There are no further witnesses."

The chairman gavels, "The matter of Kingston Re: Anderson will reconvene Friday, November 17, 2017, at which time a request for additional testimony or a motion for criminal charges or dismissal will be filed. This inquest is adjourned. Council members and Chief Banks please remain in chambers."

Primrose Priscilla

The upstairs is dark. The downstairs is minimally lit and deathly still. Ruby Norman is inside with her hand twirling circles on her baby bump. Rodriquez is outside with his night vision binoculars trained on the secluded bungalow. Dale Jacobs is sitting on the bottom stair with his gun in his hand.

Ruby *psssts* from around the upstairs corner, "Can I come sit with you? I'm really feeling something isn't right."

"That's because someone's outside."

She walks down a few stairs and pops a squat, "Did you see someone?"

"Nope, heard footfalls on the gravel drive. You can stay near, Ruby, but don't talk. If shit goes down, go to Tom's room, not yours, lock the door, and try to barricade it with a dresser or something. Do you have your burner?"

She shows him.

"Plug this number in, 207-555-2677. It's a direct line to WPD dispatch. When Donna Abbott answers, tell her there's an officer involved shooting at Tom Martin's house."

"Shooting? There's going to be a shooting?"

"If the fucker outside tries to get inside, there will be a shooting."

The fucker outside tries to get inside.
There is a shooting.

Town Hall

Chief Banks takes the call from Donna Abbott, "A bit busy, Donna."

"An alarm was triggered at Tom Martin's house. Alarm systems all over the island have had problems since the storm, but a 9-1-1 call about an officer involved shooting just came in from his address."

The chief pushes from the chambers and grabs Tom's arm, "Come on. There's been a shooting at your place."

Tom grabs Sherry and lifts her through the crowd past a smiling asshole named King. The detective motions his head when he passes Roxanne. She gets into the line rushing out and into the chief's Rover.

"What do you know, Vern?"

"Only what I told you. Call Donna."

Tom dials, "Donna, it's Tom."

"Oh, thank God it's not you. Where are you?"

"With the chief. What happened?"

"Ruby Norman called, said she is barricaded in your bedroom and there was a shooting. She said an officer was involved."

"Dale Jacobs was guarding Ruby. Shit, Donna, any other details?"

"Sorry, Tom."

"Gotta go."

The Rover screeches to a halt on the very crowded, brightly lit street. Officers are combing the woods on the right-back-side of the bungalow, and a triage officer is tending to Dale, who's sitting on the front stoop. His gun is thigh-holstered, the sleeve of his shirt is missing, and he's got a bicep bandage sporting a fair amount blood.

"What happened," the detective and chief unison.

"Some big-ass dude came in through the back door after killing the lights. The alarm went down, but came online within seconds, but he'd already made his way through the kitchen and into the living room. When he rounded the corner to go upstairs, I rounded from the top, identified myself as a cop, told him to freeze and drop his weapon. That's when he took a shot, and I took a shot. I caught an armful of wood splinters from your busted up banister and when I got to the bottom step I realized I got a piece of him. I followed the blood trail outside and took a seat on the front stoop. His blood spill isn't much, but his injury is enough to fuck up his night."

"Where's Ruby?"

"Still upstairs."

Tom leads Sherry and Roxanne inside the house and knocks on his bedroom door, "Ruby, it's Tom."

"I can't let you in. I hurt my back moving a dresser. It's sort of blocking the door."

"Can you unlock the door?"

"Yes." There's a bit of moaning and groaning before and after the click of the lock.

"Okay, move away."

Vern joins in on the heave-ho, gets the door open, lifts Ruby and deposits her onto her bed down the hall. "I'll send the triage officer up. I want you checked out, Ms. Norman. Ms. Carmichael please stay with Ruby and Sherry." He follows Tom downstairs and pulls him aside, "The shooter came up from the private beach. There's no way he could have climbed the dune, made it through the tree line, and gotten inside your place on a first go-around."

"Nope, he's been casing this place. Ruby had a bad feeling the other night, that's why I had Dale come by." Tom does some thinking. "If the guy was here Monday night when Ruby was alone, he could have taken her or killed her. Why didn't he?"

"Maybe the shooter was after Sherry Flynn? Maybe he thought she was inside?"

Tom thinks about Bartender Man, "I left a really pissed off guy at Mooring the day I showed up looking for Mr. Fuller and walked away with Mrs. Fuller. The guy's name is Rodriquez. Sherry is terrified of him. She thinks he works for Paxton, who we now know works for King."

"Let's hope there's a direct link between Rodriquez and King in the stuff Paxton left with Attorney Stuart."

The men find Dale at the kitchen table, "Suppose you're gonna grill me some, Chief."

"Not about tonight. The scene adds up to your story, but you're on the bad side of Edward Kingston III. Any idea why?"

"Can you be more specific?"

"Let's start with the hit and run. The Tacoma is an Echo vehicle."

Dale nods.

"The same Tacoma that's been surveilling Jacobs Jolly."

Dale nods.

"Whoever was inside that Tacoma has a direct link to the Kingston estate. Currently, the only person residing at Echo is Edward Kingston III."

"So?"

Silence.

Dale checks with Tom.

Silence.

Dale pushes in. "Chief, you said you think you know who was involved in my shooting. Are you thinking King shot me or paid someone to do it? What the fuck, fill in some holes."

"Why did you raise the possibility your shooting was a paid hit?"

"Maybe because I'm sitting here with part of a banister in my arm. Whoever broke in here tonight and took a shot at me was probably a paid thug after Ruby Norman. Here's a question for you, if you think Edward Kingston III is gunning for me, why the fuck isn't he behind bars?"

Silence.

"Tom, what do you think?"

"I think King is good for the hit and run. There's evidence he was drunk and behind the wheel. As for the shooting—"

Dale pushes from the table, "Fuck this. I'm out of here."

The chief stands from his lean on the counter, "I'm gonna need your weapon, Dale."

He hands it off and heads to the door.

Tom follows. "Dale, I'll give you a ride."

"Don't want a ride, Tom."

Roxanne arrives downstairs and enters the kitchen. Her eyes move slowly between the two men, "Shit, there's tension in this room."

"Yeah," they unison.

"I need to head out and put some stuff down about the inquest while it's fresh."

"Come on, I'll give you a ride to get your car."

She's no sooner belted in the F-150 when she's pushing in. "What happened back there?"

"We think we know who might be gunning for Dale, and he didn't take the news well."

"This is where you tell me—off the record, right?"

He thinks a minute. "This is so far off the record, it may never see the light of day."

"Okay."

"The person who almost hit Dale and Marin was Edward Kingston III."

A push of air is followed by an open-ended question. "Was it intentional?"

"Not sure."

A push of air is followed by a direct question. "Why on earth would The King of Whisper want to kill a rookie detective?"

"Sixty-four-million-dollar-question."

Carmichael Corner

Roxanne steps out of her Jeep.

Dale steps out of the shadows. "I need a place to stay tonight."

"Come on."

"Can this stay be off the record?"

"Sure."

Sheryll O'Brien

The Promise
Fragments of memories roll like waves...

She dropped to the ground and froze
when he saw her.
~~THAT'S HIM~~

She wondered if it was Laire
who was dumped at sea.
~~IT WAS~~

She looked through her telescope
at the moonlight.
~~WATCH LEDGE~~

She stepped from the telescope
when she heard her.
~~LOOK FOR ME~~

She moved to the window
and gazed at a crescent light.
~~WELCOME BACK MARIN~~

She settled on her cliff spot
and stared at the moon.
~~GO HOME~~

She landed hard on the rocky shore
below the cliff.
~~SAVE YOURSELF~~

Marin shoots straight up in bed, runs her hand across her cheek, wipes away silent tears that fall like tiny ice chips. She gets out of bed, opens French doors and looks out at the tiny sliver of moon.

FLASHES OF LIGHTNING
BLAZE THE SKY

The rise of mist, or spray of a wave—something that resembles the ghostly image of a teenage girl moves across the night sky.

"Laire?"

~~IT IS LAIRE MacTAVISH~~

"You tried to warn me all along. You saved me from Edward."

~~YOU NEED SAVING AGAIN~~

"From whom?"

~~THE CLOSE ONE~~

The Three Women push into the room and start clanging in Marin's ear.

"Ay Dios mío ¿qué estás pensando? It's freezing in here. Someone close the door."

"No! Don't! She's not done telling me."

"She? Who? Telling you what?" Esmé tries to take hold of her daughter.

"No! Don't! You need to leave. Laire was telling me someone is in danger."

The Three Women can't hide their
concern so they don't try.

"Jesus, Marin, did you bang your head?"

"June!" Jenny admonishes.

"What, Jenny? She's standing at an open French door – it's freezing out – and she's rambling on about a conversation she's having with a dead girl. Am I the only one who finds that fucking nutty? No offense intended, Marin."

"Get out. All of you."

"Mija—"

"Get out! If you don't believe me, then I want you to leave." She waits until the door is closed before breaking into tears, gets into bed and dials Dale's number. The call goes to voicemail. She sniffles then hangs up when she realizes she can't tell him what happened. "He won't believe me, either."

The Three Women head downstairs. Esmé busies herself building a pot of coffee, Jenny paces between rooms, and June hops onto a counter. "Any chance Marin is pulling too many fucking memory-threads and they've all twisted together into some psycho-meltdown?"

"I don't know," Esmé groans. "Where the hell is Dale?"

The J-Squad eyeball one another. "Why?"

"He should be here – with her?"

"Are you for real? You've been complaining about being pushed aside, and now you want him in the thick of things?"

"I don't know what I want, June. I only know I can't take much more of this." She. Breaks. Down.

Jenny slips from the room when June goes to Esmé's aid. She calls Tom. "Where the hell is Dale?"

"We need to talk. I'm on my way."

Tom drags his beyond-tired-ass into the kitchen at The Promise.

"What the hell is going on?" everyone says at the same time.

"You first," Tom pushes.

"Marin is upstairs having a chit-chat with Laire MacTavish," Guess Who pushes back.

He eyes the sane women in the room. One breaks down into tears, the other does a combo head-dip/shoulder-shrug.

"Shit, Jenny. Should she be alone? Upstairs? Near a balcony?"

"No, she shouldn't be alone, but she ordered us out of her room. Marin needs

Dale," she answers, her voice raising an octave or eight.

"I don't know where Dale is."

"What? Why?"

"Don't freak out—"

June is all the fuck over that, "Heads up, Detective, 'don't freak' out is a sure fire way of getting us to freak out."

He points a finger, "I'm tired. You be quiet. There was a break-in at Primrose tonight. There was gunfire exchanged between Dale and a hired hitman, we think. Dale has a minor injury to his arm, and the perp took a hit. We aren't sure how bad, but my carpet is stained sufficiently."

Esmé and Jenny plop their asses onto chairs. June quietly leans against the back door.

"After the shooting, Chief Banks shared some information on an investigation he's working, and it didn't settle well with Dale. He left in a huff. I assumed he'd head here, but he might have gone to Jacobs Jolly."

"Because he didn't want Marin to know he got shot."

"WHAT!? DALE WAS SHOT? WHEN? WHERE IS HE?"

"Oh, for fuck's sake," June blurts.

Tom approaches Marin, holds onto both arms, "Look at me. A bullet was fired in Dale's direction. It did not hit him. It hit a wooden banister and sent fragments into his upper arm. He's been tended to and is probably blowing off some steam. He'll come around when he cools off. Okay."

She nods. She tears. She leaves.

Echo
Midnight comes – midnight goes – without any texts from the mystery assassin.

The King of Whisper Island realizes something went off the rails, or he was played.

BIG TIME

Week Four – Day One
Thursday, November 16
Waning Crescent – Illumination 2%

Marin headed to the dock when the first rays of sun found her still awake in her bed. It is very safe to say the absolute last thing Marin wants to see first thing in the morning is Dale Jacobs boarding the Abenaki with the beautiful WCWI reporter, Roxanne Carmichael. "Is she why he didn't come home last night? Was he with her?"

The Three Spying Women hold mugs of coffee, sipping from time to time, and never taking their eyes off Marin. "Who's going down to talk to her?" Jenny asks.

Esmé pulls a handful of cut straws from the cabinet, "These have been getting a lot of use lately."

June groans when she draws the short straw. "I'm pretty sure you rig that shit, Esmé." She grabs her coat, walks the dock – or the plank, depending on your point of view — and follows Marin's line of sight. "Oh, for fuck's sake," she whispers when she sees Dale with another young woman at the bow of the 7 AM ferry to Portland. She pops a squat and nudges, "Want to come in from the cold?"

"Nope."

"Want to talk about anything?"

"Nope."

"Want to grab coffee and a donut?"

"I want to be left alone."

June taps Marin's thigh. "Okay." She gets up and starts back, stopping when Marin speaks.

"There's something I want to do."

"Okay."

"I'll be doing it with or without company."

"Okay."

"Do you have a tattoo?"

"Two."

"Did I know you had them because it doesn't feel like I did?"

"I don't think you knew. Esmé thought it'd be an enticement."

"Are they hidden?"

"Sometimes."

"Is one a llama?"

June cracks the fuck up. Marin does, too.

"No, there's no llama."

"Are you going to tell me what they are?"

"Not planning to."

"I'm getting a tattoo today. Will you come with me?"

"Yes."

"Will Esmé kill you?"

"There will be a discussion."

"With lots of Spanish words and flying hands."

June laughs. "I love it when she goes all loco and shit, but have you considered telling her about this?"

"I want this for myself. I don't want a big discussion about lifelong decisions and shit. Besides, I think putting a whole lot of effort into lifelong anythings on Murder Island is a colossal waste of time."

"Word. Have you decided what you're getting inked?"

"Yes."

"Are you going to tell me?"

"MMXVI"

"Roman numerals for 2016."

The daughter who misses her father tears.

"For Joe."

"And Laire. And Lan."

"You're not responsible, Marin. You know that, right?"

"I own some of it, June."

She gives a slight nod, "You're entitled to think and feel your own way about things."

"But?"

"But, nothing. Did you choose a placement?"

"Under my left breast."

"Under your heart."

"Yeah."

June wraps her arm around, "That's where one of mine is."

"Really? What is it?"

"The date I met Jenny."

"Huh. I never would have pegged you as the sentimental type."

"Only when it comes to Jenny – and maybe you."

"Where's the other one?"

"On my left ass cheek."

"What is it?"

"A pair of lips."

"Oh. My. God. I so want to see it."

"Later. Let's go piss off your mother, first."

Portland Prison

Lan feels it deep when he sees Roxanne with Dale. He ignores the push of whatever it is that moves within. His year in prison has taught him it's best to disregard emotions of free men whilst caged like an animal.

"Roxanne."

She feels it deep when he says her name, ignores her need and want of him. If she thinks she's masked her desire, she hasn't.

"What brings you across the bay, Officer Jacobs?"

Silence.

Roxanne reacts to the tension with a quick ramble, "There was an incident last night, a shooting, at Tom Martin's place."

Lan straightens in his seat and leans in.

"He's fine. Actually he wasn't at home at the time. Dale was bodyguarding an inquest witness when someone made a move on her. By the time the dust settled, Dale needed a place to—"

"Bang his boots for the night."

She shakes her head, "Settle his boots for the night."

Dale smirks.

"Not findin the humor. Guess my laugh-bone's out of practice."

Dale hitches his head toward Roxanne and Lan, "You two are ..." he stops mid-sentence, shakes his head and laughs a bit.

"Nothin on this end but appreciation for Roxanne, though I'm wonderin what's on your end, Dale."

The emotionally singed woman answers when it appears Dale won't. "Dale's with Marin Baxter."

"Seems he's with you, Roxanne."

Dale scoffs in her direction, "There's no way that guy and I could have been friends, or even friendly."

"Havin some bothers with memory are ya?"

"Yeah, and at the moment, I'm glad." He pushes from his seat, "Roxanne, I'll wait at the gate."

"Holy, the fuck, What. Was. That?" She drills Lan with her crystal-blue eyes, her long, ponytail moving in concert with her shaking head.

"I've an hour. Won't be wastin one minute talkin about the holy fuck of things. If you've got news, I'd appreciate hearin it."

"The Anderson inquest took place. There may be a decision on Friday."

"Will I be payin for another girl's murder?"

"My assessment is that the Council isn't even considering you for her disappearance."

He straightens. He listens.

"Tom presented a surprise witness. Someone who put you belly to the bar the entire time you were inside Diggers, and put Christie on the lap of another guy."

He deflates, "Same shit, Rox."

She shakes her head, "Tom pulled a thread on something you said during his visit and it paid off. You said Christie bumped against a waitress carrying drinks, a new waitress to Diggers."

He nods.

"The waitress is Sherry Flynn. She was the brand new girlfriend of Fred Fuller at the time. She's his wife now, well, she's his widow now, but she testified that you were long gone from the bar before Christie left that night, and more importantly, she said Christie spent the entire night riding the lap of another guy. Sherry was new to Whisper and couldn't ID the guy, but Tom and Chief Banks both think—"

"Banks," Lan practically spits the name, "what's his role in this?"

Roxanne squirms. "Shit. I can't tell you."

A memory bangs the prisoner's head...

"Look, Lan. I'm working the case again. I made a deal with the devil so I could get the Council to look at the cases in chronological order. That's the only way they'll be able to connect Heir to all of the crimes. I needed an extra week to put some shit together."

"Am I to put my faith in some demon? Cause if that's the path we're travelin, then my prayers to the man upstairs are misdirected."

"You keep your prayers set, let me deal with the devil."

"Is Banks workin with Tom now?"
Silence.
"Is my freedom dependin on the man who set me up and sent me up?"
Silence.
"Answer me or get out."
"Yes."
"Get out."
"Lan, please, listen."
He gets up.
She gets up, then sits back down when the guard steps their way.
"Lan, please don't do anything that might keep you here. Please."
He walks away.

Roxanne is more than pissed when she walks through the prison gates, "Don't talk to me."
"Wasn't planning on it."
Two hours later, when the Abenaki docks on Whisper she starts a sprint to her Jeep.
Dale takes hold of her arm, "This pissed shit can't be just about me."

"It's not, but you swirled the shit with Lan, walked away, and left me to try to cool him. There's a whole lot of people who don't like each other or trust each other working to get him out of prison, and you fucking waltzed in and—" She shakes her arm free, "I need to talk to Tom." She leaves him standing in the parking lot under the watchful eyes of Marin and June who witness the confrontation from across Main.

"Fuck!" He heads in their direction.

They continue their walk toward The Promise.

"Marin, we need to talk."

June halts her step. Marin continues walking.

Primrose Priscilla

Tom listens to Roxanne's story. He doesn't bother with a back and forth with her; he gets on the phone. "Vernon, I need a favor. You need to get me approved for a visit with Lan, today. Roxanne met with him earlier so his visitor allotment is used, but I need inside that prison. As a favor, I'm asking you to use whatever clout or favors owed you."

"Get on the next ferry mainland."

Tom hangs up. "Roxanne, I need you to stay with The Boarders. Shit, now I'm leaving three women unprotected in my home."

"I'll be right back, Tom." She heads to her Jeep, unlocks her glove box, takes her handgun and returns.

His eyes go to her hand, "What the fuck is that?"

"A .38 Ruger LCP. I'm licensed, capable, and smart. The alarm will stay on and no one will be allowed in. Go see Lan. Talk him the fuck down. And I'm sorry I started this mess by bringing Dale with me. I had no idea there was all that male testosterone shit between them. I know Lan was caught off guard, and Dale had a bad night, but there's some bad undercurrent between them and it knocked me off kilter."

Tom grabs his coat and heads out, "Set the alarm behind me."

Outer Banks

The chief calls Tom after he's already set sail, "You're all set. I spoke with Warden Flores and she's gonna sit on the prisoner until you get there and talk him off the ledge. What the fuck happened?"

"Roxanne brought Dale along for her weekly prison visit. It set Lan off. She said there's a bad undercurrent between the two and they verbally sparred. Dale left, but the visit went from bad to worse. Lan told Roxanne to leave. She's really concerned he's going to act out and we won't be able to get him out."

"Call when you're done." The chief gets back to work, "Edward Kingston IV, you're good for Christie and Laire, but where were you when Danielle was being strangled and Joe fell off

……. when Joe was pushed off that cliff?" He accepts that as fact and moves on. "Okay, Edward, you divided your time between Whisper and Portland. The best way to track your time at Echo is to talk to Ruby Norman. The best way to track your time in Portland is to track your comings and goings from the condo." The chief grabs the phone and makes a call, "Good afternoon, Henri. Chief Banks, here."

"You received the special delivery, I trust."

"I did. Thank you. I know this is a longshot, but is there any chance you have video for July 2016?"

"No, I'm sorry."

"Like I said, a longshot. Thanks."

"Chief, may I contact you back. I might have something that could help."

"You have my cell." He sprints to the kitchen, grabs a beer and a bag of chips and rushes back to his ringing phone. "Hello!"

The man on the phone laughs, "It's me, Henri."

"Any luck?"

"Not with tapes, but with handwritten accounts. The Claremont is a fine, upscale residence, but we do encounter occasional problems with our security camera system, something with the salty mist from the ocean. We had a particularly long stretch of camera inconsistencies during the summer of 2016. I did not want our residents to feel insecure in their homes, so I put an employee at the front desk 24/7 to monitor the lobby. I have three log books that you are welcome to. I would like them returned when you are finished reviewing them."

"Yes, of course."

"Would you like me to ferry them?"

"Actually, a detective of mine is on the mainland. Could he pick them up from you later today?"

"Oui. I am here until 11 PM."

"Perfect. Thank you Henri." The chief leaves a voicemail message for Tom asking him to swing by The Claremont to retrieve a package.

Portland

Lan is none too pleased when he's led inside the visitor's room. "Ya snuck out from under the devil's thumb did ya?"

"Sit your ass down."

"Wouldn't be obligin if I had a choice."

"I don't know what bug crawled up your ass, but you'd better ignore its bite, or shit it out, Lan. I'm this fucking close to getting your ass out of here, and you're not gonna fuck it up. Once you're on the outside, you can fuck your future with a fisticuffs with Dale Jacobs or anyone else that suits you, but you will not stand in the way of a promise I made. Do. You. Understand?" Tom doesn't wait for a response. He. Just. Leaves. As soon as he's outside, he listens to Vernon's voicemail and heads to The Claremont. As soon as that errand is finished, he heads to Mooring, "Still closed? No one here when I arrived, no one here when I leave. Wonder how long the joint's been closed." He heads to a nearby tavern and bellies up to the bar, "Hey, I'm supposed to meet a friend at Mooring. The place is closed."

"It's been closed all week. Take a look around, maybe your friend landed here."

Tom pulls a five dollar bill and slaps it onto the bar, "Thanks." The detective does his fair share of muttering on his way to the Abenaki. "Mooring has been closed for a week. That means Rodriquez has been who knows where for a week. The Abenaki went back online a week ago. Coincidence? Nope. Rodriquez is on Whisper, and he's the one who broke into my home, shot the fuck out of my banister, fragmented the shit out of Dale, and scared the hell out of Ruby. That son of a bitch better find a way off island before I find his ass."

Echo

King grabs his Colt and aims it at the man standing at his office door aiming a gun in his direction. "Get the fuck off my property."

"Go ahead and shoot. Then explain why a contract killer is dead on your lawn." Rodriquez makes a move to enter.

King points his weapon.

Rodriquez moves to the door. "Move that the fuck away from me or I'll stick it up your ass and pull the trigger."

"You're the thug who fucked me out of $500Gs?"

"I'm the thug who took a bullet and you're the asshole who's gonna stitch me up and hide me out."

"The fuck I am," he tries to push the door closed.

"If I don't make a call in two minutes informing my associate that I am safely ensconced in this beautiful estate, $10Gs of your money will be delivered to Chief Banks, another $10Gs will be delivered to Tom Martin. Attached to their bounty will be a note explaining their newfound wealth. One or the other is smart enough to dust the money for prints. They will find mine, and since you've been fucking things up for weeks, I'll assume they'll find your prints, too. Look, asshole, if I don't get off my feet and tended to, I'll be dead on this lovely doorstep, and you'll have one hell of a time moving me or explaining me. Now get the fuck out of my way."

Primrose Priscilla

Chief Banks is in the living room with Ruby when Tom gets back from the prison. Roxanne and Sherry follow Tom out of the kitchen. Tom looks at the crowd, "I don't think I've ever had this many people in this house at the same damned time, certainly not when I wasn't here." He hands off the package from The Claremont.

The chief nods. "You should sit. I have some questions for Ruby. I'm working on establishing a timeline for Heir." The trio play a quick game of parlor checkers, then grab seats. The chief notices a sweet little Ruger tucked into Roxanne's back waistband when she walks past, "Ms. Carmichael, are you carrying?"

"Yes, Chief."

"Any chance that's a .38?"

"Yes, Chief."

"Any chance you used it to put a bullet into Dale Jacobs' back."

"Nope, but check with me tomorrow."

"He pissed you off some today."

"He did."

"Better hope he doesn't end up taking another bullet. There are a lot of witnesses in this room who just heard a veiled threat."

"And I suspect there are lots of people out there who find Mr. Jacobs' objectionable enough to shoot him. I like my odds."

The men laugh.

The Boarders go all gobsmacked.

The chief gets down to business. "Ruby, I need to establish a timeline for Heir for the month of July 2016. Particularly for the nights of Danielle Rayburn's murder and Joseph Baxter's murder."

"You're reclassifying the finding from accidental fall to homicide?" Tom casually observes.

"Haven't made it official yet, Detective Martin, but my working theory is that Joe was pushed from the ledge because the killer thought Marin knew too much and wanted to make sure she and her mother stayed off the island."

"Not a bad theory, the problem is—"

"They came back."

Ruby pushes in. "I definitely know .... nope, I sort of know where Edward was the night of Danni's murder."

"Did you know Ms. Rayburn?"

"Yes. I was working the Beach Bum when she moved to Whisper in 2013. She was always in for food, and we started hanging out. I introduced her to King when he and I started our thing, and he hired her at the marina."

"Tell me about the night of her murder."

The crowd leans in.

"When I awoke that morning, I didn't know Danielle had been murdered, and I didn't know much else either. I was still in bed when Edward walked from my en suite. I panicked because we never spent time together when King was at Echo. I asked him what he was doing in my room. He laughed and said, 'Seriously? You don't remember last night?' I told him to quit fooling around and that we hadn't been together. I pulled the covers aside and saw that I'd been with someone who left a hickey or two. Then I saw two wine glasses and an empty bottle of 2005 Chateau Mouton Rothschild on my nightstand. I had a flash of a memory. King brought the bottle to my suite and had some with me. Edward swore he brought the wine and he and I shared it. I went to take a shower and when I returned Edward was gone and King was there asking if I wanted to go to Portland for the day and maybe stay overnight. I couldn't go because I didn't know for sure who I'd been with and who gave me the hickeys."

Tom addresses Vern, "If Ruby testifies that she went to bed with King but woke up with Heir, the Council's gonna want to know what time the switch took place. Ruby can't say because she was drugged. That leaves the door wide open for King to say he wasn't with her at all, leaving the implication that Heir was with her all night."

"Ruby, what time did you wake that morning?"

"I didn't look at the clock, but it was early."

"Was the sun up?"

"Yes."

"You said Edward was walking from the en suite when you woke."

"Yes."

"Had he showered?"

"No, he actually looked all disheveled."

"So Edward could have just arrived in your room?"

"I have no idea, Chief."

"Vern, Ruby gave me her calendars for 2016 and 2017. There might be notations that would help establish a timeline."

"Good. Okay Ruby, any chance you remember where Edward was July 31, 2016, from 10 PM until the next day at noon? That's the day Joe Baxter died."

"He was with me that night. King went to Peaks even though I hadn't been feeling well that day. Edward insisted he'd stay with me in my room."

"Was that odd?"

"Very. The Kingston men aren't caretakers. But that night, I remember Edward sitting at my bedside watching T.V. I'm pretty sure it was raining that night and maybe thundering. I'm not completely sure on that, but I remember Edward's phone ringing a little before 11 PM."

"Did you hear his side of the conversation?"

"He said, 'Good to know.' That's the only thing I heard before falling back to sleep. When I woke around 3 AM, he was gone."

"Alibi Number Two," Tom offers.

"Edward was working with someone."

"Or hired someone."

"About that, Vern. When I got off the Abenaki, I stopped by Mooring. It was closed up tight. On my way back to the Abenaki, I checked the place again, then I stepped into a nearby tavern and told the bartender I was supposed to meet a friend at Mooring. He said the place has been locked up tight for a week. I figure that's how long Rodriquez has been on Whisper. Pretty sure he's the one who shot up my banister."

Sherry shoots to her feet and starts flitting about the crowded room, "He's gonna kill me.

He's gonna hunt me for the rest of my life, and then he's gonna take my life."

Tom steps in front of her, "First, Rodriquez isn't going to do anything anytime soon. Dale got a piece of him so he's gonna need to lay low for a while. Second, you don't have to testify during the MacTavish inquest, or the Rayburn or Baxter ones, so we can put you someplace, get you totally off the grid. When it's time for Chief Banks to present Edward's timeline, you'll have to testify about his interactions with Fred, but that's weeks away. Whisper's a small island. Rodriquez is going to stand out like a sore thumb. We'll either get him, or he'll get off the island."

The tree sprite comes in for a landing.

Portland Prison

Lan is sitting on his slab, his back pressed against the wall. He's trying hard to ignore the moaning, pud pulling, talking, singing, and snoring of the men on his cellblock. He knows there's no use trying to grab shuteye—not because of the racket around him, but because of the shit storm raging in his head...

"Detective Jacobs, do you know the defendant, Lachlan MacTavish?"

"Yes."

"In a professional capacity?"

"Yes."

"In a personal capacity?"

"Yes."

"Let's concentrate on the professional. Did you first meet Mr. MacTavish on the morning after his teenage sister, Laire, went missing?"

"Yes."

"Explain the circumstances."

"I stopped by Watch Ledge, the home owned by Mr. MacTavish, to introduce myself."

"Is that standard police procedure?"

"No."

"Why did you break SPP?"

"I was a rookie, and I was eager to help find Laire MacTavish."

"Can't fault you there, Detective." **She smiled and nodded toward the jury.** "What time did you arrive at the MacTavish home the morning of July 22, 2016?"

"A few minutes past 7 AM."

"How quickly did Mr. MacTavish answer your knock."

"Immediately."

"Was he dressed?"

"Yes."

"Was he drunk?"

"Objection."

She nodded at the defense council. "I'll rephrase the question. In your opinion, had Mr. MacTavish been drinking prior to your visit?"

"Yes."

"Did he smell of alcohol?"

"Yes."

"Did he slur his words?"

"I don't think I'm qualified to answer that."

"Why not?"

"Mr. MacTavish has a Scottish brogue, an Americanized one, but still, I wouldn't know how to assess slurred speaking."

"Very well. Let's discuss the morning of July 27, 2016, the day Danielle Rayburn was found murdered in her Shaky Town shack. Were you on duty that morning?"

"Yes. I was set to end an 11 PM to 7 AM shift when the call came in."

"Did you work the case?"

"I was present when the senior officers and the chief worked the case."

"Were you present when the senior officers and the chief interviewed Mr. MacTavish?"

"I was."

"Where was the interview held?"

"At Watch Ledge, Mr. MacTavish's home."

"Did the defendant admit to being with Ms. Rayburn the night before and into the morning of her murder?"

"Yes."

"That's all, for now, Detective Jacobs."

Lan gets off his slab, kneels before it, rests his elbows onto it and his head into his hands, "Will this nightmare I'm livin ever end?" He feels an icy run along his cheek. He touches his cold flesh, "Laire." He begins to cry.

~~LAN ~ HOLD ON TO YA FAITH~~

Week Four – Day Two
Friday, November 17
Waning Crescent – Illumination 1%

Marin wakes to a cold, overcast, empty cottage. She rummages through her drawers, grabs rag socks, sweatpants, and a white long-sleeve T-shirt, only to realize it's Dale's. "WPD," she says as she runs her fingertip across the stitched letters on the cuff. She starts to put it back, then slips it overhead instead, grateful for the roomy size. "This should keep it from pressing against my tattoo." She shuffles to the living area, thinks about starting a fire – thinks better of it. She grabs her coat, winces when she stretches too far putting it on, bends her left elbow and sort of presses her casted hand and forearm against the bandaged area beneath her left breast. She glances at the clock, "They should be up." She pulls open the door and finds Dale kicked back on a chaise. She walks past and down the few stairs.

He bounds to his feet, "We should talk."

"No thanks, I'm good."

He reaches out. She yelps in pain.

"What? What just happened? Did I hurt your hand? Jesus, I'm sorry."

"My hand is fine."

"Then, what?"

"Nothing."

"Marin, if you're in pain, please tell me why."

"I need to go to The Promise. I'll be back in a few minutes."

Dale is still on the porch when she returns.

"You could have gone inside, Dale."

"I know." He notices the Peduzzi's pharmacy bag. He finds her eyes, "Are you alright?"

"I'm fine. It's just soap."

He follows her inside.

"I need to take care of something. And I need coffee."

He heads to the kitchen to build a pot. She heads to the bathroom, sprints back to the kitchen area, reaches for a piece of paper on the counter, pulling back at the pinch of bandage tape beneath her breast, and causing the paper to fall to the floor. Dale picks it up and reads the tattoo parlor logo.

"You got inked?"

Silence.

"That's why you have pharmacy soap. It's antimicrobial soap and antibacterial ointment."

Silence.

"You and June were coming from the parlor, yesterday," he extends his arm to hand her the paper and pushes a grunt of pain.

She suddenly remembers the shooting at Tom's bungalow. "How's your arm?"

"It's fine."

"He said you'd show up after you cooled off. Are you about done?"

"Yeah."

"You've been staying at Roxanne's house?"

"The first night."

"And last night?"

"At Jacobs Jolly, until about five this morning."

"You could have come inside."

"The November nip was part of my cooling off."

She nods and heads toward the bathroom.

"Need any help?"

"No."

"Are we alright, Marin?"

"No."

"Will we be?"

"Don't know."

Echo

King stands at the entrance of the first floor den. "It's time for you to leave," he says to the waking thug.

"I'm staying three days, so put this conversation the fuck behind us."

"You're the guy who runs Mooring."

"I quit."

"Where's Paxton?"

The thug laughs, "He's long gone. He got his ass pinched by Banks, spent several hours with the chief, the detective, and some babe, probably a lawyer, before being escorted to the ferry by the chief of *po-leece*."

"Did he take his Mercedes?"

"Nope. He left it and everything in it."

King walks to the window and lets the memory push...

"Mr. Kingston, open the door and sign the impound paperwork." **Another knock,** "Mr. Kingston, you are ordered to open this door. If you do not, forceable entry will be made."

King opened the door, signed the paperwork, and tried to slam the door. The chief stopped it with his hand, stepped close and talked low, "Paxton left the island. Before he set sail, he gave me the goods. All of the goods. On all of it. You are going down for all of it. And when you're spending the last miserable days of your life in jail, remember this." **Vernon moved closer.** "The **father** of Kathleen Beckwith's son is the one who beat your ass and put it behind bars." **He removed his hand and walked to the WPD Rover.** "Have a nice day, Mr. Kingston."

The heated bile of that exchange rises as tiny ice pellets start tapping the window. "What happened with the Ruby hit?"

"Tom Martin put a bodyguard inside without my seeing it. I was making it up the stairs to whack her when a dude rounded the corner. We played a quick game of, Let's Shoot And See Who Wins."

"Spoiler Alert, asshole. You didn't win. That means Ruby Norman will be testifying at the upcoming inquests."

"You created this mess by playing the long game. You should have gone after Banks and Martin. If they'd been eliminated, the whores never would have taken the stand, and if they did, they wouldn't have said shit."

"You can stay until you're ready for another job. The den, the kitchen, and the downstairs bath, those are your quarters."

"I could use some antibiotics."

King looks out the window at the icy mess that's forming, "It'll be a while."

Outer Banks

Vernon grabs the timeline on Edward and starts filling in things based on the information Ruby Norman provided. "According to Ruby, Heir was in her room shortly after the murder of Danielle Rayburn took place. His appearance was disheveled—Ruby showed signs of a sexual event she has no memory of. Bottom line, she provides a questionable alibi for Heir, and lots of questions about King. Let's pull this thread from the assumption that King drugged the wine he brought to Ruby's suite. Once she was out cold, he leaves her room, and Edward leaves the estate with the intent purpose of killing Danielle." He ruminates – a while. "The question is why? Why would the Kingston men want her dead? Did they review the boating logs, and was there a notation that Edward was on the waters the nights Christie Anderson and/or Laire MacTavish were dumped into the bay? Was Danielle killed because she would be called to testify about her logs? Have her logs been altered?" He scoffs, "Of course they've been altered, and without her say so, the logs will stand as evidence."

The chief flicks a switch on a corner fireplace and makes his way to the window. Icy pitter-patter against the frosted glass provides a rhythmic backdrop to his thoughts. "Did Heir need an alibi for Danielle and Joe because he knew they'd be murdered?" He takes a lean against the wall, untwists a paperclip in his hand, tosses it into a trash bin, grabs another, and goes off track for a minute. "If Dale hadn't been at Tom's, Ruby would be dead – killed by a contract killer. Hours before that, I personally escorted a different hired hitman off Whisper Island. King has some big-ass plans for people on Whisper. That's some shit I need to sort through, but it leaves me with this question, did King and/or Heir hire someone to kill Danielle Rayburn to keep her from talking OR did they just kill her to setup Lan MacTavish up to take the fall?"

He makes his way back to his desk, jots a few notes onto the legal pad and continues with Edward's timeline. "At the time of Joe Baxter's death, Heir was offering care and comfort to an ill Ruby. According to Esmé Baxter, who has been identified as the only person in contact with

Joe that night, the married couple talked by phone from 10:25 until 10:35 PM. She said Joe was going outside to commune with nature after the storm had passed; his body was found at noon the next day at the bottom of a cliff at Stony. Ruby Norman puts Edward in her bedroom suite at 11 PM when he answered a phone call. He said, 'good to know' at which point Ruby stopped paying attention or fell back to sleep. When she woke at 3 AM he was gone. For this murder, Heir has a much better alibi, though the suggestion can be made that he knew about the murder ahead of time and received notification when it was done. Again, this points to the possibility of someone working with Heir or being paid by him to whack Joe."

The chief kicks back, puts his feet onto his desk, locks his fingers behind his head, and stares at the ceiling —— for many, many minutes. When some pieces are connected, he grabs the legal pad and jots some notes.

Primrose Priscilla
Tom locks himself behind the denroom door for some Miss Prissy journal reading. In no time at all, he finishes the second tome for 1983, grabs hold of the paper he's keeping a running list on, and jots down the song she chose as 'her song' for that year, *Sexual Healing*. He laughs at the recent reference June made of this song when discussing Dale and Marin. "No matter the

generation, Priscilla, sexual healing comes round and round."

Hours into his reading, Tom turns the musical list over, "We're entering the nineties, Miss Prissy. I am so grateful for this trip down memory lane. You were a wonder, dear."

The things I hear at the quilting club and on group walks through the cemetery. I would love to tell Tom, but he isn't one for gossip. Too bad because this is *really* good gossip. Around the same time Tom and I learned he was sterile, (1989), Connie Jacobs announced that she and her husband, Matt, found out he was sterile and were considering adoption. I'm sure my face reddened when she mentioned male sterility, though no one looked my way – I think everyone was as shocked as I was that Connie talked so openly about her private issues. (A memory note here: Connie Jacobs clings to the June Cleaver image. She's all prim and proper, all starched and squeaky clean. Hearing her discuss *that* in such a public way was absolutely mind-blowing).

Anyway, Connie came to the quilting club today and announced that she is pregnant. The shock of my hearing that cannot be overstated. I was positively astounded and more than a bit bewildered. While I was centering myself, congratulations and hugs were offered, and questions of how are you feeling? .... and when are you due? .... and any preference – boy or a girl? flew the room like clay pigeons being fired from a cannon. As soon as she left, questions of how did *that* happen? .... he's sterile, right? .... and do you think Connie cheated on Matt? exploded like clay pigeons being struck by bullets. Ooo, gotta go, Tom is home and he'll know I'm gossiping! Don't know how he'll know, but he will know. (1992)

Tom has a good, long laugh for himself. "God, I loved that woman." He closes the journal and tosses it onto the bed, kicks the recliner closed and sits a few minutes listening to icy bits hit the window. "When I started this whole journal reading event it was because I wanted to see if Priscilla made note of who might have fathered Dale Jacobs. I haven't found any reference yet, but I think I know."

Outer Banks

The chief answers Donna Abbott's call.

"Sorry to send you out in this weather, Chief, but a car slid off the western cliff."

"Who the hell was out in this shit?"

"Betty Adams."

"Nurse Betty? Why was she out in this shit?"

"Officer Millhouse was first on scene. He said it looks like she was heading south and plunged off the road between Echo and the marina."

"Call Tom. Tell him I'm picking him up. ETA an hour or a day, depending on the road conditions."

The first thing out of Tom's mouth when he parks his ass in the Rover, "What the hell was she doing out in this shit?"

"No clue, but Millhouse said it looks like she was coming from Echo toward the marina."

"She could have been coming off Cliff Road."

"In this shit? There's only one person who could get that woman out on the roads today."

"King."

"Wonder what's so damned important for her to make a house call."

"Maybe we should do a wellness check on Betty's boss."

"After we check the scene."

Echo

Rodriquez sprints from the den to a walk-in pantry off the kitchen when the strobe of police lights come from the circular drive. King answers the door in the same manner as when Nurse Betty arrived, disheveled, a blanket thrown around his shoulders, and a wetness across his brow and lip courtesy of a finger-dab of water. "What's going on?" *Cough. Sniffle. Cough.*

"Mr. Kingston, there's been an accident, a fatality, not far from here. The victim is an employee of yours."

"Betty?"

The chief makes eye contact with Tom who's taken a lean against a big-ass entrance column. Vernon answers in the affirmative. "Was Betty Adams at Echo at any time today?"

"Yes."

"Can you explain the reason?"

"She came to take my temperature."

The chief of police wants to punch the fuck out of the asshole standing in front of him.

Tom pushes in, "And do you have a temperature?"

Silence.

"Any chance Nurse Betty left some antibiotics for your *temperature*?"

King turns around and shuts the door.

The lawmen get back into the Rover. "Any chance the injured hitman is inside that estate."

"Yeah."

"And he was injured enough by Dale's bullet that he needs antibiotics?"

"Yeah."

"Have you figured a way to get inside for a search?"

"Not yet."

Sand Castle

The only noise inside the cottage all day has been the icy tap on the windowpanes. There have been a few brief question and answer lobs, but Marin and Dale have yet to address the fact that instead of coming home after he was injured in a shootout, he took shelter in the home of another woman. Unable to leave and tired of the silence, Dale gets off the couch and blocks Marin's path to the kitchen, "Talk to me."

"I don't have anything to say, Dale. I'm not the one who did a disappearing act and spent the night with someone else."

"No, but you must have thoughts on it."

"I do, but I'm finding the silent treatment much more effective."

"So you're trying to, what?"

"I'm trying not to slap you."

He laughs, "So you're pissed."

"Very."

"Well, that's a start."

She folds her arms across her chest, winces when the tee comes in contact with the tattoo, unfolds her arms.

"Sore?"

"A little."

"That's my T-shirt." He gets a memory-nudge. He ignores it.

"Yeah."

"Looks good on you." He gets another memory-nudge. He ignores it.

She gets a memory-nudge and that faraway stare…

Marin stared through her telescope at the half-moon, "Perfect," she sighed. She turned her telescope easterly and found an opening through the array of flowering bushes along the cliff walk. She zoomed in tighter and tighter and watched someone in jeans, a white long-sleeve T-shirt and black ski mask move quickly in and out of view. She pulled away from the eyepiece and cautioned herself. "You've already seen too much on this island. Don't snoop. Don't." She spun the scope back toward the bay, "Ahhhh, the moon, a bringer of light." She stepped away from the scope and looked with her naked eye at its splendor. "I wish I had my sketchpad. Maybe I should tell what I know."

~~LOOK FOR ME~~

Marin stepped to the telescope, looked through the eyepiece and watched a cloud, or the rise of mist, or the spray of a wave— something that resembled ……. "Is that?" The terrified teen straightened at the ghostly image of a teenage girl. "Is that Laire MacTavish?"

Dale steps toward Marin, "God, what did you remember? You're as white as a ghost."

"Ghost?" she repeats, then shakes her head. "It's nothing."

"No, it's something."

"Yeah something from when I was living in Oxford. It would take too long to explain and it's really nothing." She grabs her backpack, tosses it onto the couch and heads to the bathroom. "I'm going to shower then camp out on the recliner. I'm working on a drawing and I want to spend some time with it. If you want to stay, you can have the bedroom." She walks away.

A piece of the real Dale breaks free…

Officer Dale Jacobs started his patrol a little after 11 PM just as a moonlight cruise on the Abenaki set sail from the docks. He looked skyward, "A half-moon, a two-hour cruise on a beautiful night, not a bad way to spend an evening." He did a slow drive down Main Street, looped around and headed to Shaky Town as per his normal routine. He pulled to a stop near Diggers, watched the comings and goings, decided a couple girls heading in might be underage, made a note on his police log as per WPD protocol, then moved along. He was nearly through the bohemian village when he recognized several vehicles, "Lan MacTavish's black Beemer parked at the Rayburn shack," and a little farther up the road, "Edward Kingston's navy Jag parked at the Beach Bum." Dale listened to dispatch then made his way out of Shaky. When he arrived cliff side, he pulled to a stop near Watch Ledge, grabbed a white, long-sleeve T-shirt and black ski mask and headed toward the bungalow.

Another piece…

He edged through the bramble toward the moving beam of light coming from the direction of Wind Ledge. He stepped between two gnarled Mountain Laurels and waited, and then he pushed. He knew his work was done when the scream ended with the thud of Joe Baxter against the rocks below.

Another piece…

The lawman moved swiftly away from the newest Whisper Island murder scene. He pushed through the bramble toward Walker Ledge, got into a WPD vehicle parked on the gravel driveway, edged it onto Cliff Road, then crept down the westerly side of the island past the Kingston estate and marina. He placed a call, "Baxter's been taken care of."

"Good to know, Dale. Now what?"

"We wait for his wife to report him missing, or for someone to find him on Stony. Though I doubt anyone will be venturing to Stonehenge tomorrow. It's supposed to piss-pour rain all day."

Edward released a devilish laugh. "The breaks keep coming our way, friend."

"We're not friends, remember?"

"Right, we're brothers."

All of the pieces fall into place. "I'm back!"

Dale swings around at the touch to his shoulder. Marin jumps back, "What?"

"What?" he shouts, then dials it back, "I'm sorry, I didn't hear you come in."

"No, I'm sorry. I thought you were talking to me. Were you recovering a memory?"

"I'm not sure."

She sighs heavily, "I hate those kinds. There's a thread, you're not sure what will unravel if you pull it, but you just have to. Then, when all the work is done, you end up not knowing if the memory is real, part of a movie, or a book, or a hallucination."

"My memories are the real deal."

He gets hard – really, really hard.

Week Four – Day Three
Saturday, November 18
New Moon – Illumination 0%

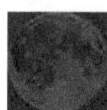

Vernon slept in—if tossing and turning and staring at walls and the ceiling constitutes as sleeping, then he slept in. He drags his ass from bed, calls Donna for an update on the Betty Adams accident, hangs up and repeats the same thing, over, and over, and over. "Damn fucking shame."

He plugs in the percolator and renders his opinion, "She shouldn't have been on the roads, certainly not for what was probably a bogus house call. That son of a fucker is leaving a trail of death and destruction in his wake. It is painfully apparent that no one is safe from Edward Kingston III." A thought bangs and sets him off in the direction of his office, "I need to push into something." He plops his ass, grabs a new yellow pad and titles it.

Whisper Crimes

- Heir killed Christie Anderson and dumped her body.
- King helped with coverup.

- o 2014: Personal in nature.

- Heir killed Laire MacTavish and dumped her body.
- King ordered the killing and helped with coverup.
  - o 2016: Personal in nature.

- Someone killed Danielle Rayburn.
- Heir and King established co-alibis with Ruby Norman.
  - o 2016: Motive unknown.

- Someone killed Joe Baxter.
- Heir established an alibi with Ruby Norman.
  - o 2016: Motive unknown.

- King put a contract on Fred Fuller.
  - o 2017: Personal in nature.

- King put a contract on Ruby Norman.
  - o 2017: Personal in nature.

- King probably put a contract on Sherry Flynn.
  - o 2017: Personal in nature.

- Someone put a bullet in the back of Dale Jacobs.

"Something here is not like the others. It's Dale Jacobs. Does his shooting have something to do with the Kingstons? All of the other crimes on this list are Kingston related. If King shot, or paid someone to kill Dale, what was the motivation? Was there a personal relationship between the two? .... between Dale and Heir? .... was Dale a dirty cop?"

He puts the pad aside, puts the gun he confiscated from Dale on top, and heads for a cup of Joe.

Echo

King spends all day getting blind drunk. The death of Nurse Betty is hitting him hard, pushing emotional bruises he hadn't yet addressed after the loss of Edward. He parks his ass behind his desk, finishes a bottle of whisky and after a few minutes of mourning the loss of a faithful servant, he passes out cold. Too bad his brain continues to function...

~~YOUR SON IS DEAD~~
~~I KILLED HIM~~

"Edward! You are my only son!" ... The body of Edward Kingston IV lifts and settles, lifts and settles, and rolls toward shore – "Dead." Without mercy.

~~RETRIBUTION~~
~~FAIRNESS BE~~
~~A SON FOR A SON~~

"Edward!" the pitiful cry, "Dead because of me," the painful truth. King raised the gun to his head—but was denied a swift end when he saw him. "Dale Jacobs!" He turned the gun on the retreating man and brought him down.

RETRIBUTION OF MY OWN

Sand Castle

Dale finds Marin under two blankets on a chaise on the porch. He steps out, the final layer of ice crunching beneath his boots, "What are you doing? It's freezing out here."

"Thinking."

He groans, "Well, this can't be good."

"Why didn't you come home after the shooting at Tom's?"

"I was pissed."

"At?"

"Whoever shot me on Stony and left me unable to chase a suspect – at the constant barrage of questions that bang in my head – and I'm pissed at you ..." He stops mid-sentence and does a little I'm-freezing-my-ass-off-twostep.

"Me?"

"Because you want an explanation, and I don't really have one, not one that you'll accept, or should accept. Can we take this inside?" He offers her a hand up. "How's your wrist?"

"Okay."

They head in, she toward the coffee perc, and he toward the fireplace. When she is sufficiently caffeinated, and he sufficiently warmed, they take seats on opposite ends of the couch.

"Marin, the other night was a shit show that could have gone very badly," he gives his head a shake, "and full disclosure, my bicep doesn't hurt from the busted banister, I pulled a muscle when I smacked the side of Tom's house."

"You're not ready for this."

He scoffs, "That message was sent loud and clear when the chief confiscated my weapon."

Silence from her.

Dawning from him.

"You're talking about us, you and me, not about the police work."

"I got really freaked about the shooting. I needed to see you, I needed to see for myself that you were alright. The not knowing was overwhelming. It felt the way it did when I was in rehab. Everyone said you were alright, but I never saw you. I figured everyone was lying to keep me from knowing how badly you were hurt, or worse. The other night brought it all back. I understand that you needed to bail. Really, I get that."

"But?"

She pulls her legs up and wraps her arms around her knees. "The shooting unleashed a tsunami of memories. Processing them left me emotionally drained. You not being here made me push through them on my own, which is good, but in order to do that, I had to push against feelings I have for you. I had to put some separation between us. I'm having some trouble getting back to where we were."

"You want me to leave?"

"Maybe."

He moves close to her, wraps his arm around her shoulders, pulls her for a kiss to the side of her head, "I guess neither of us is ready for this."

She starts to cry.

"Aw, shit, Marin, please don't cry."

After several minutes of holding on, he grabs his jacket and keys and heads toward the door, "Hey, Marin."

"Yeah."

"I'm **really** glad you didn't say you love me." He walks through the door and leaves it open behind him.

A shiver runs her spine.

WPD

Tom stops for the hug Donna Abbott needs to give him, then heads to the chief's office. "You wanted to see me."

"Yeah." The chief stands at his window looking at the sparkling bay, "I'm working a timeline for Edward. He didn't kill Danielle or Joe. He might have hired someone to do it for him, or he had help from someone."

"Who?"

He shrugs, "Not ready to say yet." The chief turns Tom's way and takes a hip on the windowsill. "Close the door."

The energy in the room changes in a heartbeat. "The legal and professional problems for me are more significant than I first let on. I will do some prison time when all is said and done."

Tom takes a seat.

"I was a good clean cop until 2014, until September 12, 2014 to be exact. That's the day King called and said Heir killed Christie Anderson in a fit of rage and dumped her body in Casco Bay."

Tom shifts in his seat and clenches his hands.

"Hold the beatdown you want to give me until I'm finished."

Tom nods.

"I'm sure you're thinking Edward Kingston III had something on me, something that would cause me to abandon my ethics, he didn't. I protected Heir because he was Kathleen Kingston's son—because he was my son."

Tom rests his forearms on his legs and hangs his head.

"You know some of my history, but here's all of it. I left Whisper in 1977 for college on the mainland. After getting my BA from Stanford, I stuck around for a law degree and an MBA. I took a job at a law firm in Palo Alto and started hating every day of my life. I spent years doing corporate law crap, decided I hated the business end of things, but liked the legal part. I liked the law part. I quit my job, moved to Maine and went to the academy. I moved back to Whisper in early '91 and met Kathleen Beckwith, a beautiful socialite from Kenilworth, Illinois. She'd come to the island for the spring and summer with her family. We met and jumped heart first into a relationship. Then King returned to Whisper, swooped in and swept her from my bed and into his."

Tom gets up and takes a lean against the door, "When did you find out Edward was your son?"

"The day Kathleen died. I visited her deathbed and she confessed, then she asked me to – she begged me to – take care of her son. I failed Kathleen and Edward. I didn't fight for that kid. I didn't save him from The King of Whisper."

"You covered up Christie Anderson's murder and the desecration of her body?"

"Yes."

"You covered up Laire MacTavish's murder and the desecration of her body?"

"Yes."

"You need to resign. If you don't, and the cases against Edward Kingston IV move through the inquest process, they will be tainted, tossed out, and no one will be held accountable – except you, Vernon."

"I know." The chief reaches inside his desk drawer, grabs a sheet of paper and tosses it onto his desk, "My letter of resignation, dated Monday, November 20, 2017. I'm going to present it to the Council at 9 AM. The inquest will be put on hold until this whole sordid mess is figured out. I'm making a recommendation that you be named my successor."

"Nope."

"You have no choice, Tom. The Council knows you and respects you, as do the citizens of Whisper. The island will need a breather from the dirty dealings that have taken place. You're the breath of fresh air this place needs. Look, I'm going to make the recommendation. I suspect the Council will make an offer. You do what you want. If you take over, you've got the inquests for MacTavish, Rayburn, and Baxter in the immediate future; probably an inquest for Fred Fuller, and a complete forensic of Heir's culpability, and his mental status during and after the crimes, most specifically his state of mind immediately preceding his death. Then you've got the Jacobs' shooting on Stony, and the hit and run attempt by Edward Kingston III, and the litany of charges of fraud, money laundering, and who the fuck knows what else."

Tom takes his seat, does the whole arm to his thighs and head hanging thing again. It is many, many, many minutes before he speaks. "Okay," he gets up and leaves the office of Vernon Banks, Chief of Police.

Sand Castle

Marin is on the deck beneath a couple blankets staring at the new moon and singing the opening line of *Moondance* over and over. "It's a wonderful night for a moon dance." She sings so she doesn't remember his green eyes, his quirky smile, his playfulness, or his easy ways. "It's a wonderful night for a moon dance." A fright-shiver runs her spine. She sits up a bit, looks at the very dark shoreline, ocean, and sky. She gets up quickly, grabs her blankets, goes inside, and locks the door.

Dale Jacobs headed to Main Street toward Shaky as soon as he left Sand Castle. He looped from the main drag and made his way to the shoreline then to the dunes that line the Baxter property. He watches Marin bolt from the porch, then moves closer, finding a perfect view inside. He keeps his eyes on her as she moves throughout the cottage, steps deeper into the shadows along the side of the house, takes a lean-to against a weathered wooden fence and watches her strip for a shower. And when she returns all dewy and flush, her hair a mess of wet waves, he hardens—and when she pulls his white, long-sleeve T-shirt on, he hardens even more—and when she falls onto the bed in tears he warns.

"Don't worry, Marin,
I'm not finished with you yet."

Week Four – Day Four
Sunday, November 19
Waxing Crescent – Illumination 1%

Tom

Spends the day behind the denroom door.

Marin

Spends the day moping at The Castle.

Roxanne

Spends the afternoon reporting
from the site of *Darling*.

Rodriquez

Spends the day preparing for a hit.

King

Spends the day preparing for a hit.

Vernon

Spends the day preparing files
for his replacement.

Dale

Spends the day planning his revenge.

Week Four – Day Five
Monday, November 20
Waxing Crescent – Illumination 4%

Dale is up early and hoofing it to Whisper Bank & Trust. He happily goes through greetings with the tellers and idle chit-chat with the manager who escorts him to the lower level. She locks him and his security box in a private room and waits outside. He knocks on the door when he's finished and steps into the hall, noticing the wide smile on the manager's face, "What?"

She waves an index card his way, "Says here that it's your birthday."

He smiles wide.

"Bet it'll be the best birthday ever," she winks.

"Why?"

"You've had a tough year, Dale. You should live it up. Do something fun, daring, bold."

He smiles wider, "I should, shouldn't I?"

Dale is having coffee at the near-empty Boardwalk when Vernon Banks crosses Main Street from the beach. "Wonder what he was doing on the sands? Don't think I remember a time when he was anywhere near the beach."

He laughs, "And I remember everything." Dale checks his watch, "Time to visit she who delivered me on this 20th day of November, 1992."

Council Chambers

The members are seated in the spectator area as per Vernon's request. He walks through a swing gate, pulls a deep breath then turns their way. He leans across the rail and hands a sealed envelope to Chairman Collins. "That is a letter of resignation from my appointment of Chief of Police of Whisper Island. I'd prefer if you wait to open it. Without going into too much detail, pursuant to my Fifth Amendment Rights, recent conduct prohibits me from continued service. It most definitely prohibits me from any further participation in the inquest matters pertaining to Edward Kingston IV."

The council sits in stunned silence—for several minutes.

The councilman speaks, "Are the matters serious enough to warrant a pause in the inquest proceedings?"

"Yes."

"There needs to be a replacement found for your position."

"Yes."

"If the Council asked Tom Martin to step into an interim role as chief, is he likely to consent?"

"Yes."

"Would he hold you and any others who are involved in any misdeed or criminal acts accountable?"

"Yes."

The chambers are sealed. Plans are made.

Echo

The security system at the estate has been offline since the Halloween nor'easter. King didn't plan it that way, but he sure has benefitted from it. He's discussing the matter with Rodriquez, "Do you have transportation?"

"A rental."

"You're leaving the island after the hit."

"Yeah."

"Take the rental onto the Abenaki and get rid of it on the mainland."

"It'll cost you."

"It always does." He goes to his wall safe, spins the dial left four rotations stopping on the number 2, turns it right three rotations stopping on the number 5, turns left twice to 19, and right once to 72, clicks it open and grabs a banded $50Gs and tosses it to Rodriquez. "I shouldn't give you a fucking penny since Ruby-fucking-Norman is still breathing, but I want you and that car off this island. If the hit goes south, Do Not come here. If you get arrested, wait it out until a bail hearing comes up."

Rodriquez calls Casco Bay Ferry Lines to check the schedule and to book a ticket under an alias. "I'll be leaving Whisper at seven. Make sure you're inside the chamber by six."

Carmichael Corner

The reporter's phone starts blowing up with calls from her station manager, her cameraman, and the various and sundry shortly before 5 PM. "Roxanne, don't forget to swing by for your Press Pass." ... "Hey, Roxi, it's Tim. No need to call back, just reminding you about the Press Pass, none of us will be allowed in without it. Forget I called, I'll grab the pass. See you in a few." ... "Hi, Roxanne, it's your mother. Just wanted to wish you good luck on tonight's inquest and to tell you I've watched your *Darling* stories. I can't wait to see what happens next. You don't need to call. I just wanted to say, I love you."

Jacobs Jolly

Marin does another knock on the back door, gets no answer, so she leaves the gift-wrapped box on the doorstep and heads back to the trolly stand.

Town Hall

Tom enters the chambers a few minutes past 5 PM. He could have been on time, but he chose not to be.

Chairman Collins swings the gate open, "Thanks for coming, Tom. You know what this is about, so we're going to cut to the chase. We need you to step in as Vern's replacement, effective immediately. An announcement of Chief Bank's resignation will be made when we gavel in and we'd like to announce that you've accepted the interim position as chief."

"I want complete authority and autonomy. I won't run a single thing by anyone on the Council. Not one thing. The first phone call or chance meeting in a hallway that suggests anyone on this Council wants to discuss or question any decision I've made will result in my immediate resignation. If you agree with those terms, put it in writing and I'll sign."

"Done." The chairman hands him a document.

Tom reads. Tom signs.

Inquest
Whisper Island, Maine

Edward Kingston IV –
Re: Laire MacTavish

Missing Person's Case

Monday, November 20, 2017

Opening Statement:
Norman Collins, Chairman, Town Council

"Before we gavel in for tonight's proceedings, I want to address the members of the press. All of the rules and regulations previously stated during my opening statement on November 13, 2017, are applicable to this evening's proceedings."

For the third time, Tom makes eye contact with Roxanne's cameraman. For the third time, he receives a shake of the head and a shrug of the shoulder. For the third time Tom scans the attendees. For the third time he notices the seat reserved for Edward Kingston III remains empty.

The chairman stands. "I have an announcement. Earlier today, Chief of Police Vernon Banks submitted his letter of resignation."

The standing room only crowd gasps, then quiets.

"The circumstances surrounding his retirement will not be disclosed at this time. Just prior to tonight's gaveling in, Thomas Martin, former detective with WPD accepted the interim position of chief and was sworn in."

The standing room only crowd offers a huge sigh of relief.

Tom leaves his seat, walks through the swinging gate at the wooden railing, gets the ear of the chairman, says a few words, and sprints from the chamber. He's on his phone before he's out of the building, "Donna, this is Chief Martin. Get a unit to Carmichael Corner."

Vernon Banks, newly resigned chief of police of Whisper Island, hears the call come over his vehicle's police radio and gets a pit in his stomach. "Ms. Carmichael didn't make it to the inquest? There's no way she would miss that hearing." He screeches to a halt on the driveway of Outer Banks, runs inside, up the stairs to his safe, removes his personal firearm, and takes a bullet to the chest before he makes it back to the first floor.

The killer of Vernon Charles Banks takes a lean against a doorjamb and watches the man painfully gasp for air and waits for the final exhale before initiating Part Two of his plan.

Tom races onto Roxanne's driveway, parks behind her Jeep, heads around back and through the open door. There are obvious signs of a struggle in the kitchen. He heads outside and points to two officers, "No one is allowed inside this cottage. No one is allowed anywhere near her Jeep." He gets inside his truck and makes a call, "Jenny, are The Boarders with you?"

"Yes."

"Are you safe?"

"Yes."

"I'm going to need some reassurances. What's your going rate for legal representation?"

"A dollar an hour. A hundred for a month. What's going on, Tom?"

"This goes in your shoe, Counselor."

"Yes."

"Roxanne Carmichael is missing."

The wind leaves Jenny, courtesy of an emotional sucker punch.

Tom gets out of his F-150 and approaches Officer Millhouse, "You may be unaware, but I was sworn in as chief of police earlier today. If you need verification, call Donna Abbott or Chairman Collins, but do it fast. I need to promote you to detective."

"I already called Donna to find out why you were directing two WPD officers, sir."

Tom slaps the young man's shoulder, "Come inside. Do not touch anything. Take a duplicate set of cell pics. Whatever I photo, you photo. They are property of WPD and should not be disseminated to anyone. Understood?"

"Yes, sir."

"If you see something that doesn't settle well, say something. Ask questions and take notes." He hands Millhouse a notebook he grabbed from his glove box. "Let's go."

Tom is on his way back to his F-150 several hours later when he realizes two things: 1) He hasn't heard from Vernon, "He'd be here if he heard the call come over the radio." 2) He didn't think to shut down the ferry system. "Rookie-fuckin mistake." He checks his watch. "Nine-thirty. Fuck." He calls Vernon's cell. He calls Vernon's house phone. He calls Donna Abbott, "Have you heard from Vernon?"

"No."

"Call his *call sign* over the radio and ask him to call me."

Tom barrel-asses to Outer Banks ——— falls to his knees at the body of Vernon Banks. He calls Donna, "I need .... I need." He removes his fingers from Vernon's pulse point.

"I need all emergency personnel
to Outer Banks.
The chief is dead."

The End

Please enjoy the teaser for the next
Twisted Threads story,

Awake on Stony Beach

Awake on
Stony Beach

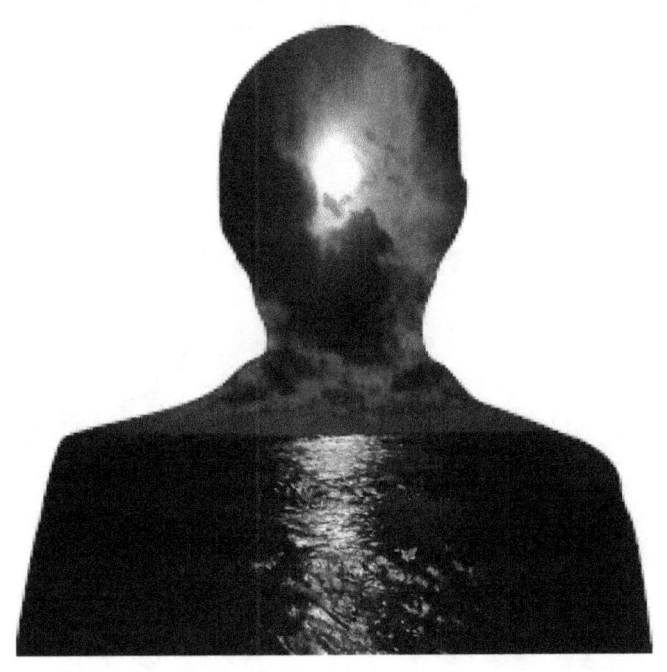

~~~ TWISTED THREADS ~~~
A Novel
SHERYLL O'BRIEN

2017
Sandy Side

Welcome Back to Murder Island

Tom Martin walks shoulder to shoulder with Lan MacTavish through prison gates without word. As soon as the gate slides closed behind them, they are flanked on either side by two Maine state troopers. The newly appointed chief and the newly released prisoner are escorted to the backseat of a black Discovery that falls in the middle of a state police caravan. Lan starts to say something. Tom shakes his head. They make the hour plus trip to the docks in Portland, press through a waiting crowd of reporters and television crews, board the reserved and empty Abenaki, and make the half-hour crossing to Whisper Island, all in complete silence. The accompanying state troopers do the whole flanking thing as the men leave the ferry. A larger and louder throng of press and public greets them with a steady stream of camera-clicking, question-shouting, and a robust round of applause. None of the spectacle means anything to Lan MacTavish. The only thing he's thinking about, the only thing pressing deep against his bruised heart, is the harsh irony that his sister, Laire, was missing when he left, and his friend, Roxanne, is missing when he returns.

ABOUT THE AUTHOR

She is not dead.

Sheryll O'Brien crafts characters without constraints. She tells them who they are, then let's them show her better versions of themselves. She gives them life and they live it beyond her wildest dreams.

Sheryll is a lifelong resident of Worcester, Massachusetts, where she is wife to the most supportive husband ever, and mother of two adult daughters, one who refuses to leave her home and the other who refuses to tell her where she lives. Of most significance, she is MammyGrams to the sweetest eight-year-old, Hadley.

Sheryll worked several years in the fundraising community of Worcester County, writing grants for non-profit organizations. She began writing for her own pleasure after surviving brain surgery and breast cancer. Happily, for her fanbase of family and friends——she is not dead.

If you have enjoyed reading my book, I would very much appreciate you taking a few minutes to write a review and post that review on amazon.com and goodreads.com.

The opinion of readers can help prospective readers make a purchasing decision.

To learn more, please visit my website, www.pullingthreadsnovella.com subscribe to my blog for updates on future projects.

I would absolutely love to hear from my readers, you can email me at,

pullingthreadsnovella@gmail.com